William Gershom Collingwood

The Life and Work of John Ruskin

Volume II

William Gershom Collingwood

The Life and Work of John Ruskin
Volume II

ISBN/EAN: 9783337056193

Printed in Europe, USA, Canada, Australia, Japan

Cover: Foto ©Raphael Reischuk / pixelio.de

More available books at **www.hansebooks.com**

THE LIFE AND WORK OF

JOHN RUSKIN

BY

W. G. COLLINGWOOD, M. A.

EDITOR OF "THE POEMS OF JOHN RUSKIN," ETC.

WITH PORTRAITS AND OTHER ILLUSTRATIONS

IN TWO VOLUMES

VOLUME II

BOSTON AND NEW YORK
HOUGHTON, MIFFLIN AND COMPANY
The Riverside Press, Cambridge
1893

CONTENTS.

APPENDIX.

LIST OF ILLUSTRATIONS

NOTE.

The following portraits of Mr. Ruskin are mentioned by Mr. M. H. Spielmann in the *Magazine of Art* for January and February, 1891: Pencil drawing, or drawings, by Sir J. E. Millais (about 1852); medallion by Mr. Charles Ashmore (1875); sketch by Pilotelle (1876); miniature by Mr. Andrews (exhib. R. A. 1877); water-color by Mr. Arthur Severn (about same time); life-size head in water-color by Mr. Herkomer (exhib. Grosvenor Gallery, 1881); portraits by Mr. Emptmeyer and Miss Webling (both exhib. R. A. 1888); bust by Mr. Conrad Dressler (1884, exhib. New Gallery, 1889); water-color head by himself in the possession of Mrs. Arthur Severn, excellently reproduced as frontispiece to Vol. I. (about 1864, the black tie perhaps indicating the recent loss of his father). To these may be added: Bust by Mr. B. Creswick (1877, presented to Prince Leopold, 1879); bust by Mr. Atkinson (1881); two life-size heads in water-color by himself, unfinished, in possession of Mrs. A. Severn; pencil study (1873 or 1874) and water-color (1875?) by himself, in possession of Prof. C. E. Norton. Also many photographs, the best known by Messrs. Elliott & Fry (1866, 1882) and Barraud (1882, 1886). The sketch at Vol. II., p. 552, is enlarged from a group photograph by Capt. Walker (1892). From photographs were copied an excellent lithograph illustrating a Bibliography by Mr. Wedderburn, in the *Examiner*, Nov. 1, 1879; engraving by W. Roffe in the Ruskin Birthday Book; etching by W. Burton in Biographical outline (Messrs. Virtue's series of "Celebrities," 1889); woodcut by T. A. Butler, *Harper's Magazine*, Feb., 1889. Caricatures in *Vanity Fair* by F. Waddy; in "Sir Isumbras crossing the Ford," by F. Sandys (Arts Club, London), etc., etc.

BOOK III.

HERMIT AND HERETIC.

(1860–1870.)

"Hush! you must not speak about it yet, but I have made a great discovery. The fact is that the strongest man upon earth is he who stands most alone."

IBSEN, Enemy of Society.

CHAPTER I.

THE TRANSITION FROM ART.

(1860–1861.)

AT forty years of age Mr. Ruskin finished " Modern Painters," and concluded the whole cycle of work by which he is popularly known as a writer on art. Since then, art has sometimes been his text, rarely his theme. He has used it as the opportunity, the vehicle, so to say, for teachings of far wider range and deeper import; teachings about life as a whole, conclusions in ethics and economics and religion, to which he seeks to lead others, as he was led, by the way of art. And in this later period, when he does speak of art in especial, the greater range of his inquiry naturally modifies his aim and standpoint; just as, in a vast wall-painting, the detail is viewed and treated otherwise than when it formed the subject of separate still-life studies. Some observers prefer the still-life; and indeed it may be good work.   But the broad treatment is the greater.

If we want to understand Mr. Ruskin, there is only one way of studying him; and that is to trace from point to point the growth of his mind.   Now all those books — "Modern Painters," "Stones of Venice," "Seven Lamps," the earlier Lectures and Letters on Art — are works of a young man, not yet forty; that is to say, before the age at which most great authors, painters, and thinkers have done their best.   They contain much that is valuable and much that is characteristic; but they are only the forecourt, not the presence-chamber.   They lead to his final conclusions, but they do not express them.   What the juvenile poems are to these works, they are to the later works, — seedlings and saplings, so like and so unlike the full-grown plant.   It is no use quarreling with the author for not composing a consistent explanation of his views; though it would have been convenient for students, who might as well wish that Plato had left them a handbook of his philosophy, or that Shakespeare had appended notes to " Hamlet."

During the time when he was preaching his later doctrines, Mr. Ruskin wished to suppress the interfering evidences of the earlier; not so much because they contained mistaken estimates and misleading statements, as because they betrayed a tone of thought which differed from the tone of his later period as much as a stained window differs from a Tintoret. He let his works on art run out of print, not for the benefit of second-hand booksellers, but in the hope that he could fix upon his audience the burden of his prophecy for the time being. But the youthful works were still read; high prices were paid for them, or they were smuggled in from America. And since the epoch of " Fors " has passed, he has agreed to the reprinting of all that early material. He calls it obsolete and trivial; others find it interestingly biographical, — perhaps even classical.

But when we read articles professing to criticise his life-work, and find that they estimate his art-theory from a few passages in " Modern Painters," Volumes I. and II., obviously immature; when, on the other hand, magazine writers analyze, as axioms of his social science, without tracing their origin and import, the winged words with which he tried, in his failing powers and forlorn hopes, to arouse the dull conscience of a Philistine public; when men of a different generation, an alien race, of traditions dissimilar and irreconcilable tempera-ment, hastily sample his paragraphs as customs-officers gauge a cargo; we turn at last to the historical method, and ask whether these things should be so. And as a geologist, puzzled at some inversion of strata, Nature's paradox, yet, on accurately plotting it out upon his map or model, sees the fitness and necessity of the pheno-menon; so, with the biographical scheme under-stood, the discrepancies and difficulties of Ruskin fall into their place and explain themselves. He at last stands revealed, and then can be criticised, as we criticise any other thinking, growing man, — say Plato, Titian, Goethe, — who has left a long life's work behind him.

This year, then, 1860, the year of the Italian kingdom, of Garibaldi, and of the beginning of the American war, marks his turning-point, from the early work, summed up, not too adequately, in Mr. Harrison's[1] " Selections," to the later work which no one has yet thoroughly examined in print.

Until he was forty, Mr. Ruskin was a writer on art; after that his art was secondary to ethics. Until he was forty he was a believer in English Protestantism; afterwards he could not reconcile current beliefs with the facts of life as he saw them, and had to reconstruct his creed from the foundations. Until he was forty he was a philanthropist, working heartily with others in a definite cause, and hoping for the amendment of wrongs, without a social upheaval. Even in the beginning of 1860, in his evidence before the House of Commons Select Committee on Public Institutions, he was ready with plans for amusing and instructing the laboring classes, and noting in them a " thirsty desire " for improvement.[2] But

---

[1] I have always understood from Mr. Ruskin that the Selections were made by Mr. W. H. Harrison; the editors of the Bibliography attribute them to Mr. Williams, of Smith, Elder & Co.

[2] It is interesting to remark, in passing, that he did not believe in lectures without intermediate study, and anticipated the illus-

while his readiness to make any personal sacrifice, in the way of social and philanthropic experiment, and his interest in the question, were increasing, he became less and less sanguine about the value of such efforts as the Working Men's College, and less and less ready to coöperate with others in their schemes. He began to see that no tinkering at social breakages was really worth while; that far more extensive repairs were needed to make the old ship seaworthy.

So he set himself, by himself, to sketch the plans for the repairs. Naturally sociable, and accustomed to the friendly give-and-take of a wide acquaintance, he withdrew from the busy world into a busier solitude. During the next few years he lived much alone among the Alps, or at home, thinking out the problem; sometimes feeling, far more acutely than was good for clear thought, the burden of the mission that was laid upon him. In March, 1863, he wrote from his retreat at Mornex to Mr. Norton: "The loneliness is very great, and the peace in which I am at present is only as if I had buried myself in a tuft of grass on a battle-field wet with blood, — for the cry of the earth about me is in my ears continually, if I do not lay my head to the very ground." And, a few months later: "I am still very unwell, and tormented between the longing for rest and lovely life, and the sense of this terrific call of human

trated courses to mixed and working-class audiences which are now the chief feature of University Extension.

crime for resistance and of human misery for help, though it seems to me as the voice of a river of blood which can but sweep me down in the midst of its black clots, helpless."

Sentences like these, passages here and there in the last volume of " Modern Painters," and still more, certain passages omitted from that volume, show that about 1860 something of a cloud had been settling over him, — a morbid sense of the evil of the world, a horror of great darkness. In his earlier years, his intense emotion and vivid imagination had enabled him to read into pictures of Tintoret or Turner, into scenes of nature and sayings of great books, a meaning or a moral which he so vividly communicated to the reader as to make it thenceforward part and parcel of the subject, however it came there to begin with. It is useless to wonder whether Turner, for instance, consciously meant what Ruskin found in his works. A great painter does not paint without thought, and such thought is apt to show itself whether he will or no. But it needs a powerful sympathy to detect and describe the thought. And when that powerful sympathy was given to suffering, to widespread misery, to crying wrongs; joined also with an intense passion for justice, which had already shown itself in the defense of slighted genius and neglected art, and to the high-strung Celtic temperament of some Highland seer and trance-prophesying bard; it was no wonder that Mr. Ruskin became like one of the hermits of old who retreated from the world to return upon it with stormy messages of awakening and flashes of truth more impressive, more illuminating than the logic of schoolmen and the statecraft of the wise.

And then he began to take up an attitude of antagonism to the world, he who had been the kindly helper and minister of delightful art. He began to call upon those who had ears to hear to come out and be separate from the ease and hypocrisy of Vanity Fair. Its respectabilities, its orthodoxies, he could no longer abide. Orthodox religion, orthodox morals and politics, orthodox art and science, alike he rejected; and was rejected by each of them as a brawler, a babbler, a fanatic, a heretic. And even when friendly Oxford gave him a quasi-academical position, that did not bring him, as it brings many a heretic, back to the fold.

In this period of storm and stress he stood alone. The old friends of his youth were one by one passing away, if not from intercourse, still from full sympathy with him in his new mood. Carlyle was not yet the admiring intimate he afterwards became. His parents were no longer the guides and companions they had been; they did not understand the business he was about. And so he was left to new associates, for he could not live without some one to love, — that is the nature of the man, however lonely in his work and wanderings.

The new friends of this period were, at first, Americans; as the chief new friends of his latest period (the Alexanders) were American, too. Mr. Charles Eliot Norton, after being introduced to him in London, met him again by accident on the Lake of Geneva — the story is prettily told in " Præterita."   And Mr. Ruskin adds, " Norton saw all my weaknesses, measured all my narrownesses, and, from the first, took serenely, and as it seemed of necessity, a kind of paternal authority over me, and a right of guidance. . . . I was entirely conscious of his rectorial power, and affectionately submissive to it, so that he might have done anything with me, but for the unhappy difference in our innate and unchangeable political faiths."   So, after all, he stood alone.

Another friend about this time was Mrs. H. Beecher Stowe, to whom he wrote on June 18, 1860, from Geneva: " It takes a great deal, when I am at Geneva, to make me wish myself anywhere else, and, of all places else, in London; nevertheless, I very heartily wish at this moment that I were looking out on the Norwood Hills, and were expecting you and the children to breakfast to-morrow.

" I had very serious thoughts, when I received your note, of running home; but I expected that very day an American friend, Mr. Stillman, who, I thought, would miss me more here than you in London, so I stayed.

" What a dreadful thing it is that people should

have to go to America again, after coming to Europe! It seems to me an inversion of the order of nature. I think America is a sort of 'United' States of Probation, out of which all wise people, being once delivered, and having obtained entrance into this better world, should never be expected to return[1] (sentence irremediably ungrammatical), particularly when they have been making themselves cruelly pleasant to friends here. My friend Norton, whom I met first on this very blue lake water, had no business to go back to Boston again, any more than you. . . .

"So you have been seeing the Pope and all his Easter performances! I congratulate you, for I suppose it is something like ' Positively the last appearance on any stage.' What was the use of thinking about *him?* You should have had your own thoughts about what was to come after him. I don't mean that Roman Catholicism will die out so quickly. It will last pretty nearly as long as Protestantism, which keeps it up; but I wonder what is to come next. That is the main question just now for everybody."

Professor Norton has remained always Mr. Ruskin's friend; Mrs. Beecher Stowe, not always. Mr. Stillman had been a correspondent about 1851, — "involved in mystical speculations, partly growing out of the second volume of ' Modern Painters,'" as he says of himself in an

---

[1] "Good Americans when they die go to Paris." — *The Autocrat of the Breakfast-Table*, quoting **T. G. Appleton**.

article on "John Ruskin" in the "Century Magazine" (January, 1888).   He tells us that he wrote to the author for counsel, and quotes a long letter in which Mr. Ruskin advises "on no account to agitate nor grieve yourself, nor look for inspirations, — for assuredly many of our noblest English minds have been entirely overthrown by doing so, — but go on doing what you are sure is quite right, — that is, striving for constant purity of thought, purpose, and word."

Nothing could have been more infelicitous, after such advice and the known tenor of Ruskin's teaching, than Mr. Stillman's picture of a mortal struggle between a man and a buck, — the buck painted, in curious misunderstanding of Pre-Raphaelite principles, from a dead buck. Nothing could more naïvely illustrate the gentle art of making enemies than Mr. Stillman's combination of anecdote and remark.   Mr. Ruskin called his buck, we are told, "filthy."   "His art-criticism is radically and irretrievably wrong." At Denmark Hill, the American visitor proved a Turner drawing to be false in tone; Mr. Ruskin (who thinks it bad manners to argue with a guest, and had fully explained the subject in his chapter on the Use of Pictures) waived the discussion. "His assumption of Turner's veracity is the corner-stone of his system, and its rejection would be the demolition of that system."   Mr. Stillman was his "guest" for the summer of 1860 in Switzerland.   He found his host "generous to extravagance;" but when he was asked to draw a group of cottages, — as Millais had been asked to draw the tiger's head, and other artists sharing Mr. Ruskin's purse and patience have been invited to share his work, — Mr. Stillman showed a ten minutes' sketch for his day's result, and explained that the subject was not worth his while. At Chamouni, Mr. Ruskin stopped his drawing of the Mer de Glace on finding, what an artist might have seen beforehand, that the lines were awkward. "Mr. Ruskin never seemed to understand style in drawing." "His influence on modern landscape-painting has been pernicious from beginning to end."

In Mr. Stillman's company at Chamouni, July, 1860, Mr. Ruskin seems to have sketched very little. Two moonlights, a new subject for him, are attributed to that summer. He was far from well; feeling for the first time, to a serious degree, the morbid depression which some of his letters of the period indicate; and turning over in his mind the thoughts he was embodying in a new series of essays on political economy. The year before, from Thun and Bonneville and Lausanne (August and September, 1859) he had written letters to Mr. E. S. Dallas, suggested by the strikes in the London building trade. In these he appears to have sketched the outline of a new conception of social science, which he was now elaborating, with more attempt at system and brevity than he had been accustomed to use.

These new papers, painfully thought out and carefully set down in his room at the Hôtel de l'Union, he used — as long before he read his daily chapter to the breakfast party at Herne Hill — to read to Mr. W. J. Stillman; and he sent them to his friend Thackeray, who accepted them for his magazine, the " Cornhill," started the year before by Smith & Elder. Mr. Ruskin had already contributed to it a paper on " Sir Joshua and Holbein," a stray chapter from Volume V., " Modern Painters." His reputation as a writer and philanthropist, together with the friendliness of editor and publisher, secured the insertion of the first three, — from August to October. Thackeray then wrote to say that they were so unanimously condemned and disliked that, with all apologies, he could only admit one more. So the series was brought hastily to a conclusion in November, and the author, beaten back as he had never been beaten before, dropped the subject, and "sulked," so he called it, all the winter.

It is pleasant to notice that neither editor nor publisher quarreled with the author who had laid them open to the censure of their public, — nor he with them. On December 21st, he wrote to Thackeray, in answer, apparently, to a letter about lecturing for a charitable purpose; and continued: " The mode in which you direct your charity puts me in mind of a matter that has lain long on my mind, though I never have had the time or face to talk to you of it. In somebody's drawing-room, ages ago, you were speaking accidentally of M. de Marvy.[1] I expressed my great obligation to him; on which you said that I could prove my gratitude, if I chose, to his widow, — which choice I then not accepting, have ever since remembered the circumstance as one peculiarly likely to add, so far as it went, to the general impression on your mind of the hollowness of people's sayings and hardness of their hearts.

" The fact is, I give what I give almost in an opposite way to yours. I think there are many people who will relieve hopeless distress for one who will help at a hopeful pinch; and when I have the choice I nearly always give where I think the money will be fruitful rather than merely helpful. I would lecture for a school when I would *not* for a distressed author; and would have helped De Marvy to perfect his invention, but not — unless I had no other object — his widow after he was gone. In a word, I like to prop the falling more than to feed the fallen."

The winter passed without any great undertakings. Mr. G. F. Watts proposed to add Mr. Ruskin's portrait to his gallery of celebrities; but he was in no mood to sit. Rossetti did, however, sketch him this year. In March he presented a series of Turner drawings to Oxford, and another set of twenty-five to Cambridge. The address of

---

[1] Louis Marvy, an engraver, and political refugee after the French Revolution of 1848.

thanks with the great seal of Oxford University is dated March 23, 1861; the catalogue of the Cambridge collection is dated May 28th. Later in the year Walter Thornbury's " Life of Turner " appeared, the book that Mr. Ruskin ought to have written. He wrote from Lucerne, December 2, 1861: "I have just received and am reading your book with deep interest. I am much gratified by the view you have taken and give of Turner. It is quite what I hoped. What beautiful things you have discovered about him! Thank you for your courteous and far too flattering references to me." It was, of course, gratifying to find somebody who did not consider Turner, as Mr. Stillman does, a miser and a satyr; and when Mr. Ruskin compliments, he compliments handsomely.

He was prevailed upon, in spite of his unfitness, to give a lecture before "a most brilliant audience," as the " London Review " reported, at the Royal Institution (April 19, 1861). Carlyle wrote to his brother John: " Friday last I was persuaded — in fact had inwardly compelled myself as it were — to a lecture of Ruskin's at the Institution, Albemarle Street. Lecture on Tree Leaves as physiological, pictorial, moral, symbolical objects. A crammed house, but tolerable even to me in the gallery. The lecture was thought to 'break down,' and indeed it quite did '*as a lecture;*' but only did from *embarras des richesses,* —

a rare case.   Ruskin did blow asunder as by gunpowder explosions his leaf notions, which were manifold, curious, genial; and in fact, I do not recollect to have heard in that place any neatest thing I liked so well as this chaotic one."

CHAPTER II.

THE PROTEST IN ECONOMICS.

(1862.)

> "Nor kind nor coinage buys
> Aught above its rate ;
> Fear, Craft and Avarice
> Cannot rear a State."
>
> EMERSON.

IT is not every traveler nowadays who knows the Salève. One goes through the Alps too quickly to linger among the foothills, and a mere three thousand feet of crag above the plain does not stop the way to aiguilles and glaciers. But the tourist of the future, after seeing Voltaire's Fernex in the morning, will perhaps pick his way among the fields beyond Carouge and through the gorge of Monnetier, or drive on his pilgrimage by Annemasse round the Petit Salève, to another shrine at Mornex. There, two thousand feet above sea-level, basking in the morning sun, and looking always over the broad valley of the Arve at Mont Blanc and its panorama, are country retreats of the modern Genevese, beneath the old mother-castle of Savoy; and there, with its shady little garden and rustic summer-house, is the chalet, or *cottage ornée*, where Mr. Ruskin went into hermitage, and wrote his " Political Economy." You can enter, now ; it is a place of public entertainment ; and in the cool, broad-windowed dining-room, you can drink a glass to the memory.

After three or four months there, he went, at the end of 1861, to Lucerne; then in February, 1862, hearing that the Turner drawings in the National Gallery had been mildewed, he ran home to see about them ; and was kept until the end of May. He found that his political economy work was not such a total failure as it had seemed. The editor of " Fraser's Magazine " thought there was something in it, and would give him another chance for the new papers he had been writing at Mornex. So, by way of a fresh start, he had his four " Cornhill " articles published in book form ; and almost simultaneously, in June, 1862, the first of the new series appeared.

The author had then returned to Lucerne; and he soon crossed the St. Gothard to Milan, where he tried to forget the harrowing of hell in a close study of Luini, and in copying the St. Catherine, now at Oxford. Mr. Ruskin has never said so much about Luini as, perhaps, he intended. A short notice in the " Cestus of Aglaia," and occasional references scattered up and down his later works, hardly give the prominence in his writings that the painter held in his thoughts.

In August he went back to Mornex, with the faithful Couttet. Mr. Ruskin had been ill at

Milan, and was going to be better among the Alps. His Working Men's College pupil, George Allen, who had been learning engraving from Le Keux, met him there with his wife and children, and, among other occupations, made himself famous as a rifle-shot at Swiss " Tirs," and as a skillful carpenter helped to mend Savoyard cottages.

In September the second article appeared in " Fraser." " Only a genius like Mr. Ruskin could have produced such hopeless rubbish," says a newspaper of the period. Far worse than any newspaper criticism was the condemnation of Denmark Hill. His father, whose eyes had glistened over early poems and prose eloquence, strongly disapproved of this heretical economy. It was a bitter thing that his son should turn prodigal of a hardly earned reputation, and be pointed at for a fool. And it was intensely painful for a son " who had never given his father a pang that could be avoided," as old Mr. Ruskin had once written, to find his father, with one foot in the grave, turning against him. He went home in November for a few weeks; in December the third paper appeared. History repeated itself, — as usual, with variations. This time not only the public but the publisher interfered; and with the fourth paper the heretic was gagged. A year after, his father died; and these " Fraser " articles were laid aside until the end of 1871, when they were taken up again, and published on New Year's Day, 1872, as " Munera Pulveris." [1]

It will surely be asked, Why was there so great a noise about a few articles on a theoretical subject like political economy?

We are so accustomed nowadays to free speculation and outspoken theorizing — even to bold experiments in socialism and kindred systems — that it is rather difficult for us to see what the " harm " was in these essays, until we put ourselves at the point of view of the time — thirty years ago — when they were written, in order to see how it was they terrified people, disturbed consciences, and seemed like an eclipse-portent. It was not just that they attacked a theory. They aimed at the working creed, the comfortable scheme of all society, the sanction of property as then held and constituted, and the justification of life as then lived.

People had been asking why there were poverty and misery, vice and crime. When Ruskin was still a verse-writing little lad the poor-laws had been blamed for great part of it, and in 1834 had been overhauled, by the light of political economy, and hopefully reconstituted. Later, great schemes of charity had been not only set going, but energetically worked. And still there were poverty and vice. People cried to their gods, the all-powerful Laws of Competition, Supply and De-

[1] The title is an allusion to Horace, Odes, I. xxviii. 3 ; as *Unto this Last* refers to Matthew xx. 14.

mand, and the rest, to step in and save them: with absolute faith that if the right sacrifice were offered, the right formula preferred, the great religion of Adam Smith would make the world what its priests declared it, in desperate faith, to be, — the best of all possible worlds. Imagine what some virtuous Norseman felt, when the first Christian missionary stood up and said: "The vice you deplore, the barbarity you lament, is not to be cured by sacrifice to your idols, or recital of Runes; it is only to be done away by throwing down Thor and unlearning the Sagas of Blood; and by taking to heart the White Christ and His Gospel of forgiveness." Ruskin said exactly that. He said that the reason of poverty and vice was nothing else — discounting human frailty — than the mistaken creed in which the virtuous world had been comforting itself, justifying itself, these fifty years or more.

"Autres temps, autres mœurs," they say: we may say, too, Other times, other truths. Monasticism was a grand movement, for the age of St. Benedict; but when the monasteries became a scandal, they needed reform upon reform. The political economy of the orthodox school was, in its origin, a fine advance upon the cruder notions dating from Machiavelli. It had suggested a wider view of life, the wealth no longer of tyrants or narrow oligarchies, but of broader-based society. It had initiated the habit of mind which regards the welfare of the state, — no longer "l'état c'est

moi," but as the aggregate of population, strug-
gling onwards, or back, to a Greek ideal of true
political philosophy. But the stock-in-trade of
truth with which it started was becoming used
up. The history of philosophy shows that every
movement, however popular and practical, has
its origin and its support in some metaphysical theory. The details of public business are
worked by rule of thumb, and by opportunism;
but the great national ideal, the spirit of the
age, is the outcome of some thinker's theory
which has prevailed. Now the old political
economy was the outcome of eighteenth-century
philosophy; of the éclaircissement, the school of
rough generalizations; the mood of mind which
takes the line of least resistance, and hastens to
deductive conclusions from introspection, or from
too scanty survey of the infinite multiplicity of
facts which it has not time nor patience to sift.
It assumed " whatever is, is right ; " and whatever
was, at the moment, the phase of prevailing activity, it took for the eternal and immutable order
of things. In this case, the commercial and
manufacturing industries, a new and magnificent
development of civilization, it assumed to be
normal. It generalized too rapidly upon the tendencies which the growing trade and material
progress of England brought into play, as if these
were the only objects, the only facts of life ; as if
output of cotton and coal, for example, were an
end of existence. And it deduced rules by which

the output might be increased, and formulated Division of Labor, Competition, and so forth, as the means to its end.

This was parallel to the old orthodoxy in art, with which Mr. Ruskin had to deal in his youth. Then there had been a similar system of thought, based on an outworn metaphysic, the Platonism of the Renaissance, applied to the making of pictures. Certain ideals, archetypes, had been assumed as ultimate truths; and rules for painting had been deduced from them. Mr. Ruskin had shown that the scientific method of the modern age could be applied to this province of thought; that " particular fact " was to be regarded as the starting-point, and that, after due induction of principles, new values were to be given to the words truth, beauty, and imagination. The old rules, fallaciously supposed universal laws, he set aside, not without opposition; and ended in securing the acceptance of Turner and Naturalism.

John Stuart Mill had shown the logical side of that movement in 1843; but just as Ruskin, by sympathy with romanticism, had been attracted over to the reactionary school for a time, so Mill, by his sympathy with liberalism, the descendant of the éclaircissement, had allowed himself to be less true to the modern scientific method in his political economy. He advanced beyond Bentham; but still on the same lines. Carlyle had exemplified the opposite school of thought, a school whose tradition had been kept alive in Germany. Dr. Arnold of Rugby, the friend of Niebuhr and Bunsen, wrote to Mr. James Marshall from Fox How (January 23, 1840): "My differences with the Liberal Party would turn, I think, chiefly on two points. First, I agree with Carlyle, in thinking that they greatly over-estimate Bentham, and also that they overrate the political economists generally; not that I doubt the ability of these writers, or the truth of their conclusions, as far as regards their own science, — but I think that *the summum bonum of their science, and of human life, are not identical;* and therefore, many questions in which free trade is involved, and the advantages of large capital, etc., although perfectly simple in an economical point of view, become, when considered politically, very complex; and *the economical good* is very often, from the neglect of other points, made in practice a *direct social evil.*" [1]

What Arnold said privately in 1840, Ruskin said publicly in 1860. What he had done for Turner, he did for Carlyle: he analyzed the principles of those two great men, and laid the foundations of a new system, in the first case of an art theory, in the second case of a social theory, which they had illustrated in concrete examples.

As long as he kept to the political economy of art, spectators could look on with comfort, and applaud him when he fought for the rights of the workman. It was only against architects and

---

[1] Stanley's *Life of Arnold*, letter 223. The italics are mine.

master-builders that his first attack was directed; it was only for art craftsmen that he fought, before 1860. But then he suddenly changed his front; bore down upon all employers, fought for all laborers; attacked not only the wrongs of one class, but the whole series of public evils. He began by a destructive criticism of the whole economy of the commercial school; as the champion, not of modern painters, but of modern thinkers; of a scientific method of economy, as opposed to the academic; of the broad view, based on the complex facts of life, as against the narrow view, based only on such facts as appeared to the commercial mind, nursed in eighteenth-century traditions.

He showed, as others have since shown more calmly and completely, after he broke the ground for them, that the old economy did not take in the whole facts of the case, as any true science does, and must do. It was not true to the data, he said, to assume a state of normal immorality, as Adam Smith seemed to do, in declaring that the only calculable motive for work was the fear of losing pay. It was not true to human nature to neglect the many phases of honesty and loyalty which really existed, and by which, in actual life, society was upheld, and successful trade and manufacture were made possible. Again; to lay down as "laws" mere generalizations which the will of any man could set aside, was a misunderstanding of the meaning of "law" in modern science. He showed that competition, for example, was not a " law," but only a phase of commercial society. If it were a law, properly so called, it would be universal and inevitable, like the attraction of gravitation; whereas in many cases it was actually set aside, at the will of one man or company of men, for coöperation; and in other cases, he showed, it stopped progress and the flow of wealth which it was supposed to promote. Supply and demand, again, was not a " law " in the sense of being a necessary condition of all production: witness the supply of art and poetry irrespective of demand; of the means of life, lamentably falling short of it. Only by intellectual jugglery could it be made out that Albert Dürer, doing his best work for next to nothing, was his own consumer; or that the bitter cry of starvation was not an effectual demand.

He concluded that the orthodox political economy was not a true science, but that it stood to the real economy in the relation of alchemy to chemistry, — as a pseudo-science, needing reformation and reconstruction. Further, that it was not a *political* economy at all; it was only a commercial economy; since it dealt one-sidedly with the aspects and advantages of the trading classes only, not with those of the community at large; and with the trading class in one age only, in one society and form of civilization only, regardless of what might be learned of the spirit in which other commercial nations, such as the Venetians, had conducted their enterprises.   And when the so-called laws of this so-called science were taken as practical rules for life and conduct, and clashed, as they often did, with plain morality, or were made the shield of selfishness, the pretext of political crime (as in the case of the employment of children in mills, the selling of dangerous or bad wares to savages, and so on), then he pressed the conclusion that it was a superannuated creed, no better than a heathenism in whose name all manner of evils might be speciously justified, — "tantum religio potuit suadere malorum."

Destructive criticism like this was only the preface to his work. He had two things yet to do: to rearrange definitions of the terms and statements of real laws; and to reconstruct ideals of life and conduct in harmony with them.

Here, however, he stumbled his readers on the threshold — though that, they say, is a good omen. The morbid excitement under which he labored often obscured the lucidity of his exposition and the conclusiveness of his reasoning, leading him to speak, like one of the prophets of old, in a trance; not, like a wise diplomatist, buttonholing his hearer, but holding only the skirts of the spirit that carried him whither he hardly knew, and assuredly would not willingly have gone. But however he was misunderstood at the time, the question for us is, What is the burden of the prophecy, however strangely delivered? what is the drift of his teaching?

The difficulties fall under two heads: first, the strange use of familiar terms, unavoidable in the reconstruction of a study; for example, when he means by "value" not *commercial* value, but intrinsic, and by "money" not merely the means of exchange, but "the documentary expression of legal claim to labor," which may be destroyed, and yet the claim may exist; and so on. In the second place, his protest against the assumption of immorality as the normal condition of human intercourse led him to assume, as most people would feel, a rather higher standard of principle than poor humanity is accustomed to practice. Instead of replacing the old theories by a new one instantly acceptable and applicable, he drew up, with axiom and theorem, a scheme of economy which was "a system of conduct founded on the sciences, directing the arts, and impossible except under certain conditions of moral culture." Puzzling as this was to the British business man, it was not absurd. It was like practical geometry, which deals with ideally perfect triangles and circles, not with crooked sticks; but may be useful in building and engineering, more than if it assumed that all wood is warped and all iron flawed. Ruskin's economy points to an ideal; it calls on practical legislation to accept the principle, "I ought, therefore I can," and to drag the world up to a moral standard; whereas the old economy's influence was the reverse. And in practical issues he was fully cognizant of human infirmities, and of the necessity for gradual evolution to the "moral culture" he speaks of.

The various ideals and proposals which resulted, in general culture, education, ethics, and social science, we must notice one by one as they come into view in the various books of the period. A few points, especially economical, may be mentioned. These first two books did not suggest anything directly revolutionary. They upheld free trade; they did not decry interest; they declined to accept socialism. But they objected to the fixing of price by competition — as they did to competition in any shape; and thought that, if trade and labor could be paid as "professions" are paid, common consent would soon fix a normal standard of wages. The basis of the valuation of labor would be, not the labor market and the rights of capital, but a consensus that equal industry is worth equal remuneration; regard being had, in the case of skilled labor, to arrears of work involved in the worker's actual capacity. It is sometimes said that Mr. Ruskin thought that "landscape artists and laboring men ought to be paid alike." What he did hold was that in any trade or class the wages should be fixed by a commonly accepted tariff, and not altered except by common consent.

For those who failed to get work under such conditions, he thought that the government should provide, by an extension of existing systems of industrial schools and reformatories, and by a reconstruction of the prison and poor laws. This was not part of his ideal commonwealth, but a means of effecting a transition to it. He wished to see the ignorant taught, the idle employed, and the penniless pensioned, by the public; as indeed they practically are; but more kindly, more educationally. As supplementary to private enterprise, he would have the wreckage and breakage of society taught in government schools and employed in government workshops, under compulsion, if necessary; as a kind of moral hospital for the cure of idleness and vice and pauperism, — a desperate remedy for a desperate evil, but one which, after all, it seems we are adopting, in schemes for home colonization and the rescue of the "submerged tenth."

Here is a true anecdote. When the General of the Salvation Army was working at the scheme which lately met with such an outcry of acceptance, he told the Rev. H. V. Mills, the first promoter of the home-colony plan, that he was entirely ignorant of political economy, and asked for a book on the subject. Mills gave him " Unto this Last."

CHAPTER III.

(1863.)

"In delectu autem narrationum et experimentorum melius hominibus
cavisse nos arbitramur quam qui adhuc in historia naturali versati sunt."
BACON, *Instauratio Magna.*

OUR hermit among the Limestone Alps of
Savoy differed in one respect from his predeces-
sors. They, for the most part, saw nothing in
the rocks and stones around them except the
prison walls of their seclusion; he could not be
within constant sight of the mountains without
watching them and thinking over them, and the
wonders of their scenery and structure. And it
was well for him that it could be so. The terrible depression of mind which his social and
philanthropic work had brought on, found a relief in the renewal of his old mountain-worship.
After sending off the last of his " Fraser " papers,
in which, when the verdict had twice gone against
him, he tried to show cause why sentence should
not be passed, the strain was at its severest. He
felt, as few others not directly interested felt, the
sufferings of the outcast in English slums and
Savoyard hovels; and heard the cry of the op-

pressed in Poland and in Italy: and he had been silenced. What could he do but, as he said in the letters to Mr. Norton, "lay his head to the very ground," and try to forget it all among the stones and the snows?

He wandered about, geologizing, and spent a while at Talloires on the Lake of Annecy, where the old abbey had been turned into an inn, and one slept in a monk's cell and meditated in the cloister of the monastery, St. Bernard of Menthon's memory haunting the place, and St. Germain's cave close by in the rocks above. About the end of May Mr. Ruskin came back to England, and was invited to lecture again at the Royal Institution. The subject he chose was " The Stratified Alps of Savoy."

At that time many distinguished foreign geologists were working at the Alps; but little of conclusive importance had been published, except in papers imbedded in Transactions of various societies. Professor Alphonse Favre's great work did not appear until 1867, and the " Mechanismus der Gebirgsbildung " of Professor Heim not till 1878; so that for an English public the subject was a fresh one. To Mr. Ruskin it was familiar: he had been elected a Fellow of the Geological Society in 1840, at the age of twenty-one; he had worked through Savoy with his Saussure in hand nearly thirty years before, and, many a time since that, had spent the intervals of literary business in rambling and climbing with the hammer and notebook. Indeed, on all his travels, and even on his usual afternoon walks, he was accustomed to keep his eyes open for the geology of any neighborhood he was in; and his servant regularly carried a bag for specimens, which rarely came home empty. The notebooks of the "Modern Painters" period contain infinite memoranda and diagrammatic sketches, of which a very small fraction have been used. In the field he had compared Studer's meagre sections, and consulted the available authorities on physical geology, though he had never entered upon the more popular sister-science of palæontology. He left the determination of strata to specialists: his interest was fixed on the structure of mountains — the relation of geology to scenery; a question upon which he had some right to be heard, as knowing more about scenery than most geologists, and more about geology than most artists. His dissent from orthodox opinions was not the mere blunder of an ill-informed amateur; it was a protest against the adoption of certain views which had become fashionable chiefly owing to the popularity of the men who had propounded them. Parallel with the state religion in England there has been a state science; the prestige of the science bishops has been no doubt as wisely used as that of the church bishops: it has certainly prevailed with their own inferior clergy and laity in much the same way. Mr. Ruskin, who had been the admirer, and to some extent

the personal pupil, of several of the leading geologists of the last generation, questioned the infallibility of the more recent school. Science, of
course, always welcomes investigation up to a certain point, and so, as the " Journal de Genève "
reported, "la foule se pressait dans les salles de
l'Institut royale de Londres, pour entendre la
lecture des fragments d'un ouvrage scientifique,
dont l'auteur compte parmi les écrivains les plus
estimés de l'Angleterre. M. Ruskin s'est fait
connaître depuis longtemps par des publications
remarquables sur l'art en général et la peinture
en particulier, mais il se présentait cette fois à
son auditoire sous un nouveau jour. C'était le
géologue que l'on venait entendre, et l'événement
a prouvé qu'il n'était point inférieur au littérateur
et au critique."

The main object of this lecture was to draw
attention to a series of mountain and valley
forms which he wished to contrast with those
more familiar to English geologists, not only with
regard to their aspect, but still more with regard
to their origin. The great discovery of the extension of glaciers, the work of an ice-age and
the phenomena of denudation, as opposed to the
theories of half a century back, had taught that
mountain forms were, roughly speaking, not *re-
poussé* work on the earth's surface, but chased
and sculptured into it. Saussure and his generation had seemed to think that every hill or group
of hills had been thrust up independently; and

that every valley or fissure had been burst open by a convulsion. A later school had taken the tiny valleys in our clay hills, and the chines in chalk downs, as their type, and referred the modeling of the whole earth's surface to the erosive action of water. In 1863 a third group of investigators was accustomed to explain everything by glacial action. They imagined our Lake district mountains, for example, to be carved by ice out of an enormous dome, two thousand feet higher than Sca-fell; and the Alps themselves to be the remnants of a similar Titanic mound, into which the glaciers had planed the valleys and gouged the lake-basins. A few voices were raised here and there against the theory; but as it was taught by the heads of the Geological Survey, men whose work in other respects was of the highest value and their attainments and characters unimpeachable, the glacial origin of "scenery" was accepted by the public with its usual docility.

In the Alps of Savoy, Mr. Ruskin wished to give an instance of a group of mountains whose forms, unlike those of Britain, could be shown to depend far more upon internal structure and original elevation than upon unassisted erosion, though erosion played its own part. He showed how they could never have been a formless mound; but had been elevated in a consistent series of wave-like ridges; cut across and carved into by erosion, but separated also longitudinally by the actual trenches between the waves. So that the old Saussurian theory, modified by Lyell's doctrine of denudation, might still form the basis of an explanation more true to facts than the glacial theory, which breaks down when it is applied to the combes and vallons, or longitudinal valleys.

He went on to give reasons for his belief that the erosive power of glaciers had been greatly overrated. In defending the "viscous theory" of Professor James Forbes (Principal Forbes), his old acquaintance, he held that a great mass of ice was not a rigid body which slid or was thrust violently over the rock surface, rasping it with imbedded stones, and digging into the valley bottoms to excavate basins. Judging from the curves it takes, as seen in sections, — and it must be remembered that curvature had been his specialty, — he considered it as flowing, like a mass of thick honey; and therefore powerless for erosion, except on a slope, where its normal viscous flow was accelerated by gravitation, or became an actual sliding over rocks already inclined and comparatively smooth. These, and occasional upstanding knolls, it could more or less polish, he allowed; but the universal presence of glacier-scoring and *roches moutonnées* he considered to be evidences of the very limited erosive power of ice, not proofs of its universal and overwhelming agency. The Savoy Alps, therefore, owe their form, first to upheaval, next to aqueous erosion, and last, in a very minor degree, to glacial action.

Though the extension of glaciers is nowadays more firmly believed than ever, and their presence traced in many parts of the world where they were unsuspected before, still it is very generally admitted by the younger school that their erosive power was overstated by the geologists of thirty years ago, and that the origin of lake-basins is a problem which cannot be solved by the application of any single formula. And a more detailed research into the structure of mountains shows that the simple denudation of a chalk hill is not a sufficient analogy for their very complex phenomena. Mr. Ruskin pointed out the importance of metamorphism in the elevation and curvature of these cretaceous strata, anticipating recent studies (on which see further in our eighth chapter); and he suggested that this action was continuous, — certainly not catastrophic, as another art writer turned geologist, the great Viollet le Duc, twelve years later implied in the opening words of his work on Mont Blanc.[1]

As examples of Savoy mountains this lecture described in detail the Salève, on which Mr. Ruskin had been living for two winters, and the Brezon, the top of which he had tried to buy from the commune of Bonneville — one of his many plans for settling among the Alps. The commune thought he had found a gold-mine up there, and

[1] " La croûte terrestre, refroidie *au moment* du plissement qui a formé le massif du Mont Blanc, n'avait pas encore atteint le degré de dureté qu'elle a acquis depuis."

raised the price out of all reason. Other attempts to make a home in the châteaux or chalets of Savoy were foiled, or abandoned, like his earlier idea to live in Venice. But his scrambles on the Salève led him to hesitate in accepting the explanation given by Alphonse Favre of the curious northwest face of steeply inclined vertical slabs, which he suspected to be created by cleavage, on the analogy of other Jurassic precipices. The Brezon — *brisant*, breaking-wave — he took as a type of the billowy form of limestone Alps in general, and his analysis of it was serviceable and substantially correct.

This lecture was followed in 1864 by desultory correspondence with Mr. Jukes and others in the " Reader," in which he merely restated his conclusions, too slightly to convince. Had he devoted himself to a thorough examination of the subject — but this is in the region of what might have been. He was more seriously engaged in other pursuits, of more immediate importance. Three days after his lecture he was being examined before the Royal Academy commission, and after a short summer visit to various friends in the north of England, he set out again for the Alps, partly to study the geology of Chamouni and North Switzerland, partly to continue his drawings of Swiss towns at Baden and Lauffenburg, with his pupil John Bunney. But even there the burden of his real mission could not be shaken off, and though again seeking health and a quiet mind, he could not quite keep silence, but wrote letters to English newspapers on the depreciation of gold (repeating his theory of currency), and on the wrongs of Poland and Italy ; and he put together more papers, never published, in continuation of his " Munera Pulveris."

But this desultory habit, by which Mr. Ruskin's strength was broken up into many channels, — while it prevented his doing any one great work with convincing thoroughness in his later period, — was not by any means an unbalanced misfortune. It is quite impossible for a man who has no feeling for art and no interest in science to regard life as a whole, — especially modern life : and this Mr. Ruskin was better fitted than any of his contemporaries to do.

In the last century, Samuel Johnson, great thinker as he was, found his influence decisively limited by his ignorance of the arts, and his consequent inability to take into his purview a whole range of emotions, activities, and influences which are really important in the sphere of ethics, as motives of action and indices of character. So in this century, Johnson's spiritual successor, Carlyle, from a similar lack of sympathy with art and an indolence in acquiring even the rudiments of physical science, — from a strange want of ear for poetry and eye for nature, — was left short-handed, short-sighted, in many an enterprise. In framing an ideal of life he is narrow, ascetic, rude, as compared with the wider and more refined culture of a Ruskin.

BADEN, SWITZERLAND
By John Ruskin, 1863

Something of this contempt for scientific facts and theories which he had never faced, and easy admission of mysteries he cared not to solve, is traceable in a letter written soon·after the period we have been describing, and in sequel to the Savoy Alps discussion. I print it, with a few others of his, from the originals, as illustrating the intercourse of our British Elijah with his Elisha. Since about 1850, Carlyle had been gradually becoming more and more friendly with Mr. Ruskin; and now that this social and economical work had been taken up, he began to have a real esteem for him, though always with a patronizing tone, which the younger man's open and confessed discipleship accepted and encouraged. This letter especially shows both men in an unaccustomed light: Ruskin, hating tobacco, sends his "master" cigars; Carlyle, hating cant, replies rather in the tone of the temperance advocate, taking a little wine for his stomach's sake : —

CHELSEA, 22 *February*, 1865.

DEAR RUSKIN, — You have sent me a munificent Box of Cigars; for wh^h what can I say in ans^r? It makes me both sad and glad. *Ay de mi.*

> "We are such stuff,
> Gone with a puff —
> Then think, and smoke Tobacco!"

The Wife also has had her Flowers; and a letter wh^h has charmed the female mind. You forgot only the first chapter of "Aglaia;" don't forget; and be a good boy for the future. The Geology Book was n't *Jukes;* I found it again in the

Magazine, — reviewed there : " Phillips,"[1] is there such a name ? It has ag^n escaped me. I have a notion to come out actually some day soon ; and take a serious Lecture from you on what you really know, and can give me some intelligible outline of, ab^t the Rocks, — *bones* of our poor old Mother ; wh^h have always been venerable and strange to me. Next to nothing of rational could I ever learn of the subject. That of a central fire, and molten sea, on wh^h all mountains, continents, and strata are spread floating like so many hides of leather, knocks in vain for admittance into me these forty years : who of mortals can really believe such a thing ! And that, in descending into mines, these geological gent^n find themselves approaching *sensibly* their central fire by the sensible and undeniable *increase of temperature* as they step down, round after round, — has always appeared to argue a *length of ear* on the part of those gent^n, wh^h is the real miracle of the phenomenon. Alas, alas : we are dreadful ignoramuses all of us ! Ans^r nothing ; but don't be surprised if I turn up some day.

Yours ever,

T. CARLYLE.

---

[1] " Jukes," — Mr. J. B. Jukes, F. R. S., with whom Mr. Ruskin had been discussing in the *Reader*. " Phillips," — the Oxford Professor of Geology, and a friend of Mr. Ruskin's.

CHAPTER IV.

IDEALS OF CULTURE.

(1864.)

WIDER aims and weaker health had not put an end to Mr. Ruskin's connection with the Working Men's College, though he did not now teach a drawing-class regularly. He had, as he said, "the satisfaction of knowing that they had very good masters in Messrs. Lowes Dickinson, Jeffrey, and Cave Thomas," and his work was elsewhere. He was to have lectured there on December 19, 1863; but he did not reach home until about Christmas; better than he had been, and ready to give the promised address on January 30, 1864. Beside which he used to visit the place occasionally of an evening to take note of progress, and some of his pupils were now more directly under his care.

This more than ten years' connection with a very practical work of education must not be forgotten when we try to estimate his ideals of culture and social arrangements, which hasty readers are apt to suppose the table-talk of an arm-chair philosopher. So energetic a man, one who spent no time in the ordinary recreations of life, — more the pity, ultimately, for his own usefulness and happiness in later periods, — so busy a mind, found opportunity for many occupations. And he does not deserve to be rated as a dilettante or a visionary, simply because other folk cannot imagine how he managed to do more work than they.

It was from one of these visits to the college, I am told, on February 27th, that he returned, past midnight, and found his father waiting up for him, to read some letters he had written. Next morning the old man, close upon seventy-nine years of age, was struck with his last illness ; and died on the 3d of March. He was buried at Addington Church, near Shirley in Surrey, not far from Croydon; and the legend on his tomb records : " He was an entirely honest merchant, and his memory is to all who keep it dear and helpful. His son, whom he loved to the uttermost, and taught to speak truth, says this of him."

Mr. John James Ruskin, like many other of our successful merchants, had been an open-handed patron of art, and a cheerful giver, not only to needy friends and relatives, but also to various charities. For example, as a kind of personal tribute to Osborne Gordon, his son's tutor, he gave £5000 toward the augmentation of poor Christ-Church livings. His son's open-handed way with dependants and servants was learned

John James Ruskin

from the old merchant, who, unlike many hard-
working money-makers, was always ready to give,
though he could not bear to lose. In spite of
which he left a considerable fortune behind him,
— considerable when it is understood to be the
earnings of his single-handed industry and steady
sagacity in legitimate business, without indul-
gence in speculation. He left £120,000, with various other property, to his son. To his wife he
left his house and £37,000, — and a void which
it seemed at first nothing could fill. For of late
years the son had drifted out of their horizon,
with ideas on religion and the ordering of life so
very different from theirs; and had been much
away from home, — as he would say, selfishly, but
not without the greatest of all excuses, necessity.
And so the two old people had been brought
closer than ever together; and she had lived
entirely for her husband. But, as Mr. Ruskin
quotes from a remark of Browning's about a true
woman, — " Put a stick in anywhere, and she will
run up it," — so the brave old lady did not faint
under the blow, and fade away, but transferred
her affections and interests to her son. Before
his father's death the difference of feeling between them, arising out of the heretical economy,
had been healed. Old Mr. Ruskin's will treated
his son with all confidence in spite of his unor-
thodox views and unbusiness-like ways. And for
nearly eight years longer his mother lived on, to
see him pass through this probation period into

such recognition as an Oxford professorship implied, and to find in her last years his later books "becoming more and more what they always ought to have been to" her.

At the same time, her failing sight and strength needed a constant household companion. Her son, though he did not leave home as yet for any long journeys, could not be always with her. Only six weeks after the funeral he was called away for a time. Before going he brought his pretty young Scotch cousin, Miss Joanna Ruskin Agnew, to Denmark Hill, for a week's visit. She recommended herself at once to the old lady, and to Carlyle, who happened to call, by her frank good-nature and unquenchable spirits; and her visit lasted seven years, until she was married to the son of the Ruskins' old friend, Consul Severn of Rome. Even then she was not allowed far out of their sight, but settled in the old house at Herne Hill: "nor virtually," says Mr. Ruskin in the last chapter of "Præterita," "have she and I ever parted since."

All through that year he remained at home, except for short necessary visits, and frequent evenings with Carlyle. And when, in December, he gave those lectures in Manchester which afterwards, as "Sesame and Lilies," became his most popular work, we can trace his better health of mind and body in the brighter tone of his thought. We can hear the echo of Carlyle's talk in the heroic, aristocratic, Stoic ideals, and the insistence

on the value of books and free public libraries,[1]—
Carlyle being the founder of the London Library.
And we may suspect that his thoughts on women's
influence and education had been not a little
directed by those months in the company of " the
dear old lady and ditto young " to whom Carlyle
used to send his love.

These lectures were the following up of his
economic writing in this sense, — that he had required a certain *moral culture* as the necessary
condition for realizing his plans. It was as if one
should say, " Here is an engine; on these principles it works; but it must be kept clean, oiled,
and polished." He did not demand, — and this is
important to note, — he did not demand a state of
society hopelessly unlike the present, such as the
altruistic guild-brethren of Mr. Morris's Epoch of
Rest, or the clockwork harmony of Mr. Bellamy's
American Utopia. He took human nature as it
is, but at its best; not, as the older economists
did, at its worst. He tried to show how the best
could be brought out, and what the standards
should be towards which education and legislation
should direct immediate public attention. " Sesame and Lilies " puts in popular form his explanation of the phrase "certain conditions of
moral culture," in " Munera Pulveris."

[1] The first lecture, " Of Kings' Treasuries," was given December 6, 1864, at Rusholme Town Hall, Manchester, in aid of a
library fund for the Rusholme Institute. The second, " Of Queens'
Gardens," was given December 14th, at the Town Hall, King
Street, now the Free Reference Library, Manchester, in aid of
schools for Ancoats.

His father's charity had made him life governor of various institutions and schools; and the yearly budget of petitions from forlorn gentility begging for its children to be educated, at other people's cost, into *getting on*, had struck him as a sign of the times. His teaching at the Working Men's College had not been given that the men might *get on*, — that one should scramble on the shoulders of others and make them carry him, and envy him, and applaud him. Mr. Ruskin's views of literary education were not that it was a means of success in the world, and getting into good society; but that it was in itself the best society into which one could get.   The real use of books is that they afford actual intercourse with great men, and afford it freely to those whose minds are sensitive to accurate thinking, whose feelings are capable of sympathy with fine natures.

Again, the use of book-learning is not information for the sake of satisfying curiosity, nor yet because " knowledge is power," even in the higher sense that it gives the means of material and mechanical advantages. Mr. Ruskin does not wish people to be educated either for the sake of outwitting their neighbors, or for the sake of inventing labor-saving appliances. His view was that of the Greek thinkers who aimed at making their pupils " philosophers; " or of those moderns who preached " plain living and high thinking."

In the lecture on " Kings' Treasuries " he illustrated the kind of study he desired to see : the intelligent analysis of words and thoughts and feel-ings of great authors, as opposed to perfunctory reading or superficial information-gathering. By such habits the student becomes a scholar; he ac-customs himself to think as well as to remember; he takes a higher tone of mind, one that is ele-vated above rash opinion and petty self-interest; a broad view of life, in which its tangled plan is more or less unrolled, and its lights and shades fall into their due keeping. On such a view is based justice; for moral judgments are based on intellectual. The scholar who converses with the great minds of all ages, though he may be poor and unfashionable in the world's eyes, looks at life otherwise than as a nation of shopkeepers looks at it. And so, while modern society has no real appreciation of literature, science, art, nature, and the problem of human intercourse, he alone is fully civilized man: the rest are incomplete de-velopments, comparatively barbarians.

The object of a wise economy is to elevate the whole race; to cultivate the *pianta umana;* to breed the human animal. Production is its pur-pose, — not only of the means of life, but of the life to which food and clothing, necessaries and luxuries, art and literature, and all the rest, are subservient. Ruskin would like to see, for ex-ample, an order of chivalry for both sexes, — to bring definitely before the public, as he showed later on, in " Time and Tide," the necessity of this *homiculture*, if we may coin a word for the antithesis of the — virtual — homicide by which the ends of life are defeated in the mistaken social economics of the vulgar struggle for it.

Given mankind as it is, real equality is impossible. There must be some who are less capable of higher culture, as the race is constituted; not only some who are less fitted to become scholars, but many who are in every respect inferior developments, lower organisms. There must, he thinks, be leaders, and natural "kings and queens" of the world they live in. They have no right to pride in their higher gifts, but the superiority cannot be denied, and need not be decried. He would not have political and social power *given* to them; he is not in that sense a Tory: but he says that they *have* the power, as it is; and he calls on them to use it, with full sense of their responsibility.

For example, in his second lecture, on "Queens' Gardens," he discusses the position of women. They do not need to assert the rights, or claim the education of men. They have their rights, as it is, if they use them. They do, as a matter of fact, teach and guide, he declares, — counsel and command, the actors in practical affairs. And the education they need should indeed be in the same subjects as those studied by young men, but in a different spirit; still less than men seeking for mere information, and still more exercising their judgment, especially in matters of the deepest seriousness, as in religion and morality; not hoping to create in art, or discover in science, but to set the standards of taste and the limits of ambition; to determine the direction and to award the prize of men's endeavors. And, most of all, they should be brought to a full sense of their duties to their neighbors: so that they might not live for themselves and their narrow immediate circle in a round of worldly amusements and religious observances; but be the helpers and heroines of the state in which they live.

" Sesame and Lilies " has become the author's most popular book. In various forms it has run through fourteen English editions, and of all his works it is the most widely read in America and abroad. It would be idle to give testimonies of this and that reader to the stimulus toward a higher life which these lectures have afforded; but two things we may notice.

In the first place, they are a real and all-round advance upon the panacea-systems of Utopian theorists. They strike at the root of the evil. They give no recipe for millennial perfection; no ascetic rule of conduct. But they aim at a balanced and healthy progress, to which each in his sphere can contribute by the simple recognition of his duty, and the reasonable service of whatever divine or human authority he may honestly and thoughtfully accept.

In the next place, they are within reach. They ask no centuries of previous development, nor return to a state of nature. For that reason they do not appeal to the Romantic spirit, of which, by inadequate criticism, Mr. Ruskin is supposed to be the exponent. They are essentially modern in their readiness to take advantage of modern opportunities. They acknowledge evolution toward a higher humanity in accordance with the severest anthropology: —

> "Titanic forces taking birth
>   In divers seasons, divers climes;
> For we are Ancients of the Earth
>   And in the morning of the times."

CHAPTER V.

LESSONS IN EDUCATION.

(1865.)

" Si cette enfant m'était confiée je ferais d'elle, non pas une savante, car je lui veux du bien, mais une enfant brillante d'intelligence et de vie et en laquelle toutes les belles choses de la nature et d'art se refléterait avec un doux éclat. Je la ferais vivre en sympathie avec les beaux paysages, avec les scènes idéales de la poésie et de l'histoire, avec la musique noblement émue. Je lui rendrais aimable tout ce que je voudrais lui faire aimer." — ANATOLE FRANCE, *Le Crime de Sylvestre Bonnard.*

IMPROVED health and quiet life at home made these years prolific of literary work; and the political economy found its relief, and at the same time its sequel, in a study of education. This question was now chiefly before Mr. Ruskin, both as bearing on his ideals of culture, and consequent public standards of life and conduct, and as pressed upon him, we may believe, by the presence of a young lady whose studies he was in some measure called upon to direct. And so it happens that some of the most thoughtful work of his central period was given to illustrate methods of teaching, in harmony with the broad views of life which his most emphatic writings had been endeavoring to expound.

In 1864 a new series of papers on art was begun, the only important work upon art of all these ten years, and this, definitely connected with the question of education. These papers ran in the " Art Journal " from January to July, 1865, and from January to April, 1866, under the title of " The Cestus of Aglaia," by which was meant the Girdle, or restraining law, of Beauty, as personified in the wife of Hephæstus, " the Lord of Labor." Their intention was to suggest, and to evoke by correspondence, " some laws for present practice of art in our schools, which may be admitted, if not with absolute, at least with a sufficient consent, by leading artists." As a first step the author asked for the elementary rules of drawing. For his own contribution he showed the value of the " pure line," such as he had used in his own early drawings, learned originally from Cruikshank etchings and Prout lithographs, and practiced—with what success can be judged from such drawings as the Rouen reproduced in the " Poems." Later on, he had adopted a looser and more picturesque style of handling the point; and in the " Elements of Drawing " he had taught his readers to take Rembrandt's etchings as exemplary. But now he felt that this "evasive " manner, as he called it, had its dangers. It had, in fact, originated the ordinary type of popular free draughtsmanship, degenerating sometimes into that black blotting and scribbling with which Mr. Ruskin's ideals of delicacy, purity, dignity, to say nothing of the actual fineness of organic form, have nothing in common. And so these papers attempted to supersede the amateurish object lessons of the earlier work by stricter rules for a severer style; prematurely, as it proved, for the chapters came to an end before the promised code was formulated; though they contained interesting — if rather free — criticism of current art, and many passages of lively wit and pretty description. The same work was taken up again in " The Laws of Fésole; " but the use of the pure line, which Mr. Ruskin's precepts failed to enforce, was, in the end, taught to the public by the charming practice of Mr. Walter Crane and Miss Greenaway.

A lecture at the Camberwell Working Men's Institute on " Work and Play " was given on January 24, 1865; which, as it was printed in " The Crown of Wild Olive," we will notice further on. Various letters and papers on political and social economy and other subjects hardly call for separate notice: with the exception of one very important address to the Royal Institution of British Architects, given April 15th, " On the Study of Architecture in our Schools."

In appearing before a body of men whom, as an undergraduate, he had audaciously criticised, and with whom he had been more or less at war ever since, Mr. Ruskin was, as it were, in the enemy's camp. But while apologizing for the liberties which he had taken with their works and aims, he stood up for his principles. He had called for Naturalism as against the blind following of Renaissance-Classic tradition; but he tried to show that his advocacy of Naturalism did not extend to "the mere cast of a flower, or the realization of a vulgar face, carved without pleasure, by a workman who is only endeavoring to attract attention by novelty, and then fastened on, or appearing to be fastened, as chance may dictate, to an arch, or a pillar, or a wall." In short, the artistic treatment of natural form was his requirement. He admitted that much good work had been done in England and France; but he felt that modern city life was adverse to a great school of architecture; modern culture, sated and jaded, did not know its own wants, and had no real hearty aims,—in the Carlylean sense, no religion. What was wanted in the teaching of young architects was far beyond any technical system; it was the rediscovery of sincerity, a higher tone in the whole conduct of life. And secondarily, they needed a much wider general culture, both artistic and literary, but more select standards of style. He would exclude the mass of mediæval and modern and oriental examples from the school museum, and concentrate the mind of the student wholly upon the study of natural form, and upon its treatment by the Greeks between 500 and 350 B. C., with the best Florentine work and a few carefully chosen examples of thirteenth-century Gothic.[1]

---

[1] I am told on good authority that casts from real leaves and other natural forms were unknown in drawing schools until Mr.

Advice of this sort does not commend itself to the " practical " man, who looks on education as the means to turning out craftsmen able to supply a given public demand.   That, however, was not Mr. Ruskin's meaning of the word. He could not give recipes for the reconstruction of society ; but he could point to the need of it; and, after all, a good diagnosis is the first step to a cure.   And yet he was not idle in attempting to find some remedy. He had been making experiments in artistic education for many years at the Working Men's College; and now, from time to time, he was trying experiments in general education of another sort, much more pleasant, though no less practical.

About the end of October, 1859, I believe, he had been introduced by the Bishop of Oxford to a Miss Bell, who, with her partner Miss Bradford, kept a girls' school at Winnington Hall, near Northwich in Cheshire. It was not an ordinary school — still less a *pensionnat de demoiselles* of the type described in " Le Crime de Sylvestre Bonnard," [1] in which the pettiness and tyranny of

Ruskin used them at the Working Men's College as models to draw from.   They were introduced into the Government School of Design after an inspection of the Great Ormond Street classes by the Marlborough House head-master.

[1] The quotation at the head of that chapter is one marked with approval by Mr. Ruskin, who was greatly interested in the book on its appearance, not only for its literary charm and tender characterization, but "as finding there some image of himself" in the old Membre de l'Institut with his " bon dos rond " and his passion for missals, and Gothic architecture, and Benedictine monks, and

the worst kind of schoolmistress of — let us hope
— a bygone age are pilloried. The principles of
Winnington were advanced; the theology —
Bishop Colenso's daughter was among the pupils.
Friends and patrons whose names were thought
to be an undeniable guarantee gave the place a
high character. And the managers were pleased
to invite the celebrated art-critic to visit whenever
he traveled that way, whether to lecture at provincial towns, or to see his friends in the north, as
he often used. And so between November, 1859,
and May, 1868, after which the school was removed, he was a frequent visitor; and not only
he, but other lions whom the ladies entrapped, —
mention has been made in print (in " The Queen
of the Air ") of Charles Hallé, whom Mr. Ruskin
met there in 1863, and greatly admired.

Mr. Ruskin could not be idle on his visits; and
as he is never so happy as when he is teaching
somebody, he improved the opportunity by experiments in a system of education "tout intime et
parfaitement incompatible avec l'organisation des
pensionnats les mieux tenus," and yet permitted
there for his sake. Among other things, he devised singing dances for a select dozen of the
girls, with verses of his own writing, " noblement
émues ; " one, a maze to the theme of " Twist ye,
twine ye," based upon the song in " Guy Manner-

natural scenery; and his defiance of the Code Napoléon and the
ways of the modern world; with many another touch for which one
could have sworn he had sat to the painter.

ing," but going far beyond the original motive in its variations weighted with allegoric thought : —

> " Earnest Gladness, idle Fretting,
> Foolish Memory, wise Forgetting ;
> *And trusted reeds, that broken lie,*
> *Wreathed again for melody. . . .*
>
> " *Vanished Truth, but Vision staying;*
> Fairy riches, lost in weighing ;
> And fitful grasp of flying Fate,
> *Touched too lightly, traced too late.*"

Deep as the feeling of this little poem is, there is a nobler chord struck in the Song of Peace, the battle-cry of the good time coming ; in the faith — who else has found it ? — that looks forward to no selfish victory of narrow aims, but to the full reconciliation of hostile interests and the blind internecine struggle of this perverse world, in the clearer light of the millennial morning. " Thine arrows are sharp in the *hearts* of the King's enemies, whereby the people fall *under thee.*" " Yea, in all these things we are *more than conquerors,* through Him that loved us."

> " Put off, put off your mail, ye kings, and beat your brands to dust ;
> A surer grasp your hands must know, your hearts a better trust :
> Nay, bend aback the lance's point, and break the helmet bar, —
> A noise is on the morning winds, but not the noise of war !
>
> " Among the grassy mountain-paths the glittering troops increase :
> They come ! they come ! — how fair their feet — they come that
>   publish peace ;
> Yea, Victory ! *fair Victory ! our enemies' and ours,*
> And all the clouds are clasped in light, and all the earth with
>   flowers.

"Ah! still depressed and dim with dew, but yet a little while
And radiant with the deathless Rose the wilderness shall smile,
And every tender living thing shall feed by streams of rest,
Nor lamb shall from the fold be lost, nor nursling from the nest."

These dances were not mere play. They were taught as lessons, and practiced as recreation. "On n'apprend pas en s'amusant," says the villain of the story to M. Bonnard. "On n'apprend qu'en s'amusant," he replies, — vigorously underlined and side-lined by Mr. Ruskin. "Pour digérer le savoir, il faut l'avoir avalé avec appétit." The art of teaching is to stimulate that appetite in a natural and healthy way. "On n'est pas sur la terre pour s'amuser et pour faire ses quatre cents volontés," says the objector, again ; to which he answers: "On est sur la terre pour se plaire dans le beau et dans le bien, et pour faire ses quatre cents volontés quand elles sont nobles, spirituelles et généreuses. Une éducation qui n'exerce pas les volontés est une éducation qui déprave les âmes. Il faut" — here the pencilmarks are very thick — "il faut que l'instituteur enseigne à vouloir."

"Je crus voir," continues M. Bonnard, "que maître Mouche m'estimait un pauvre homme ;" and I observe that Mr. Ruskin's method of teaching, as illustrated in "Ethics of the Dust," has been variously pooh-poohed by his critics. It has seemed to some absurd to mix up theology, and crystallography, and political economy, and mythology, and moral philosophy, with the chatter of school-girls and the romps of the playground. But it should be understood, before reading this book, which is practically the report of these Winnington talks, that it is printed as an illustration of a method. The method is the kindergarten method carried a step, many steps, further. With very small children it is comparatively easy to teach as a mother teaches; but with children of larger growth it is not the first-comer who can replace the wise father, whose conversation and direction and example would form an ideal education. Still, an experiment like this was worth making. It showed that play-lessons need not want either depth or accuracy; and that the requirement was simply capacity on the part of the teacher.

The following letter from Carlyle was written in acknowledgment, I suppose, of an early copy of the book, of which the preface is dated Christmas, 1865: —

CHELSEA, 20 *December*, 1865.

DEAR RUSKIN, — Don't mind the *Bewick*;[1] the indefatigable Dixon has sent me, yesterday, the Bewick's "Life" as well (hunted it up from the "Misses Bewick" or somebody, and threatens to involve me in still farther bother about nothing) — and I read the greater part of it last night before going to bed. Peace to Bewick: not a great man at all; but a very true of his sort, a well completed, and a very *enviable*, — living there in communion with the skies and woods and brooks, not here in do with the London Fogs, the roaring witchmongeries and railway yellings and howlings.

[1] Bewick was being studied by Mr. Ruskin in connection with the problem of the pure line, for *The Cestus of Aglaia.*

The " Ethics of the Dust," wh^h I devoured with^t pause, and intend to look at ag^n, is a most shining Performance!   Not for a long while have I read anything tenth-part so radiant with talent, ingenuity, lambent fire (sheet — and *other* lightnings) of all commendable kinds!   Never was such a lecture on *Crystallography* before, had there been nothing else in it, — and there are all manner of things.   In power of *expression* I pronounce it to be supreme ; never did anybody who had *such* things to explain explain them better.   And the bit of Egypt^n mythology, the cunning *Dreams* ab^t Pthah, Neith, &c, apart from their elucidative quality, wh^h is exquisite, have in them a *poetry* that might fill any Tennyson with despair.   You are very dramatic too ; nothing wanting in the stage-direct^{ns}, in the pretty little indicat^{ns} : a very pretty stage and *dramatis personæ* altogeth^r.   Such is my first feeling ab^t y^r Book, dear R. — Come soon, and I will tell you all the *faults* of it, if I gradually discover a great many.   In fact, *come* at any rate !

Y^{rs} ever,   T. CARLYLE.

The Real Little Housewives, to whom the book was dedicated, were not quite delighted — at least, they said they were not — at the portraits drawn of them, in their pinafores, so to speak, with some little hints at failings and faults which they recognized through the mask of *dramatis personæ.* Miss " Kathleen " disclaimed the singing of " Vilikins and his Dinah," and so on.   It is difficult to please everybody.   The public did not care about the book ; the publisher hoped Mr. Ruskin would write no more dialogues : and so it remained, little noticed, for twelve years.   In 1877 it was republished and found to be interesting, and in the next twelve years 8000 copies were called for.

The break-up of Winnington was not the end

of Mr. Ruskin's educational experiments. He has described in " Præterita " how he played the part of drawing-master to a pair of little girls, during this period; and no doubt some day we shall have the reminiscences of many another pupil on whom he has spent his time and affectionate advice, for the love of the work. Not only at Winnington, but at very many schools and colleges for girls and for boys, he has placed the most valuable collections of minerals, the most carefully chosen series of prints and pictures, in the hope of making it easy for others to carry out his plans: which are, after all, only what Rousseau had formed, long before, and a long series of educational theorists and experimenters have attempted, in their different ways. But Mr. Ruskin's system, if it can be called a system, reaches farther, attempts more ; is closely bound up with a general scheme of life and politics, — Platonic in its breadth of view. His work in this kind was the suggesting and exemplifying a course of action for others to follow out. He could not very well undertake to devote himself to school-teaching. The advantage of his method would never be thoroughly brought out unless continued and confidential relations were set up between the teacher and the taught. And while, for a bright and intelligent mind, it is a liberal education in itself just to live in his company, not even Mr. Ruskin can make a silk purse out of a sow's ear.

But none of the advanced educationists of the

present day will doubt, if I read aright the tendency of the last twenty years, that his view of the function of the teacher is sound in the main points. To break down the wall between the schoolroom and the playground; to widen the range of subjects, and at the same time to replace a superficial breadth by accurate dealing with concrete facts; to consider each study in its relation to the whole aim and purpose of life; to set good literature and worthy art, healthy nature and sincere thought, before the pupil from the very beginning, — this is what he has taught as the first step to that "certain moral culture," the higher development of the human race, through which — and by no panaceas of statesmanship or party victories — the "time of wrath" may one day be past, "and the Wolf be dead in Arcady, and the Dragon in the Sea."

CHAPTER VI.

PUBLIC MORALITY.

(1865–1866.)

HERRICK.

MENTION has been made of an address to working men at the Camberwell Institute, January 24, 1865. This lecture was published in 1866, together with two others,[1] under the title of " The Crown of Wild Olive,"—that is to say, the reward of human work, a reward "which should have been of gold, had not Jupiter been so poor," as Aristophanes said.

What work is thus rewarded? the speaker asked. What reward is to be hoped for? And how does it influence, how ought it to influence, the aims and the conduct of the various classes of men who make up the active world, the three great distinct castes of laborers, traders, and soldiers? In fact, these three lectures, on Work, Traffic, and War, — one before a suburban institute, one at a great manufacturing centre, and one

---

[1] Republished in 1873, with a fourth lecture added, and a Preface and notes on the political growth of Prussia, from Carlyle's *Frederick*.

addressed to the young soldiers of Woolwich, — sketch out Mr. Ruskin's political ethics in sequel to his economy and educational ideals.

In the loose way we have of saying "one man's play is another man's work," and other phrases of the sort, we often forget the real distinction between work and play, which ought to fix the first principles of our conduct in life. Unless we know, to begin with, whether we are working or playing, whether a given action is a necessary step in our progress towards a determined end, we cannot form a clear notion of our duties. And Mr. Ruskin pointed out that, in many cases, occupations and aims that were really play were put forward as work, and took an importance in the public mind and code of morality far beyond the importance given to the real work by which human life is made possible. For example, the whole scheme of orthodox political economy — was it the laws of work? or only rules of a game? Mr. Ruskin had labored to prove that it was not a true analysis of the real process of human provision for all human needs; that is to say, it was not a scientific account of work; and now, approaching the subject from the other side, he showed that the great occupation of money-making, which was the end and aim of British political economy, was, after all, only play on a large scale. Not only was the so-called science not a science, but the so-called work was not work.

True work, he said, meant the production (taking the word "production" in a broad sense) of the means of life; not the using of them as mere counters for gambling. So that a great part of commerce, as it is generally practiced, is not work, and deserves no consideration, still less justification, by political science. On the other hand, if true work were properly understood and its laws made plain, it would appear that every one·ought to take some share in it, according to his powers: some working with the head, some with the hands; but all acknowledging idleness and slavery to be alike immoral. And as to the remuneration, he said, as he had said before in "Unto this Last," justice demands that equal energy expended should bring equal reward. He did not consider it justice to cry out for the equalization of incomes,[1] for some are sure to be more diligent and saving than others; some work involves a great preliminary expenditure of energy in qualifying the worker, as contrasted with unskilled labor. But he did not allow that the possession of capital entitled a man to unearned increment; and he thought that, in a community where a truly civilized morality was highly developed, the general sense of society would recognize an average standard of work and an average standard of pay for each class. Where all took their share, many hands would make light work. Where all re-

---

[1] Though in *Time and Tide*, Letter II., he approved the idea of a maximum limit to incomes.

ceived their fair reward, although absolute equality would be impossible, great inequality could not prevail, and the struggle for life would be minimized.

Such was his first suggestion for an organization of labor, extremely ridiculous twenty-five years ago; not quite so ridiculous now.[1] Though it demands a higher state of public morality than we can attain in a moment, it does not demand, like many other schemes and Utopias, a totally different human nature; nor on the other hand does it propose to bring the kingdom of heaven to our doors by act of Parliament. It leaves untouched most rights of property, and all those sentiments which the tradition of ages has taught us to be inseparable from humanity; while it recognizes and only calls for the higher development of the better feelings of mankind, in opposition to a system which seemed to deny them, and cynically to proclaim, " Evil, be thou my good."

In the next two lectures he spoke of the two great forms of play, the great games of money-making and war. He had been invited to lecture at Bradford, in the hope that he would give some useful advice towards the design of a new

---

[1] It will be worth the reader's while to compare these views of Mr. Ruskin's with those of the clearer-headed of the modern socialists, such as Dr. Albert Schäffle, former Minister of Finance in Austria, of whose *Quintessence of Socialism* (Eng. tr., Sonnenschein, 1891) M. de Laveleye said it was the only publication he knew that explained the scheme of collectivism and treated it in a scientific way.

exchange which was to be built; in curious for-getfulness, it would appear, of his work during the past ten years and more. It might have been expected, after all he had written, that he would have remarks to make on the architecture of an " exchange," of all places, which an unprepared audience would hardly welcome; and indeed the picture he drew them of an ideal " Temple to the Goddess of Getting-on " was as daring a sermon as ever prophet preached. But when he came to tell them that the employers of labor might be true captains and kings, the leaders and the helpers of their fellow-men, and that the function of commerce was not to prey upon society but to provide for it, there were many of his hearers whose hearts told them that he was right, and whose lives have shown, in some measure, that he did not speak in vain.

Still stranger, to hearers who had not noted the conclusion of his third volume of " Modern Painters," was his view of war, in the address to the Royal Military Academy at Woolwich, in December, 1865. The common view of war as destroyer of arts and enemy of morality, the easy acceptance of the doctrine that peace is an un-qualified blessing, the obvious evils of battle and rapine and the waste of resources and life through-out so many ages, have blinded less clear-sighted and less widely-experienced thinkers to another side of the teaching of history, which Mr. Ruskin dwelt upon with unexpected emphasis. He showed that in Greece and Rome and in the Middle Ages, war had brought out the highest human faculties, and in doing so had stimulated the arts. This was not the case, he said, in civil wars, such as that waging in America; though perhaps we may now see that even there the great war did eventually develop national virtues and powers hardly known before. But he showed that, as Bacon said, "No Body can be healthful without *Exercise*, neither Naturall Body, nor Politique: and certainly, to a Kingdom or Estate, a Iust and Honourable Warre, is the true *Exercise*." As little John Ruskin had written in 1828, "'T is vice, not war, that is the curse of man;" but the aim of public morality was to limit war to "just and honorable" occasions, and to confine it to those on either side who had a direct interest in it, and could wage it in a just and honorable manner.

It is curious that Ruskin the Goth, who had begun by attacking the "Greek" tradition in art, should now be of all men the most complete exponent of the Greek spirit in policy. They had permitted only their freemen, their gentlemen, to fight; their public morality called a slave a slave, but did not expect him, or allow him, to share in the terrible, fascinating game. And Mr. Ruskin showed how that policy was rewarded. But modern war, horrible, not from its scale, but from the spirit in which the upper classes set the lower to fight like gladiators in the arena, he denounced; and called upon the women of England, with whom, he said, the real power of life and death lay, to mend it into some semblance of antique chivalry, or to end it in the name of religion and humanity.

These lectures, though in the main drift of them consistent with the logical development of Mr. Ruskin's "message," were written with too evident warmth of feeling. A slip or two in names and statements, a passage or two in which the cohesion of thought is not easily apparent, ought not, however, to deter a thoughtful reader from examining for himself the grounds, and weighing the conclusions, of Ruskin's political ethics.

In the "New Review" for March, 1892, there appeared a series of "Letters of John Ruskin to his Secretary," which, as the anonymous contributor remarked, illustrate "Ruskin the worker, as he acts away from the eyes of the world; Ruskin the epistolographer, when the eventuality of the printing-press is not for the moment before him; Ruskin the good Samaritan, ever gentle and open-handed when true need and a good cause make appeal to his tender heart; Ruskin the employer, considerate, generous, — an ideal master." As a vignette portrait of Mr. Ruskin in one phase of his private life, the letters are very interesting; though it would have been wiser to have suppressed names and even initials which unpleasantly refer to innocent persons still living, or else to have given a fuller explanation of the circumstances of the correspondence.

Charles Augustus Howell became known to Mr. Ruskin (in 1864 or 1865) through the circle of the Pre-Raphaelites; and, as the editor of the letters mildly puts it, "by his talents and assiduity" became the too-trusted friend and protégé of Mr. Ruskin, Mr. Gabriel Rossetti, and others of their acquaintance. It was he who proposed and carried out the exhumation, reluctantly consented to, of Rossetti's manuscript poems from his wife's grave, in October, 1869; for which curious service to literature let him have the thanks of posterity. But he was hardly the man to carry out Mr. Ruskin's secret charities, and long before he had lost Rossetti's confidence he had ceased to act as Mr. Ruskin's secretary. I should be glad enough to keep to the rule *de mortuo nil nisi bonum* if it were not more important to be just to the living than polite to the dead, and these letters in the "New Review" raise a point. Under the name of B—— a libellous allusion seems to be made to a young gentleman of considerable talent; though perhaps he had mistaken his vocation in studying art, and he had certainly shown a want of worldly wisdom in marrying contrary to the wishes of his family. Howell proposed to get him assistance from Mr. Ruskin, which, as Sam Weller said of Messrs. Dodson & Fogg, was "werry kind" of him. Mr. Ruskin, in September, 1866, was not only more than usually out of health,— on November 3d he writes to Howell, "You can't at all think what complicated and acute worry I 've been living in the last two months. I 'm getting a little less complex now, only steady headache instead of thorn fillet." But he was besieged with calls upon his purse; and wrote at last: " Tell B—— it 's absolutely of no use his trying to see me (I don't even see my best friends at present, as you know), and nothing is of the least influence with *me* but plain facts plainly told and right conduct." To which the editor adds: " How many impostors who may read this last letter will smile at the declaration which concludes it? For Mr. Ruskin's judgment has notoriously been victimized many a time and oft at the expense of his heart — and pocket." Quite true; but it should be more explicitly stated that the impostor in this case was not Mr. B——, who was, equally with Mr. Ruskin and many other men of note, the victim of the "talents and assiduity " of the private secretary.

Pleasanter revelations are the anecdotes about the canary which was anonymously bought at the Crystal Palace Bird Show (February, 1866) for the owner's benefit — and bestowed by Mr. Howell on his cousin; about the shopboy whom Mr. Ruskin was going to train as an artist; and about the kindly proposal to employ the aged and impoverished Cruikshank upon a new book of fairy tales, and the struggle between admiration for the man and admission of his loss of power, ending in the free gift of the hundred pounds promised.

In April, 1866, after writing the Preface to "The Crown of Wild Olive," and preparing the book for publication, Mr. Ruskin was carried off to the Continent for a holiday with Sir Walter and Lady Trevelyan, her niece Miss Constance Hilliard (Mrs. Churchill), and Miss Agnew (Mrs. Severn), for a thorough rest and change after three years of unintermitting work in England. They intended to spend a couple of months in Italy. On the day of starting, Mr. Ruskin called at Cheyne Walk with the usual bouquet for Mrs. Carlyle, to learn that she had just met with her death, in trying to save her little dog, the gift of Lady Trevelyan. He rejoined his friends, and they crossed the Channel gayly, in spite of what they thought was a little cloud over him. At Paris they read the news. "Yes," he said, "I knew. But there was no reason why I should spoil your pleasure by telling you."

After the proper interval he wrote to Carlyle. The letter of condolence brought the following reply, addressed " Poste Restante, Milan : " —

CHELSEA, LONDON, 10 May, 1866.

DEAR RUSKIN, — Y[r] kind words from Dijon were welcome to me : thanks. I did not doubt y[r] sympathy in what has come ; but it is better that I see it laid before me. You are y[r]self very unhappy, as I too well discern ; heavy-laden, obstructed and dispirited ; but you have a great work still ahead ; and will gradually have to gird y[r]self up ag[st] the *heat of the day*, wh[h] is coming on for you, — as the night too is coming. Think valiantly of these things.

After giving way to his grief, — "my life all laid in ruins, and the one light of it as if gone out," — he continues : "Come and see me when you get home; come oftener and see me, and speak *more* frankly to me (for I am very true to y^r highest interests and you) while I still remain here. You can do nothing for me in Italy; except come home improved," — in health and spirits ; and so on.

But before this letter reached Mr. Ruskin, he too had been in the presence of death, and had lost one of his most valued friends. Their journey to Italy had been stopped by the illness of Lady Trevelyan at Neuchatel. In a few days it was all over ; and Mr. Ruskin, much more sensitive to such a loss than he permits himself to own, or wishes others to suspect, — take this for the statement of one who has watched him in bereavement, — "lifted up his eyes to the hills," as he always did for help in trouble ; and tried to fix his mind, as a relief and a resource, upon his old puzzle of Alpine geology. Howell was not the man for him to open his heart to in such an event. In a week he could write, with the stoicism he affects when he least feels it : " I 've had a rather bad time of it at Neuchatel, what with death and the north wind ; both devil's inventions as far as I can make out. But things are looking a little better now, and I had a lovely three hours' walk by the lake shore, in cloudless calm, from five to eight this morning, under hawthorn and chestnut, —

here just in full blossom, — and among other pleasantnesses too good for mortals, as the north wind and the rest of it are too bad. We don't deserve either such blessing or cursing, it seems to poor moth me."

From Thun he went to Interlaken and the Giessbach, with his remaining friends; and he occupied himself closely in tracing Studer's sections across the great lake-furrow of central Switzerland, — "something craggy for his mind to break upon," as Byron said when he was in trouble. At the Giessbach there was not only geology and divine scenery, enjoyable in lovely weather, but an interesting figure in the foreground, the widowed daughter of the hotel landlord, beautiful and consumptive, but brave as a Swiss girl should be. They all seem to have fallen in love with her, so to speak, the young English girls as much as the impressionable art critic; and the new human interest in her Alpine tragedy relieved, as such interests do, the painfulness of the circumstances through which they had been passing. Her sister Marie was like an Allegra to this Penserosa; bright and brilliant in native genius. She played piano-duets with the young ladies; taught Alpine botany to the savants, — for Sir Walter, too, was a man of science; guided them to the secret dells and unknown points of view; and with a sympathy unexpected in a stranger, beguiled them out of their grief, and won their admiration and gratitude. Marie of the Giessbach was often referred to in letters of the time, and for many years after, with warmly affectionate remembrances.

In June, 1866, the professorship of poetry at Oxford was vacant; and Mr. Ruskin's friends were anxious to see him take the post. He, however, felt no especial fitness or inclination for it, and the proposal fell through. Three years later he was elected to a professorship that at this time had not been founded. "Tout vient à qui sait attendre."

After spending June in the Oberland, he went homewards through Berne, Vevey, and Geneva, to find his private secretary with a bundle of begging letters, and his friend Carlyle busy with the defense of Governor Eyre.

In 1865 an insurrection of negroes at Morant Bay, Jamaica, had threatened to take the most serious shape, when it was stamped out by the high-handed measures of Mr. Eyre. After the first congratulations were over another side to the question called for a hearing. The Baptist missionaries declared that among the negroes who were shot and hanged *in terrorem* were peaceable subjects, respectable members of their own native congregations, for whose character they could vouch; and they added — if I remember aright stories in which I had certain personal interest at the time — that the gravity of the situation had been exaggerated by private enmity and jealousy of their work and creed. And sympathizers at home pointed out that the executions were not

even "judicial" murders, since Mr. Eyre was not
governor of Jamaica, and really had no right to
take extreme measures.   A strong committee was
formed under Liberal auspices, supported by such
men as John Stuart Mill and Thomas Hughes,
the author of "Tom Brown's Schooldays," —
men whose motive was above suspicion, — to bring
Mr. Eyre to account.

Carlyle, who admired the strong hand, and had
no interest in Baptist missionaries, accepted Mr.
Eyre as the saviour of society in his West Indian
sphere; and there were many, both in Jamaica
and at home, who believed that, but for his prompt
action, the white population would have been
massacred with all the horrors of a savage rebellion.   Mr. Ruskin had been for many years the
ally of the Broad Church and Liberal party; he
had supported the candidature of Mr. Mill and
Mr. Hughes in Westminster and Lambeth.   But
he was now coming more and more under the personal influence of Carlyle; and, when it came to
the point of choosing sides, declared himself, in a
letter to the "Daily Telegraph" (December 20,
1865) a Conservative and a supporter of order;
and joined the Eyre Defense Committee with a
subscription of £100.   The prominent part he
took, for example, in the meeting of September,
1866, was no doubt forced upon him by his desire
to save Carlyle, whose recent loss and shaken
nerves made such business especially trying to
him.   Letters of this period remain, in which Car-

lyle begs Ruskin to "be diligent, I bid you!"—
and so on, adding, " I must absolutely *shut up* in
that direction, to save my sanity." And so it fell
to the younger man to work through piles of
pamphlets and newspaper correspondence, to interview politicians and men of business, and —
what was so very foreign to his habits — to take a
leading share in a party agitation.

But in all this he was true to his Jacobite instincts. He had been brought up a Tory; and
though he had drifted into an alliance with the
Broad Church and philosophical Liberals, he was
never one of them. Now that his father was gone,
perhaps he felt a sort of duty to own himself his
father's son; and the failure of liberal philanthropy to realize his ideals, and of liberal philosophy to rise to his economic standards, combined with Carlyle to induce him to label himself
Conservative. But his conservatism could not be
accepted by the party so called. Fortunately, he
did not need or ask their recognition. He took
no real interest in party politics, and has never in
his life voted at a Parliamentary election. He
only meant to state in the shortest terms that he
stood for loyalty and order.

CHAPTER VII.

(1867.)

> " Yea, the voiceless wrath of the wretched
> And their unlearned discontent,
> We must give it voice and wisdom,
> Till the waiting-tide be spent."
> WILLIAM MORRIS, *Poems by the Way.*

" DEAR Ruskin," writes Carlyle from Mentone [1] (February 15, 1867), " if the few bits of letters I have written from this place had gone by the *natural* priority and sequence, this would have been the first, or among the very first; and indeed it is essentially so,— the first that I have written except upon compulsion, or in answer to something written. My aversion to writing is at all times great. But I begin to feel a great want of having some news from you, at least of hearing that you are not fallen *unwell;* and there is no other method of arousing you to your duty."

He goes on to tell how " the impetuous Tyndall tore me out from the sleety mud abysses of London, as if by the hair of the head; and dropped

---

[1] The letter mentioned in *Time and Tide,* letter 6: " I heard from him last week at Mentone," etc.

me here;" and then follows a long story about the place and the people.   At last:—

"Often I begin to think of my route home ag[n], and what I shall next do then. . . . The only point I look forward to with any fixed satisfact[n] as yet, is that of having Ruskin again eve[y] Wedn[y] ev[g], and tasting a little human conversat[n] once in the week, if oftener be not practicable! . . . Adieu, my Friend, I want a little Note from you *quam primum*.   I send many regards to the good and dear old lady, and am ever,

"Y[rs] gratefully,

"T. CARLYLE."

One reason why Mr. Ruskin had not written was, perhaps, that he had already begun the series of letters published as "Time and Tide by Weare and Tyne," which is the same thing as saying that he was engaged upon a new and important book.   These letters were addressed to Thomas Dixon, a working cork-cutter of Sunderland, whose portrait by Professor Legros is familiar to visitors at the South Kensington Museum.   He was one of those thoughtful, self-educated workingmen in whom as a class Mr. Ruskin had been taking a deep interest for the past twelve years, an interest which had purchased him a practical insight into their various capacities and aims, and the right to speak without fear or favor.   At this time there was an agitation for parliamentary reform, and the better representation of the working classes;

and it was on this topic that the letters were begun, though the writer went on to criticise the various social ideals then popular, and to propose his own. He had already done something of the sort in " Unto this Last; " but " Time and Tide " is much more complete, and the result of seven years' farther thought and experience. His " Fors Clavigera " is a continuation of these letters, but written at a time when other work and ill-health broke in upon his strength. " Time and Tide " is not only the statement of his social scheme as he saw it in his central period, but, written as these letters were,[1] — at a stroke, so to speak, — condensed in exposition and simple in language, they deserve the most careful reading by the student of Ruskin.

The earlier letters are mainly a criticism of popular ideals, and the panaceas which were prescribed for the body politic. There was parliamentary reform, about which he says that it would be useless without a much more complete and generally accepted programme than existed, while, on the other hand, if such a programme could be adopted, there would be little need of parliamentary reform to carry it. There was coöperation, good so far as it went; but leaving untouched the competition between different societies in the same place or trade, and giving no guarantee to the workman against mismanagement and failure.

---

[1] During February, March, and April, 1867, and published in the *Manchester Examiner* and the *Leeds Mercury*.

Competition as a principle he denounced; national competition, on which the theory of trade was based, meant national animosity, and the recurrent necessity of war meant standing armaments and heavy taxation; individual competition, the struggle for life, he considered barbarous; and the whole object of morality, of government, of civilization was to make it unnecessary. The mere preaching of thrift, and content in a life of toil, he did not approve; for man is made for joy as well as sorrow, and for play as well as work, and one of his complaints against modern society was that no good amusements were to be had; on the other hand, he discouraged improvident marriage, while pointing out that, as things went, public opinion and public charity put a premium on self-indulgence. Another panacea was education, whose supporters, he said, were in this dilemma; that if it were effectual in raising everybody to the rank of gentlemen and scholars, who would do the dirty work? if it — as he believed — tended to widen the difference between more and less able persons, what good would be got by those who were left behind in the race? Religion, in an age of doubt, could not be made the basis of reform; waiting on providence was foolish, for vice and crime and folly will never disappear of themselves, and must be kept in check by some kind of law and order. And lastly, while he could not entertain the idea that any man had a right to take rent, or any other form of unearned increment, he considered it useless to divide the land among a shifting and growing population. Such, put briefly, were Mr. Ruskin's criticisms on the popular ideals of 1867.

Then he proceeded to construct his own ideal, as Plato had done in his " Republic," only within much less fanciful limits. He points out repeatedly that this *is* an ideal, and not a suggestion for immediate adoption ; and yet it differs from other people's Utopias in being far nearer realization. It is, indeed,—though he does not definitely say so, —based on a system which has already worked well, the system by which the barbarian Teutonic tribes and degraded Latin races of the lower empire were gradually developed into the great kingdoms of Europe, evolving the religion, laws, arts, and sciences which the Renaissance found at its coming. And if it be true that we are now in much the same position, *mutatis mutandis*, as in Charlemagne's days, — our degenerate " upper classes " with their Renaissance culture and traditions representing the Roman element, and our discontented " lower classes " with their restlessness and vitality and overwhelming preponderance representing the invaders, — if the problem be to weld these into a new cohesion, and out of them to create a new civilization, then it was surely well thought of, to apply the ancient cure, *mutatis mutandis*, to the parallel case.

To state the ideal constitution as shortly and conveniently as possible, we might put it under four heads, though the author does not so divide it; but he seems to have adopted, and adapted, from the Middle Ages their guild system, their chivalry, their church, and something of their feudal scheme.

To get entirely rid of competition, he proposed an organization of labor akin to the ancient guilds, which he regarded as the combination, in each trade and in every kind of manufacture, agriculture, and art, of all the masters with all the men. But while the old guilds were local, he would have them universal. By their own rules, and for their own advantage, they would secure good workmanship, honest production ; they would fix fair wages for their men and provide against the bankruptcy of their members who were masters. Retail trade would be neither precarious nor degrading if it were carried on by the salaried officers of the guild. The workman, holding a well-defined position, and possessing some share of control, through the trade council, over his work and his wages, would have no ground for discontent. And the masters — for Carlyle's Elisha had no idea of a world without masters — would be " captains of labor," the friends and not the enemies of their men; with their superior talents recognized and used, not without a certain pecuniary advantage, but without that disproportion of income, and of responsibility, which is the plague of modern commerce and manufacture.

Book-learning, we saw, was not Mr. Ruskin's notion of education; and while he would have

everybody educated, he would not make every boy
and girl learned, for, as Sylvestre Bonnard says,
he wishes them well. The physical and moral
education he proposes would make finer creatures
of them; would go a long way, of itself, to eradi-
cate disease and stupidity and vulgarity. To do
this more effectually he proposed to regulate marriage by permitting it only to those young people
who had qualified themselves by attaining a certain standard of general physical and moral culture, — " bachelors " and " rosières " they might
be dubbed, on the analogy of chivalry. To in-
sure the sufficient and yet frugal bringing up of a
family, he would secure them an income from the
state, if necessary, for the first seven years; or, if
they were of the wealthier class, keep them down
to that income, and reserve the surplus for their
use later on. Indeed he would limit all incomes
to some fixed maximum; on attaining which, if a
man were independent, he might retire, to pursue
his own hobbies or to serve the state. But in
his polity it would be the part of gentlefolks —
for some would still be unavoidably both wealthier
and more refined than others — to set the example
of plain living and high thinking.

As to the church, that, as in the " Notes on
Sheepfolds," was to be strictly a state-church, in
the sense that such officers as it possessed would
be salaried by the government, and that their
work would be in harmony with the state, not
opposed to it, nor independent of it, in sects and

schisms. These clergy would be confined to pastoral care, and have no right to preach their varying views of dogma. Names, of course, matter nothing in schemes of this sort; but in calling these officers " bishops " and suggesting that they should have the oversight of a hundred families each, Mr. Ruskin points to the practice of the primitive church. Though at this time he had renounced any definite belief in ordinary religion, he did not think that human nature, as a whole, would or could become completely irreligious; but he leaves it quite open to the families of his ideal state whether they will admit the ministrations of their bishops, or not.

Finally, he adapted the feudalism of the Middle Ages, in the sense that the whole body politic would be distinctly organic, and not anarchic; that its organization would be based on a military scheme. He had said, in " The Crown of Wild Olive," that a military despotism is the only cure for a diseased society; and while minimizing the occasions and opportunities for war, he felt that, to effect the development of the present "dark age" into a more perfect civilization, some use of force would be necessary in the administration. Believing strongly in human nature, he did not pretend that everybody is virtuous. Laws must be made, and laws must be administered; and to do this effectively requires the strong hand. In his state every man would be a soldier (as in Switzerland); but just as in the guilds some would necessarily be differentiated into mastership, so, in the whole of society, individuals and families would rise into eminence and take the lead. And as the captains, judges, bishops, and schoolmasters would be salaried state officials, so to these distinguished men and families he would be glad to assign such moderate incomes as might keep them in the public service, with such estates in land as might afford them the means of exemplifying the arts and graces of life; not to be landlords, but only the tenants of the state, just as the agriculturists, through their guild (if I understand rightly) are to have the use of the soil rent-free.

I trust I have fairly, though too briefly, represented the gist of this book, and, as I take it, the central work of the life of John Ruskin. I do not see my way to labeling his political system with a name, any more than his artistic system. As to criticising it, that must be done by the reader (after reasonable study of the original work) from his own standpoint; and standpoints are too many and too various to enumerate. I would only remark that, as I said, the scheme has the support of a historical analogy; that it is in harmony with modern scientific views of the evolution of mankind; that it is elastic enough to give play to the varying aims of individuals and classes; and that, since it does not premise universal virtue, nor promise universal happiness, it is not rightly described as Utopian.

Before this work was ended, Carlyle had come

back to Chelsea, and was begging his friend, in the warmest terms, to come and see him. Shortly afterward, a passage which Mr. Ruskin would not retract gave offense to Carlyle. But the difference was healed, and later letters reveal the sage of Chelsea just as kindly and affectionate as ever. It is a poor friendship that is broken by a free speech; and this friendship between the two greatest writers of their age, between two men, we may add, of vigorous individuality, outspoken opinions, and widely different tastes and sympathies, is a fine episode in the history of both.

In May, Mr. Ruskin was invited to Cambridge to receive the honorary degree of LL. D., and to deliver the Rede Lecture. The "Cambridge Chronicle" of May 25, 1867, says: "The body of the Senate House was quite filled with M. A.'s and ladies, principally the latter, whilst there was a large attendance of undergraduates in the galleries, who gave the lecturer a most enthusiastic reception." A brief report of the lecture was printed in the newspaper; but as it was never otherwise published, and the manuscript seems to have been lost, all but the first page, I take the liberty of copying the opening sentences as a specimen of that academical oratory which Mr. Ruskin then adopted, and used habitually in his earlier lectures at Oxford.

The title of the discourse was " The Relation of National Ethics to National Arts:" " In entering on the duty to-day intrusted to me, I should hold it little respectful to my audience if I disturbed them by expression of the diffidence which they know that I must feel in first speaking in this Senate House; diffidence which might well have prevented me from accepting such duty, but ought not to interfere with my endeavor simply to fulfill it. Nevertheless, lest the direction which I have been led to give to my discourse, and the narrow limits within which I am compelled to confine the treatment of its subject, may seem in any wise inconsistent with the purpose of the founder of this lecture, or with the expectations of those by whose authority I am appointed to deliver it, let me at once say that I obeyed their command, not thinking myself able to teach any dogma in the philosophy of the arts which could be of any new interest to the members of this university: but only that I might obtain the sanction of their audience for the enforcement upon other minds of the truth which — after thirty years spent in the study of art, not dishonestly, however feebly — is manifest to me as the clearest of all that I have learned, and urged upon me as the most vital of all I have to declare."

He then distinguished between true and false art, the true depending upon sincerity, whether in literature, music, or the formative arts; he reinforced his old doctrine of the dignity of true imagination as the attribute of healthy and earnest minds; and energetically attacked the commercial art-world of the day, and the notion that drawing-schools were to be supported for the sake of the gain they would bring to our manufacturers. " Mr. Ruskin concluded his lecture," says the " Chronicle," " with a very fine peroration, the first part of which he addressed to the younger members of the academic body, the second to the elder. On the younger men he urged the infinite importance of a life of virtue and the fact that the hereafter must be spent in God's presence or in darkness. Their time in this miracle of a universe was but as a moment; with one brief astounded gaze of awe they looked on all around them, — saw the planets roll, heard the sound of the sea, and beheld the surroundings of the earth; they were opened for a moment as a sheet of lightning, and then instantly closed again. Their highest ambition during so short a stay should be to be known for what they were, — to spend those glittering days in view of what was to come after them. Then on the Masters of this, which had for years been preëminent as the school of science, he urged that their continued prosperity must rest on their observance of the command of their Divine Master, in whose name they existed as a society, — ' Seek ye first the kingdom of God and his righteousness.' . . . All mere abstract knowledge, independent of its tendency to a holy life, was useless. . . . His concluding remarks were an eloquent exhortation to the seniors diligently to perform the solemn trust given to them in the proving of youth, — ' Lead them not into temptation, but deliver them from evil.'

"Long and hearty cheers greeted the learned lecturer from all parts of the Senate House as he resumed his seat."

In this lecture we see the germ of the ideas, as well as the beginning of the style, of the Oxford inaugural course, and the "Eagle's Nest;" something quite different in type from the style and teaching of the addresses to working men, or to mixed popular audiences at Edinburgh or Manchester, or even at the Royal Institution. At this latter place, on June 4th, Sir Henry Holland in the chair, he lectured on "The Present State of Modern Art, with reference to advisable arrangement of the National Gallery," repeating much of what he had said in "Time and Tide" about the taste for the horrible and absence of true feeling for pure and dignified art in the theatrical shows of the day, and in the admiration for Gustave Doré, then a new fashion. Mr. Ruskin could never endure that the man who had illustrated Balzac's "Contes Drôlatiques" should be chosen by the religious public of England as the exponent of their most sacred aspirations and ideals.

In July he went to Keswick for a few weeks, from whence he wrote the rhymed letters to his cousin at home, quoted (with the date wrongly given as 1857) in "Præterita" to illustrate his "heraldic character" of "Little Pigs" and to shock exoteric admirers. Like, for example, Rossetti

and Carlyle, Mr. Ruskin is fond of playful nick-
names and grotesque terms of endearment. He
does not stand upon his dignity with intimates;
and he is ready to allow the liberties he takes,
much to the surprise of strangers. And when
these things creep into print, or are reflected in
passages of comical vituperation, half jest, half
earnest, the public is scandalized, not knowing its
man and his ways.

I wish I had not to chronicle so many illnesses;
but it seems as though Mr. Ruskin could never
go through any spell of hard work, or emotional
strain of any kind, without suffering for it in a
physical illness. He has been called a valetudi-
narian; but it would have been better for him if he
could have merited the name, and taken care of
himself. Now, on returning from Keswick he
was ill again, and more seriously than the "hot
muffins" and hasty lunch "before ascending Red
Pike," which the "Little Pigs" record, can account for. He was attacked, he says in his notice
of Arthur Burgess, with the first warnings of his
later illness, in giddiness and mistiness of the head
and eyes; drawing and thinking were stopped for
the time. But after spending the latter part of
September at a health resort, under the care of
Dr. Powell, he was able to return home, prepare
"Time and Tide" for publication, and write the
preface on December 14th. On the 19th the
book was out, and immediately bought up. A
month later the second edition was issued.

CHAPTER VIII.

(1868.)

" And whenever the way seemed long,
    Or his heart began to fail,
  She would sing a more wonderful song,
    Or tell a more marvellous tale."
                                LONGFELLOW.

OF less interest to the general reader, though too important a part of Mr. Ruskin's life and work to be passed over without mention, are his studies in mineralogy. We have heard of his early interest in spars and ores; of his juvenile dictionary in forgotten hieroglyphics; and of his studies in the field and at the British Museum. He had made a splendid collection, and knew the various museums of Europe as familiarly as he knew the picture-galleries. In the " Ethics of the Dust " he had chosen crystallography as the subject in which to exemplify his method of education; and in 1867, after finishing the letters to Thomas Dixon, he took refuge, as before, among the stones, from the stress of more agitating problems.

In the lecture on the Savoy Alps in 1863 he had referred to a hint of Saussure's, that the contorted beds of the limestones might possibly be due to some sort of internal action, resembling on a large scale that separation into concentric or curved bands which is seen in calcareous deposits. The contortions of gneiss were similarly analogous, it was suggested, to those of the various forms of silica. Mr. Ruskin did not adopt the theory, but put it by for examination, in contrast with the usual explanation of these phenomena as the simple mechanical thrust of the contracting surface of the earth.

In 1863 and 1866 he had been among the Nagelflüh of Northern Switzerland, studying the pudding-stones and breccias. He saw that the difference between these formations, in their structural aspect, and the hand-specimens in his collection of pisolitic and brecciated minerals was chiefly a matter of size; and that the resemblances in form were very close. And so he concluded that if the structure of the minerals could be fully understood, a clue might be found to the very puzzling question of the origin of mountain-structure.

Hence his attempt to analyze the structure of agates and similar banded and brecciated minerals, in the series of papers in the "Geological Magazine;"[1] an attempt which, though it was never properly completed, and fails to come to any general conclusion, is extremely interesting[2] as

[1] August and November, 1867; January, April, and May, 1868; December, 1869; and January, 1870; illustrated with very fine mezzotint plates and woodcuts.

[2] See the testimony of Prof. Rupert Jones, F. R. S., in the *Proceedings of the Geologists' Association*, vol. iv., No. 7.

an account of beautiful and curious natural forms too little noticed by ordinary scientific mineralogists.

Mr. Ruskin began by naming the different ways in which solid rocks became fragmentary; of which one was by homogeneous segregation, as seen in oölites and pisolites; and another, by segregation of distinct substances from a homogeneous paste. He showed how this latter way might explain some curious conditions of jasper; how an example of brecciated malachite proved that the banded structure was not prior to the fractures, but that both tendencies were at work together; and how in many forms of agate the same phenomena made it impossible to believe that simple successive deposition, and violent concussion from without, wholly explained their origin. He thought that enough attention had not been drawn to the processes of segregation; and suggested that many conglomerates might not be merely a collection of pebbles, but concretionary, like orbicular granite (Napoleonite) and other nodule-structures in metamorphic rock.

On these analogies he suspected that some contortions and faults on a large scale might not be the result of mechanical violence, but colossal phenomena of retractation and contraction; and even that many apparent strata had been produced by segregation. This idea, he said, had been suggested to him by a paper of Mr. George Maw, the son of the Mr. Maw who took him to task years before about reflections in water. I have not seen the paper alluded to, and I should not like to fix Mr. Ruskin's heresies on its author, who is so well known in the world of science by his work in geology and botany, and to the public by the encaustic tiles and lustre pottery of his firm. But while palæontology makes it evident that the great limestone strata of the Alps are the result of successive deposition, it does seem probable that Mr. Ruskin was right in his hesitation to accept the compression-theory of mountain origin.[1]

In the following papers, written during 1868, he described the different states of semi-crystalline silica, and the two great families of agates, and drew attention to the complexity of the laws under which they had been formed, and the insufficiency of the old theory. Meanwhile the conditions of crystallization were becoming the subject of a new school of research, led by Dr. Clifton Sorby, to which Mr. Ruskin looked with eagerness for the clearing up of his difficulties; but his Oxford professorship, with the many new enterprises of the next ten years, forced him to lay aside the agate question as a serious study. And though from time to time the results of the new investigations were kindly communicated to him by Dr. Sorby and Mr. Clifton Ward, and followed by him in the published memoirs of

---

[1] See *The Origin of Mountain-Ranges*, by T. Mellard Reade, C. E., F. G. S., etc. (1886).

the microscopic mineralogists; though Professor Chandler Roberts helped him in the chemistry of gelatinous states of silica, Mr. Henry Willett in the study of flints, and many others in various departments; he never was able to bring himself to handle the modern microscope and work out the whole business afresh, from the modern point of view. He had to leave his pet study, very reluctantly, to younger men; not without parting cautions against hasty theorizing, nor without claims for a wider scope in their view of the subject.

The student who cares to make himself acquainted with the spirit in which Mr. Ruskin approached one department of the subject should take the "Catalogue of a Series of Specimens in the British Museum (Natural History), illustrative of the more common forms of Native Silica, arranged [presented for the most part] and described by John Ruskin, F. G. S.," and spend a few hours at Cromwell Road with the pamphlet in his hand, over the mineral cases, just as tourists in Venice are seen comparing his notes with the pictures in the Academy. And as the shilling catalogue is by no means abstruse, and the specimens are more beautiful than most picture-shows, the unscientific reader would not find his time lost in learning something new about nature, and something new to most readers, I suspect, about Ruskin.

One other outcome of the analogy between

minerals and mountains was Mr. Ruskin's skepticism in the matter of cleavage and jointing, which he thought insufficiently studied and explained by the holders of the mechanical theory, and suspected to be rather akin to crystalline cleavage, both in aspects and in origin. Not to dwell on these details, I merely note that a great recent authority, Professor Prestwich,[1] says, after weighing the evidence: " The system of joints, therefore, seems to me to be not a simple mechanical action, but one combined with a condition of crystallization; and though, from the influences of other mechanical forces to which the rocks have been exposed, and from the varying proportions of their constituent ingredients, we cannot expect the angles to present the exact definition which a crystal of the pure mineral would have, still there is every appearance of the plane-lines of shrinkage and jointing having been guided in many cases, if not in all, by planes of crystalline cleavage, in consequence of these being those of least resistance."

We must now recover the thread of our story and carry it hastily over the year spent chiefly, though by no means wholly, in these mineral researches. And first to tell a characteristic anecdote, preserved in " Arrows of the Chace." " The ' Daily Telegraph ' of January 21, 1868, contained a leading article upon the following facts: It appeared that a girl, named Matilda Griggs,

---

[1] *Geology* (1886), vol. i., p. 283.

had been nearly murdered by her seducer, who, after stabbing her in no less than thirteen places, had then left her for dead. She had, however, still strength enough to crawl into a field close by, and there swooned. The assistance she met with in this plight was of a rare kind. Two calves came up to her, and, disposing themselves on either side of her bleeding body, thus kept her warm and partly sheltered from cold and rain. Temporarily preserved, the girl eventually recov- ered, and entered into recognizances, under a sum of forty pounds, to prosecute her murderous lover. But 'she loved much,' and, failing to prosecute, forfeited her recognizances, and was imprisoned by the Chancellor of the Exchequer for her debt. 'Pity the poor debtor,' wrote the 'Daily Tele- graph,' and in the next day's issue appeared the following letter, probably not intended for the publication accorded to it : —

" ' Sir, — Except in " Gil Blas," I never read of anything Astræan on the earth so perfect as the story in your fourth article to-day. I send you a cheque for the Chancellor. If forty, in legal terms, means four hundred, you must explain the farther requirements to your impulsive public. — I am, Sir, Your faithful servant,   J. Ruskin.' "

The writer of letters like this naturally had a large correspondence, beside that which a circle of private friends and numberless admirers and readers elicited. About this time it grew to such a pitch that he was obliged to print a form excusing him from letter-writing on the ground of stress of work. And indeed this year, though he did not publish his annual volume, as usual, he was fully occupied with frequent letters to newspapers, several lectures and addresses, a preface to the reprint of his old friend Cruikshank's "Grimm," and the beginning of a new botanical work, "Proserpina," in addition to the mineralogy, and, I believe, a renewed interest in classical studies. Of the public addresses the most important was that on "The Mystery of Life and its Arts," delivered in the theatre of the Royal College of Science, Dublin (May 13th), and printed in "Sesame and Lilies."

Early in September he left home with Mr. William Ward, his former assistant at the Working Men's College, and, after traveling up the Meuse, spent a month at Abbeville, where he was visited by Mr. C. E. Norton, and by Mr. George Allen, then employed by him in engraving. For the past five years Mr. Ruskin had found very little time for drawing; it was twenty years since his last sketching of French Gothic, except for a study (now at Oxford) of the porch at Amiens, in 1856. He took up the old work where he had left it, after writing the "Seven Lamps," with fresh interest and more advanced powers of draughtsmanship, as shown in the picture engraved as frontispiece to his "Poems," and in the pencil study of the Place Amiral Courbet, now in the drawing school at Oxford. And, returning home, he gave an account of his autumn's work in the lecture at the Royal Institution, January 29, 1869, on the " Flamboyant Architecture of the Valley of the Somme." This lecture was never published in full; but part of the original text is printed in the third chapter of the work we have next to notice, " The Queen of the Air."

CHAPTER IX.

GREEK FAITHS AND CHRISTIAN MYTHS.

(1869.)

"For when the Gentiles, which have not the law, do by nature the things contained in the law, these, having not the law, are a law unto themselves." ROM. ii. 14.

IN spite of a "classical education" and the influence of Aristotle upon the immature art-theories of his earlier works, Mr. Ruskin was known, in his younger days, as a Goth, and the enemy of the Greeks. When he began life, his sense of justice made him take the side of modern painters against classical tradition; his sympathy, much wider than that of ordinary critics, led him to praise Gothic architecture, and his common-sense prompted him to recommend it as a domestic style more convenient than the pseudo-classic of the decadent Renaissance. Later on, when considering the great questions of education and the aims of life, he entirely set aside the common routine of Greek and Latin grammar as the all-in-all of culture. But this was not because he shared Carlyle's contempt for classical studies.

In " Modern Painters," vol. iii., he had followed out the indications of nature-worship, and tried

to analyze in general terms the attitude of the
Greek spirit towards landscape scenery, as betrayed in Homer and Aristophanes and the poets
usually read. Since that time his interest in
Greek literature had been gradually increasing.
He had made efforts to improve his knowledge
of the language; and he had spent many days in
sketching and studying the terra-cottas and vases
and coins at the British Museum. He had also
taken up some study of Egyptology, through
Champollion and Bunsen and Birch, in the hope
of tracing the origin of Greek decorative art.
At that stage of archæological discovery it was
not so clearly seen as it is to-day that Egypt was
only one factor in the development of Greece.
The discoveries at Hissarlik and Mycenæ, and in
Cyprus and elsewhere, had not shown the Aryan
and Assyrian parentage of many Greek customs
and myths and forms of art. Comparative mythology, twenty-five years ago, was a department of
philology, introduced to the English public chiefly
by Professor Max Müller. Under his influence
Mr. Ruskin entered step by step upon an inquiry
which afterwards became of singular importance
in his life and thought.

In 1865 he had told his hearers at Bradford
that Greek religion was not, as commonly supposed, the worship of beauty, but of wisdom
and power. They did not, in their great age,
worship Venus, but Apollo and Athena. And
he regarded their mythology as a sincere tradition,

effective in forming a high moral type and a great school of art. In the " Ethics of the Dust " he had explained the myth of Athena as parallel to that of Neith in Egypt; and in his fable of Neith and St. Barbara he had hinted at a comparison, on equal terms, of ancient and mediæval mythology. He ended by saying that, though he would not have his young hearers believe " that the Greeks were better than we, and that their gods were real angels," yet their art and morals were in some respects greater, and their beliefs were worth respectful and sympathetic study.

" The Queen of the Air " is his contribution to this study. Like much of his work, it is only a fragment indicating what he would have done, and began to do. Ever since, he has been accumulating material for farther investigation of the vast, bewildering sphere which embraces, too amply for one man's review, the orbits of art, and science, and ethics, and religion, as they rise and set upon his limited horizon, and roll, in a mazy dance, by laws that elude his reckonings, round some " far-off, divine event, to which the whole creation moves."

On March 9, 1869, his lecture at University College, London, on " Greek Myths of Cloud and Storm," began with an attempt to explain in popular terms how a myth differs from mere fiction on the one hand and from allegory on the other, being " not conceived didactically, but didactic in its essence, as all good art is." He showed that

Greek poetry dealt with a series of nature-myths with which were interwoven ethical suggestions; that these were connected with Egyptian beliefs, but that the full force of them was only developed in the central period of Greek history, and their interpretation was to be read in the sympathetic analysis of the spirit of men like Pindar and Æschylus. "The great question," he said, "in reading a story is, always, not what wild hunter dreamed, or what childish race first dreaded it; but what wise man first perfectly told, and what strong people first perfectly lived by it. And the real meaning of any myth is that which it has at the noblest age of the nation among whom it was current." This, of course, is a higher view than that of the anthropological and archæological specialist; but at the same time, the historical method is necessary as a preliminary and a check upon the tendency to fanciful interpretation, which Mr. Ruskin, in common with the whole philological school, does not escape. With certain amendments, however, his work is most valuable, as an exposition of the system of Greek religion, the worship of four groups of nature-powers, in earth, water, fire and air; and rising out of a low animism and fetishism into high moral and intellectual conceptions.

He traced with appreciation the development of the notion of Athena, as the chief power of the air, from her character of actual atmosphere to that of the breath of human life; and thence to the higher belief in a divine spirit, indistinguish-able at first, and among simple folk always, from the material breath in the nostrils of man; but leading up to healthy views of morality and sincere faith in Omnipresent Deity, not far remote in its practical outcome from that which we have received from the Hebrews.

In the next chapter he worked out, as a sequel to his lecture, two groups of animal-myths: those connected with birds, and especially the dove, as type of Spirit, and those connected with the serpent in its various significances. These two studies were continued, more or less, in " Love's Meinie " and in the lecture printed in " Deucalion," as the third group, that of plant-myths, was carried on in " Proserpina." The volume contained also extracts from the lecture on the Architecture of the Valley of the Somme, and two numbers of the " Cestus of Aglaia," and closed with a paper on the Hercules of Camarina, read to the South Lambeth art school on March 15th. This study of a Greek coin had already formed the subject of an address at the Working Men's College, and anticipated the second course of Oxford lectures. For the rest, " The Queen of the Air " is marked by its statement, more clearly than before in Mr. Ruskin's writing, of the dependence of moral upon physical life, and of physical upon moral science. He speaks with respect of the work of Darwin and Tyndall; but, as formerly in the Rede lecture, and afterwards in the

"Eagle's Nest," he claims that natural science should not be pursued as an end in itself, paramount to all other conclusions and considerations; but as a department of study subordinate to ethics, with a view to utility and instruction. In later times it was this principle which guided Mr. Ruskin in the view he took of vivisection, and other forms of scientific research. Premising that science was subordinate to ethics, when the two clashed, as he held they did in some cases, science, he thought, was to give way.

Before this book was quite ready for publication, and after a sale of some of his less treasured pictures at Christie's, Mr. Ruskin left home for a journey to Italy, to revisit the subjects of "Stones of Venice," as in 1868 he had revisited those of the "Seven Lamps." At Vevey, on the way, he wrote his preface (May 1st). On the 8th he reached Verona after seventeen years' absence, and on the 10th he was in Venice. There, walking round the Academy, and looking at the works of the old painters with a fresh eye, and with feelings and thoughts far different from those with which he had viewed them as a young man, in 1845, he saw beauties he had passed over before, in the works of a painter till then little regarded by connoisseurs, and entirely neglected by the public. Historians of art like Crowe and Cavalcaselle [1] had indeed examined Carpaccio's works and in-

[1] Their *History of Painting in North Italy*, containing a detailed account of Carpaccio, was published in 1871.

vestigated his life, along with the lives and works of many another obscure master; artists like Mr. Hook and Mr. Burne‑Jones had admired his pictures; Mr. Ruskin had mentioned his backgrounds twice or thrice in "Stones of Venice." But no writer had noticed his extraordinary interest as an exponent of the mythology of the Middle Ages, as the illustrator of poetical folk‑lore derived from those antique myths of Greece, and newly presented by the genius of Christianity.

This was a discovery for which Mr. Ruskin was now ripe.   He saw at once that he had found a treasure‑house of things new and old.   He fell in love with St. Ursula as, twenty‑four years earlier, he had fallen in love with the statue of Ilaria at Lucca; and she became, as time after time he revisited Venice for her sake, a personality, a spiritual presence, a living ideal, exactly as the Queen of the Air might have been to the sincere Athenian in the pagan age of faith.   The story of her life and death became an example, the conception of her character, as read in Carpaccio's picture, became a standard for his own life and action in many a time of distress and discouragement.   The thought of " What would St. Ursula say?" led him — not always, but far more often than his correspondents knew — to burn the letter of sharp retort upon stupidity and impertinence, and to force the wearied brain and overstrung nerves into patience and a kindly answer.   And later on, the playful credence which he accorded to the myth has deepened into a renewed sense of the possibility of spiritual realities, when he learned to look, with those mediæval believers, once more as a little child upon the unfathomable mysteries of life.

But this anticipates the story; at the time, he found in Carpaccio the man who had touched the full chord of his feelings and his thoughts, just as, in his boyhood, Turner had led him, marveling, through the fire and cloud to the mountain-altar; and as, in his youth, Tintoret had interpreted the storm and stress of a mind awakening to the terrible realities of the world. It was no caprice of a changeful taste, or love of startling paradox, that brought him to "discover Carpaccio;" it was the logical sequence of his studies, and widening interests, and a view of art embracing far broader issues than the connoisseurship of "Modern Painters," or the didacticism of "Seven Lamps," or the historical research of "Stones of Venice."

Soon after "The Queen of the Air" was published Carlyle wrote : —

CHELSEA, Augt 17th, 1869.

DEAR RUSKIN, — Y^r excell^t kind and loving little note from Vevey reached me ; but nothing since, not even precise news at second hand, wh^h I much desired. The blame of my not answering and inciting was not mine, but that of my poor rebellious right-hand, — wh^h often refuses altog^r to do any writing for me that can be read ; having already done too much, it probably thinks ! [1]

---

[1] Carlyle was then losing the use of his hand, and this letter is scribbled in blue pencil.

. . . What I wish now is to know if you are at home, and to see you instantly if so.   Inst^{tly}!   For I am not unlikely to be off in a few days (by *Steamer Some* whither) and ag^n miss you.   Come, I beg, *quàm primùm !*

Last week I got y^r " Queen of the Air," and read it.   *Euge, Euge.*   No such Book have I met with for long years past. The one soul now in the world who seems to feel as I do on the highest matters, and speaks *mir aus dem Herzen*, exactly what I wanted to hear ! — As to the natural-history of those old myths I remained here and there a little uncert^n ; but as to the meanings you put into them, never anywhere.   All these things I not only " agree " with, but w^d use Thor's Hammer, if I had it, to enforce and put in action on this rotten world.   Well done, well done !—and pluck up a heart, and continue ag^n and ag^n.   And don't say " most g^t tho^ts are dressed *in shrouds :"* many, many are the Phœbus Apollo celestial arrows you still have to shoot into the foul Pythons, and poisonous abominable Megatheriums and Plesiosaurians that go staggering ab^t, large as cathedrals, in our sunk Epoch ag^n. . . .

CHAPTER X.

THE CALL TO OXFORD.

(1869-1870.)

THE main object of this journey to Venice was, however, not to study mythology, but to continue the revision of old estimates of architecture, and after seventeen years to look with a fresh eye at the subjects of " Stones of Venice." Beside some preliminary sketches of Carpaccio's St. Ursula, Mr. Ruskin was busy with drawings of Venetian buildings; but he soon removed to Verona, for careful studies of the Scaliger tombs and of Lombard architecture. Much of the work of this year is in pencil, or in pencil with a wash of quiet tint; but he began to paint also in realistic color, more freely than before; sometimes with Chinese white, and sometimes in pure water-color, without the pen-outline; but tending to much greater completeness and elaboration. Up to 1863 his sketching had been that of a chiaroscuro draughtsman, sometimes rising into very fine broad masses of abstract color, based upon the light and shade, and sometimes indulging in color-experiments. Then came a period during which he drew and painted very little. Then, after 1868, he resumed his sketching in quite a new spirit, akin to the naturalistic color of Carpaccio, in the same sense, and to the same extent, as his earlier style had been akin to the strong light-and-shade style of Tintoret; not consciously imitating either master, at either time, but reflecting in his landscape-method the feeling which had led him to sympathize with them.

As assistants in this enterprise of recording the monuments of Venice and Verona, and of recording them more fully and in a more interesting way than by photography, he took with him Arthur Burgess and John Bunney, his former pupils. Mr. Burgess was the subject of a memoir by Mr. Ruskin in the " Century Guild Hobby Horse " (April, 1887), appreciating his talents and lamenting his loss. Mr. Bunney, who had traveled with Mr. Ruskin in Switzerland in 1863, and had lately lived near Florence, thenceforward settled in Venice, where he died in 1882, after completing his great work, the St. Mark's now in the Ruskin Museum at Sheffield. A memoir of him by Mr. Wedderburn appeared in the catalogue of the Venice Exhibition at the Fine Art Society's Gallery in November, 1882.

The restorations of Sta. Anastasia and other acts of vandalism made it evident that no time was to be lost in securing these records. They painted hard for about three months at Verona; Mr. Ruskin often sleepless at night with anxiety and excitement. When he had been about six weeks at this work, he was invited by his friends, through the Dean of Christ Church, to stand for the professorship of fine art, lately founded at Oxford, as similar chairs were at the universities of Cambridge and London, by the bequest of Felix Slade, Esq.

Six years earlier, while being examined before the Royal Academy commission, he had been asked: " Has it ever struck you that it would be advantageous to art if there were at the universities professors of art who might give lectures and give instruction to young men who might desire to avail themselves of it, as you have lectures on geology and botany?" To which he had replied: "Yes, assuredly. The want of interest on the part of the upper classes in art has been very much at the bottom of the abuses which have crept into all systems of education connected with it. If the upper classes could only be interested in it by being led into it when young, a great improvement might be looked for; therefore I feel the expediency of such an addition to the education of our universities." His interest in the first phase of university extension, and his gifts of Turners to Oxford and Cambridge, had shown that he was ready to go out of his way to help in the cause he had promoted. His former works on art, and reputation as a critic, pointed to him as the best-qualified man in the country for such a post. Though he had figured as a heretic some years before, his Rede lecture and recent studies in Greek mythology in the school of Max Müller could be set off against the escapades of "Unto this Last" and the "Crown of Wild Olive." There was no doubt that the election would be a popular one, and creditable to the university. On the other hand, Mr. Ruskin as professor would have a certain sanction for his teaching, he believed; the title and the salary of £358 a year were hardly an object to him; but the position, as accredited lecturer and authorized instructor of youth, opened up new vistas of usefulness, new worlds of work to conquer; and he accepted the invitation. On August 10th he was elected Slade professor,[1] and, about the same time, honorary student of his old college, Christ-Church.

He returned home by the end of August to prepare himself for his new duties. During the last period he had been giving, on an average, half a dozen lectures a year, which amply filled

[1] The electors were the Very Reverend Dr. Liddell, Dean of Christ-Church, Dr. Acland, and the Rev. G. Rawlinson, being three of the curators of the university galleries; the Rev. H. O. Coxe, Bodley's Librarian; Sir Francis Grant, President of the Royal Academy of London; George Grote, Esq., President of University College, London, and R. Fisher, Esq., one of the executors of the will of the late Felix Slade, Esq., the donor.

his annual volume. Twelve lectures were required of the professor. Many another man would have read his twelve lectures and gone his way; but Mr. Ruskin was not going to work in that perfunctory manner. He undertook to revise his whole teaching; to write for his hearers a completely new series of treatises on art, beginning with first principles and broad generalizations, and proceeding to the different departments of sculpture, engraving, landscape-painting, and so on; then taking up the history of art, — an encyclopædic scheme, for which, no doubt, he was qualified, which he could have carried out if he had found nothing else to do. But he took this Oxford work, not as a substitute for other occupation, exonerating him from farther claims upon his energy and time, nor as a by-play that could be slurred. He tried to do it thoroughly, and to do it in addition to the varied work already in hand, under which, as it was, he used to break down, year after year, after each climax of effort.

This autumn and winter, with his first and most important course in preparation, he was still writing letters to the " Daily Telegraph," being begged by Carlyle to come, — " the sight of your face will be a comfort," says the poor old man, — and undertaking lectures at the Royal Artillery Institution, Woolwich, and at the Royal Institution, London. The Woolwich lecture, given on December 14th, was that added to later editions of the " Crown of Wild Olive," under the title of " The Future of England." The other, February 4, 1870, on " Verona and its Rivers," involved not only a lecture on art and history and contemporary political economy, but an exhibition of the drawings which he and his assistants had made during the preceding summer.

Four days later he opened a new period in his career with his inaugural lecture in the Sheldonian Theatre at Oxford.

BOOK IV.

PROFESSOR AND PROPHET.

(1870–1892.)

"Essa è la luce eterna di Sigieri,
Che leggendo nel vico degli strami
Sillogizzò invidiosi veri."

DANTE, *Paradiso*, x. 136.

CHAPTER I.

FIRST OXFORD LECTURES.

(1870–1871.)

"Cannot we hire some Abelard to lecture to us?"
THOREAU, *Walden.*

ON Tuesday, February 8, 1870, the Slade professor's lecture-room was crowded to overflowing with members of the university, old and young, and their friends, who flocked to hear, and to see, the author of "Modern Painters." The place was densely packed long before the time; the ante-rooms were filled with personal friends of Mr. Ruskin, hoping for some corner to be found them at the eleventh hour; the doors were blocked open, and besieged outside by a disappointed multitude.

Professorial lectures are not usually matters of great excitement; it does not often happen that the accommodation is found inadequate. After some hasty arrangements Sir Henry Acland pushed his way to the table, announced that it was impossible for the lecture to be held in that place, and begged the audience to adjourn to the Sheldonian Theatre. At last, welcomed by all Oxford, the Slade professor appeared, to deliver his inaugural address.

Those earlier courses are still fresh in the memory of many a young hearer who has forgotten, in the stress of busy life, much else of what he saw and learned at Oxford, twenty years ago. We undergraduates used to run out to the museum or to the drawing school, where the lectures were given, in a scrambling hurry from our ethics or prose class, or of an afternoon leaving the hasty luncheon, — and giving up the river, — grumbling at the awkward hours which, as the professor often told us, he could never arrange to suit everybody. And when we reached the place it was to find half the seats taken by earlier comers, whose broad hats, then in the fashion, were completely in the way of seeing the lecturer and the illustrations he had brought. But still we went, crowds of us; for there was always something to interest, and a dim sense that it was an opportunity which might soon be lost, of hearing one that spoke with authority, and not as the dons.

It was not strictly academic, the way he used to come in, with a little following of familiars and assistants, — exchange recognition with friends in the audience, arrange the objects he had brought to show, — fling off his long-sleeved Master's gown, and plunge into his discourse. His manner of delivery had not altered much since the time of the Edinburgh lectures. He used to begin by reading, in his curious intonation, the carefully-written passages of rhetoric, which usually occupied only about the half of his hour. By and by he would break off, and with quite another air extemporize the liveliest interpolations, describing his diagrams or specimens, restating his arguments, reënforcing his appeal. His voice, till then artificially cadenced, suddenly became vivacious; his gestures, at first constrained, became dramatic. He used to act his subject, apparently without premeditated art, in the liveliest pantomime. He had no power of voice-mimicry, and none of the ordinary gifts of the actor. A tall and slim figure, not yet shortened from its five feet ten or eleven by the habitual stoop, which ten years later brought him down to less than middle height; a stiff, blue frock-coat; prominent, half-starched wristbands, and tall collars of the Gladstonian type; and the bright blue stock which every one knows for his heraldic bearing; no rings or gewgaws, but a long thin gold chain to his watch, — a plain old-English gentleman, neither fashionable dandy nor artistic mountebank.

But he gave himself over to his subject with such unreserved intensity of imaginative power, he felt so vividly and spoke so from the heart, that he became whatever he talked about, never heeding his professorial dignity, and never doubting the sympathy of his audience. Lecturing on birds, he strutted like the chough, made himself wings like the swallow; he was for the moment a cat, in explaining that engraving was the art of scratch. If it had been an affectation of theatric display, we "emancipated schoolboys," as the Master of University used to call us, would have seen through it at once, and scorned him. But it was so evidently the expression of his intense eagerness for his subject, so palpably true to his purpose, and he so carried his hearers with him, that one saw in the grotesque of the performance only the guarantee of another and serious side.

If one wanted more proof of that, there was his face, still young-looking and beardless ; made for expression, and sensitive to every change of emotion. A long head, with enormous capacity of brain, veiled by thick wavy hair, not affectedly lengthy, but as abundant as ever, and darkened into a deep brown, without a trace of gray ; and short light whiskers growing high over his cheeks. A forehead not on the model of the heroic type, but as if the sculptor had heaped his clay in handfuls over the eyebrows, and then heaped more. A big nose, aquiline, and broad at the base, with great thoroughbred nostrils and the "septum" between them thin and deeply depressed ; and there was a turn down at the corners of the mouth, and a breadth of lower lip, that reminded one of his Verona griffin, half eagle, half lion; Scotch in original type, and suggesting a side to his character not all milk and roses. And under shaggy eyebrows, ever so far behind, — κατηρεφεῖς, — the fieriest blue eyes, that changed with changing expression, from grave to gay, from lively to severe ;

John Ruskin in 1871

that riveted you, magnetized you, seemed to look through you and read your soul; and indeed, when they lighted on you, you felt you had a soul of a sort. What they really saw is a mystery. Some, who had not persuaded them to see as others see, maintained that they saw only what they looked for; others, who had successfully deceived them, that they saw nothing. No doubt they might be deceived; but I know that they often took far shrewder measurements of men — I do not say women — than they revealed.

For the inaugural course, he was, so to speak, on his best behavior, guarding against too hasty expression of individuality. He read careful orations, stating his maturest views on the general theory of art, in picked language, suited to the academic position. The little volume, now published at five shillings, is most valuable as giving Ruskin on Art at his best. It is not discursive or entertaining, like " Modern Painters," and contains no pictures with either pen or pencil; but it is crammed full of thought and the results of thought; and for any one whose general knowledge is equal to interpreting it, the most valuable guide. One understands why the public which loves its " Modern Painters " does not read the " Lectures on Art," but it is surely an oversight on the part of the would-be critics of Ruskinism to ignore the restatement, in a serious course of lectures before an educated audience, of views which youthful works either failed to expound, or expounded in a loose and inadequate manner.

The Slade professor was also expected to organize and superintend the teaching of drawing, and his first words in the first lecture expressed the hope that he would be able to introduce some serious study of art into the university, which, he thought, would be a step toward realizing some of his ideals of education. He had long felt that mere talking about art was a makeshift, and that no real insight could be got into the subject without actual and practical dealing with it. He found a South Kensington school in existence at Oxford, with an able master, Mr. Alexander Macdonald; and, though he did not entirely approve of the methods in use, tried to make the best of the materials to his hand, to add to and enlarge the scope of the system. The South Kensington system had been devised for industrial designing, primarily; Mr. Ruskin's desire was to get undergraduates to take up a wider subject, to familiarize themselves with the technical excellences of the great masters, to study nature, and art in its different processes, drawing, painting, and some forms of decorative work, such as, in especial, goldsmiths' work, out of which the Florentine school had sprung. He did not wish to train artists, but, as before in the Working Men's College, to cultivate the habit of mind that looks at nature and life, not analytically, as science does, but for the sake of external aspect and expression. By these means he hoped to breed a race of judicious patrons and critics, the best service any man can render to the cause of art.

And so he got together a mass of examples in addition to the Turners which he had already given to the university galleries. He placed in the school a few pictures by Tintoret, some drawings by Rossetti, Holman Hunt, and Burne-Jones, and a great number of fine casts and engravings. He arranged a series of studies by himself and others, as " copies," fitted, like the Turners in the National Gallery, with sliding frames and cabinets for convenient reference and removal. After spending most of his first Lent term in this work, he went home for a month to prepare a catalogue, which was published the same year, the school not being finally opened until October, 1871. During these first visits to Oxford he was the guest of Sir Henry Acland; after two years he took rooms of his own in Corpus, vacated by the Rev. Henry Furneaux, who gave up his fellowship on marrying Mr. Arthur Severn's twin sister. Professor Ruskin, already honorary student of Christ-Church and D. C. L., was elected to an honorary fellowship at Corpus Christi College with Mr. Alfred Hunt, a former fellow, the landscape painter.

This work well begun, he went abroad for a vacation tour with a party of friends, — as in 1866: Lady Trevelyan's sister, Mrs. Hilliard, to chaperone the same young ladies, and three servants of his own. They started on April 27th; stayed awhile at Meurice's to see Paris; and at Geneva, to go up the Salève, twice, in bitter black

east wind.   Then across the Simplon to Milan
and Venice, where he made the careful drawing
given to the Oxford schools (engraved in Cook's
" Studies in Ruskin,") but little more ; for this was
to be a holiday, and he devoted himself to his
company.   After a month at Venice and Verona —
where he recurred to his scheme against inunda-
tion, then ridiculed by " Punch," but afterwards
taken up seriously by the Italians — they went to
Florence, and met Professor Norton.   In the end
of June they turned homewards, by Pisa and
Lucca, Milan and Como, and went to visit their
friend Marie of the Giessbach.

At the Giessbach they spent a fortnight, enjoy-
ing the July weather and glorious walks,[1] in the
middle of which war was suddenly declared between Germany and France.   The summons of
their German waiter to join his regiment brought
the news home to them, as such personal examples do, more than columns of newspaper print;
and as hostilities were rapidly beginning, Mr.
Ruskin, with the gloomiest forebodings for the
beautiful country he loved, took his party home
straight across France, before the ways should be
closed.

August was a month of feverish suspense to
everybody ; to no one more than to Mr. Ruskin,
who watched the progress of the armies while he
worked day by day at the British Museum prepar-

---

[1] During one of which occurred the adventure of the snake, that
showed presence of mind, told in the *Eagle's Nest*, § 101.

ing lectures for next term. This was the course on Greek relief-sculpture, published as " Aratra Pentelici." It was a happy thought to illustrate his subject from coins, rather than from disputed and mutilated fragments ; and he worked into it his revised theory of the origin of art, — not Schiller's nor Herbert Spencer's, and yet akin to theirs of the " Spieltrieb," — involving the notion of doll-play: man as a child, recreating himself, in a double sense ; imitating the creation of the world, and really creating a sort of secondary life in his art, to play with, or to worship. This book, too, the critics of Ruskin have unanimously over-looked; except for the last lecture of the series (published separately), in which the professor compared — as the outcome of classic art in Renaissance times — Michelangelo and Tintoret, greatly to the disadvantage of Michelangelo. This heresy against a popular creed served as text for some severe criticism of Mr. Ruskin's art-teaching by followers of the academic school ; but, as he said in a prefatory note to the pamphlet, readers " must observe that its business is only to point out what is to be blamed in Michelangelo, and that it assumes the fact of his power to be generally known," and he refers to Mr. Tyrwhitt's " Lectures on Christian Art " for the opposite side of the question.

Meanwhile the war was raging. Mr. Ruskin was asked by his friends to raise his voice against the ravage of France ; but, as he replied, it was inevitable. At last, in October, he read how Rosa Bonheur and Edouard Frère had been permitted to pass through the German lines, and next day came the news of the bombardment of Strasburg, with anticipations of the destruction of the cathedral, library, and picture galleries, foretelling, as it seemed, the more terrible and irreparable ruin of the treasure-houses of art in Paris. His heart was with the French, and he broke silence in the bitterness of his spirit, upbraiding their disorder and showing how the German success was the victory of "one of the truest monarchies and schools of honor and obedience yet organized under heaven." He hoped that Germany, now that she had shown her power, would withdraw, and demand no indemnity. But that was too much to ask.

Before long Paris itself became the scene of action, and in January, 1871, was besieged and bombarded. So much of Mr. Ruskin's work and affection had been given to French Gothic that it was not to be thought of that his beloved Sainte Chapelle should be actually under fire, — to say nothing of the horror of human suffering in a siege. He joined Cardinal (then Archbishop) Manning, Professor Huxley, Sir John Lubbock, and Mr. James Knowles in forming a "Paris Food Fund," which shortly united with the lord mayor's committee for the general relief of the besieged. The day after writing on the Sainte Chapelle he attended the meeting at the Mansion

House, and gave a subscription of £50. He followed events anxiously through the storm of the commune and its fearful ending, angered at the fratricide and anarchy which no Mansion House help could avert or repair.

It was no time for talking on art, he felt; instead of the full course, he could only manage three lectures on landscape, and these not so elaborately prepared as to make them worth printing. Before Christmas he had been once more to Woolwich, where Colonel Brackenbury invited him to address the cadets at the prize-giving of the science and art department, in which the Rev. W. Kingsley, an old friend of Mr. Ruskin's and of Turner's, was one of the masters. Two of the lectures of " The Crown of Wild Olive " had been given there, with more than usual animation, and enthusiastically received by crowded and distinguished audiences, among whom was Prince Arthur (the Duke of Connaught), then at the Royal Military Academy. This time it was the " Story of Arachne," an address on education and aims in life ; opening with reminiscences of his own childhood, and pleasantly telling the Greek myths of the spider and the ant, with interpretations for the times. This lecture still remains in manuscript.

The three lectures on landscape, or rather, the contrast of the Greek and Gothic spirits as seen chiefly in landscape painters, were briefly reported in the " Athenæum." In these he dwelt on the necessity of human and historic interest in scenery; and compared Greek " solidity and veracity " with Gothic " spirituality and mendacity," Greek chiaroscuro and tranquil activity with Gothic color and " passionate rest." Botticelli's Nativity (now in the National Gallery) was then being shown at the Old Masters' Exhibition, and Mr. Ruskin took it, along with the works of Cima, as a type of one form of Greek art. Rubens and Rembrandt he considered as less refined developments of the same spirit.

In the greatest painters, he said, the excellences of the two schools were united: Titian and Tintoret were Gothic colorists approaching the Greek ideal; Holbein and Turner were chiaroscurists of the Greek type, blossoming into color. In landscape, he said, there was little that perfectly illustrated the Gothic spirit. The Pre-Raphaelite Brotherhood and their school tried to revive it, but they undervalued the difficulty of their art, and took refuge in dramatic sensation instead of making themselves the competent exponents of real beauty; and failed.

This 1871 was an eventful year in Mr. Ruskin's home life. In April his cousin, Miss Agnew, who had been seven years at Denmark Hill, was married to Mr. Arthur Severn, and left her friends as sheep without a shepherdess. Mr. Ruskin, who had added to his other worries the additional labor of " Fors Clavigera," went for a summer's change to Matlock. July opened with cold, dry, dark weather, dangerous for out-of-door sketching. One morning early — for he was always an early riser — he took a chill while painting a spray of wild rose before breakfast (the drawing now in the Oxford schools). He was already overworked, and it ended in a severe attack of internal inflammation which nearly cost him his life. He was a difficult patient to deal with. Though one of his best friends is a physician and another a surgeon, he usually prefers to be his own doctor as long as he can, and believes more in diet and exercise than in medicine. The local practitioner who attended him still tells how he refused remedies, and in the height of the disease asked what would be *worst* for him. I understood at Matlock that the answer was " sherry ; " Mr. Ruskin himself says it was "beef!" Anyhow, he took it ; and, to everybody's surprise, recovered.[1]

But it had been a painful scare to his friends, especially to those who could get no news. Car-

---

[1] Mrs. Arthur Severn, in a note on the proof, says : " It was a slice of cold roast beef he hungered for, at Matlock (to our horror, and dear Lady Mount Temple's, who were nursing him) ; there was none in the hotel, and it was late at night ; and Albert Goodwin went off to get some, somewhere, or anywhere. All the hotels were closed ; but at last, at an eating-house in Matlock Bath, he discovered some, and came back triumphant with it, wrapped up in paper ; and J. R. enjoyed his late supper thoroughly ; and though we all waited anxiously till the morning for the result, it had done no harm ! And when he was told pepper was bad for him, he dredged it freely over his food in defiance ! It was directly after our return to Denmark Hill he got Linton's letter offering him this place (Brantwood). There are, I believe, ten acres of moor belonging to Brantwood."

lyle, who had been in the Highlands, with his right hand useless, and his amanuensis, Miss Aitken, far away, was surprised and distressed at the silence of his friend, and at last wrote anxiously: "There came the most alarming rumors of your illness at Matlock; and both Lady Ashburton and myself (especially the latter party, for whom I can answer best) were in a state really deserving pity on your account, till the very newspapers took compassion on us, and announced the immediate danger to be past. . . . Froude has returned, and is often asking about you; as indeed are many others, to whom the radiant qualities which the gods have given you and set you to work with, in such an *element*, are not unknown. Write me a word at once, dear Ruskin."

During the illness at Matlock his thoughts reverted to the old " Iteriad " times of forty years before, when he had traveled with his parents and cousin Mary from that same " New Bath Hotel," where he was now lying, to the Lakes; and again he wearied for the heights that look adown upon the dale. " The crags are lone on Coniston." If he could only lie down there, he said, he should get well again.

He had not fully recovered before he heard that Mr. W. J. Linton, the poet and wood-engraver, wished to sell a house and land at the very place: £1500, and it could be his. Without question asked he bought it at once; and as it would be impossible to lecture at Oxford so soon after his

BRANTWOOD, FROM CONISTON WATER

Mr. Ruskin's Home from 1872

illness, he set off, before the middle of September, with his friends the Hilliards to visit his new possession. They found a rough-cast country cottage, old, damp, decayed; smoky-chimneyed and rat-riddled; but "five acres of rock and moor and streamlet; and," he wrote, "I think the finest view I know in Cumberland or Lancashire, with the sunset visible over the same."

The spot was not, even then, without its associations; the Sandys family of old, Gerald Massey the poet, Mr. Linton, and his wife Mrs. Lynn Linton the novelist, had lived and worked there, and the last inhabitants had adorned it outside with revolutionary mottoes, — "God and the people," and so on. It had been a favorite point of view of Wordsworth's; his "seat" was pointed out in the grounds. Tennyson had lived for a while close by; his "seat," too, was on the hill above Lanehead.

But the cottage needed thorough repair, and that cost more than rebuilding, not to speak of the additions of later years, which have ended by making it into a mansion surrounded by a hamlet. And there was the furnishing; for Denmark Hill, where Mrs. Ruskin lived, was still to be headquarters. Mr. Ruskin gave carte-blanche to the London upholsterer with whom he had been accustomed to deal; and such expensive articles were sent that when he came down for a month next autumn, he reckoned that, all included, his country cottage had cost him not less than £4000.

But he was not the man to spend on himself without sharing his wealth with others. On November 22d, Convocation accepted a gift from the Slade professor of £5000, to endow a mastership of drawing at Oxford, in addition to the pictures and " copies " placed in the schools; he had set up a relative in business with £15,000, which was promptly lost; and at Christmas he gave £7000, the tithe of his remaining capital, to the St. George's Fund; of which more hereafter.

On November 23d he was elected Lord Rector of St. Andrews University by 86 votes against 79 for Lord Lytton. After the election it was discovered that, by the Scottish Universities' Act of 1858, no one holding a professorship at a British university was eligible. Professor Ruskin was disqualified, and gave no address; and Lord Neaves was chosen in his place.

Mrs. Ruskin was now ninety years of age; her sight was nearly gone, but she still retained her powers of mind, and ruled with severe kindliness her household and her son. Her old servant Anne had died in March. Anne had nursed John Ruskin as a baby, and had lived with the family ever since, devoted to them, and ready for any disagreeable task, "so that she was never quite in her glory," " Præterita " says, " unless some of us were ill. She had also some parallel speciality for *saying* disagreeable things, and might be relied upon to give the extremely darkest view of any subject, before proceeding to ameliorative action upon it. And she had a very creditable and republican aversion to doing immediately, or in set terms, as she was bid; so that when my mother and she got old together, and my mother became very imperative and particular about having her teacup set on one side of her little round table, Anne would observantly and punctiliously put it always on the other; which caused my mother to state to me, every morning after breakfast, gravely, that if ever a woman in this world was possessed by the Devil, Anne was that woman."

But this gloomy Calvinism was tempered with a benevolence quite as uncommon. It was from his parents that Mr. Ruskin learned never to turn off a servant, and the Denmark Hill household was as easy-going as the legendary "baronial" retinue of the good old times. A young friend asked Mrs. Ruskin, in a moment of indiscretion, what such a one of the ancient maids did, — for there were several without apparent occupation about the house. Mrs. Ruskin drew herself up and said, "She, my dear, puts out the dessert."

And yet, in her blindness, she could read character unerringly. That was, no doubt, why people feared her. When Mr. Secretary Howell, in the days when he was still the oracle of the Ruskin-Rossetti circle, had been regaling them with his wonderful tales, after dinner, she would throw her netting down and say, "How *can* you two sit there and listen to such a pack of lies?"

She objected strongly, in these later years, to the theatre; and when sometimes her son would wish to take a party into town to see the last new piece, her permission had to be asked, and was not readily granted, unless to Miss Agnew, who was the ambassadress in such affairs of diplomacy. But while disapproving of some of his worldly ways, and convinced that she had too much indulged his childhood, the old lady loved him with all the intensity of the strange fierce lioness nature, which only one or two had ever had a glimpse of. And when (December 5, 1871) she died, trusting to see her husband again, — not to be near him, not to be so high in heaven, but content if she might only *see* him, she said, — her son was left "with a surprising sense of loneliness." He had loved her truly, obeyed her strictly, and tended her faithfully; and even yet hardly realized how much she had been to him. He buried her in his father's grave, and wrote upon it, " Here beside my father's body I have laid my mother's; nor was dearer earth ever returned to earth, nor purer life recorded in heaven."

CHAPTER II.

FORS CLAVIGERA BEGUN.

(1871–1872.)

FLORIAN.

ON January 1, 1871, was issued a small pamphlet, headed " Fors Clavigera," in the form of a letter to the working men and laborers of England, dated from Denmark Hill, and signed " John Ruskin." It was not published in the usual way, but sold by the author's engraver, Mr. George Allen, at Heathfield Cottage, Keston, Kent. It was not advertised; press-copies were sent to the leading papers; and of course the author's acquaintance knew of its publication. Strangers, who heard of this curious proceeding, spread the report that in order to get Ruskin's latest you had to travel into the country, with your sevenpence in your hand, and transact your business among Mr. Allen's beehives. So you had, if you wanted to see what you were buying; for no arrangements were made for its sale by the booksellers: sevenpence a copy, carriage paid, no discount, and no abatement on taking a quantity.

By such pilgrimages, but more easily through the post, the new work filtered out, in monthly installments, to a limited number of buyers. After three years the price was raised to tenpence. In 1875, the first thousands of the earlier numbers were sold. " The public has a very long nose," Mr. Ruskin once said, "and scents out what it wants, sooner or later." A second edition was issued, bound up into yearly volumes, of which eight were ultimately completed. Meanwhile the work went on, something in the style of the old Addison " Spectator; " each part containing twenty pages, more or less, by Mr. Ruskin, with added contributions from various correspondents.

" Fors Clavigera " is practically a continuation of " Time and Tide," and addressed, not to " working men " only, but to the workers of England, those who, like Thomas Dixon, had ears to hear, in whatever rank of life. Its name, like itself, is mystic, and changes content as it goes on, — the Fate or Force that bears the Club, or Key, or Nail: that is, in three aspects, — as following, or fore-ordaining, deed (or courage), and patience, and laws, unknown or known, of nature and life; so that the " Third Fors," that plays so large a part in this later period, is simply fortune. The general sense of the title expresses the general drift of the work; to show that life is to be bettered by each man's honest effort, and to be borne, in many things he cannot better, by his wise resignation; but that above all, and through all, and in all, there works a Power outside of him, to will and to do, to reward and to punish, eventually, by laws which, if he choose, he may partially understand, and, for the remainder, may trust.

To read " Fors " is like being out in a thunderstorm. At first, you open the book with interest, to watch the signs of the times. While you climb your mountain — shall we say the Old Man of Coniston? — at unawares there is a darkening of the cloud upon you, and the tension of instinctive dread, as image after image arises of misery, and murder, and lingering death, with here and there a streak of sun in the foreground, only throwing the wildness of the scene into more rugged relief; and through the gaps you see broad fields of ancient history, like lands of promise left behind. By and by the gloom wraps you. The old thunder of the Ruskinian paragraph, shortened now to whip-lash cracks, reverberates unremittingly from point to point, raising echoes, sounding deeps ; allusions, suggestions, intimations, stirring the realm of chaos, that ordinarily we are glad to let slumber, but now terribly discern, by flashes of thought, most unexpectedly arriving. Fascinated by the hammer - play of Thor, berserking among rime-giants, — customs that " hang upon us, heavy as frost," — you begin to applaud ; when a sudden stroke rolls your own standpoint into the abyss. But if you can climb forward, undismayed, to the summit, the storm drifts by; and you see the world again, all new, beneath you, — how rippling in Thor's laughter, how tenderly veiled in his tears!

Here is a short passage for a sample of the style. It opens hesitatingly : —

" Did you chance, my friends, any of you, to see, the other day, the 83d number of the 'Graphic,' with the picture of the Queen's concert in it? All the fine ladies sitting so trimly, and looking so sweet, and doing the whole duty of woman, — wearing their fine clothes gracefully; the pretty singer, white-throated, warbling ' Home, Sweet Home' to them, so morally and so melodiously? Here was yet to be our ideal of virtuous life, thought the 'Graphic!' Surely we are safe back with our virtues in satin slippers and lace veils; and our kingdom of Heaven is come again, *with* observation, and crown diamonds of the dazzlingest. Cherubim and seraphim in toilettes of Paris (bleu - de - ciel, vert d'olivier de Noé, mauve de colombe-fusillée), dancing to Coote and Tinney's band; and vulgar hell shall be didactically portrayed accordingly (see page 17[1]); wickedness going its way to *its* poor home, bitter sweet. Ouvrier and petroleuse, prisoners at last, glaring wild on their way to die.

" Alas! of these divided races, of whom one was

---

[1] Of the number of the *Graphic*, that is to say. Need I point out the imaginative symbolism in the names of colors suggested? It would take a page to analyze them.

appointed to teach and guide the other, which has indeed sinned deepest, — the unteaching, or the untaught? which now are guiltiest, — these who perish, or those who forget?

"Ouvrier and petroleuse; they are gone their way — to their death. But for these, the Virgin of France shall yet unfold the oriflamme above their graves, and lay her *blanches* lilies on their smirched dust. Yes, and for these, great Charles shall rouse his Roland, and bid him put ghostly trump to lip, and breathe a point of war; and the helmed Pucelle shall answer with a wood-note of Domrémy; yes, and for these the Louis they mocked, like his Master, shall raise his holy hands, and pray God's peace."

Carlyle could have uttered the growl with which the first paragraph of this passage ends; but only one man, since the prophets of old who wept over Jerusalem, could so directly, so magically, have beguiled you into his sympathy, and thrilled you with his wail.

But it is not all rhapsodic or elegiac; a great part of "Fors," contrasting with the prevailing gloom, is a coruscating play of wit, dazzling with side-glances of allusion which indeed require sharp watching to catch, and more erudition than the unassisted general reader is supposed to contribute to his reading. It is not so much in the form of epigram, here in "Fors;" though there is epigram, as thus: "I am not an unselfish person, nor an Evangelical one; I have no particular pleasure in doing good; neither do I dislike doing it so much as to expect to be rewarded for it in another world." Then again of the sort of journalism he would like to see: "I cannot say whether it would ever pay well to sell it; but I am sure it would pay well to read it, and to read no other." Or, in a more serious mood, the wit still dominating the form of expression: —

"Now, my religious friends, I continually hear you talk of acting for God's glory, and giving God praise. Might you not, for the present, think less of praising, and more of pleasing Him? He can perhaps dispense with your praise; your opinions of his character, even when they come to be held by a large body of the religious press, are not of material importance to Him."

Yet the charm of "Fors" is neither in epigram nor in anecdote, but in the sustained vivacity that runs through the texture of the work; the reappearance of golden threads of thought, glittering in new figures, and among new colors; and throughout all the variety of subject a unity of style unlike the style of his earlier works, where flowery rhetorical passages are tagged to less interesting chapters, separately studied sermonettes interposed among the geology, and Johnson, Locke, Hooker, Carlyle — or whoever happened to be the author he was reading at the time — frankly imitated. It was always cleverly done; but artificial, like the composition of a Renaissance painter who inserts his *bel corpo ignudo* to catch the eye. In " Fors," however, the whole web is of a piece; all sparkling with the same life; though as it is gradually unwound from the loom it is hard to judge the design. That can only be done where it is reviewed as a whole. But as a sample of his tapestry-stitch in its lighter figures, take such a passage as this : —

" The day before yesterday, a friend, who thinks my goose pie not an economical dish! sent me a penny cookery-book, a very desirable publication, which I instantly sat down to examine. It starts with the great principle that you must never any more roast your meat, but always stew it; and never have an open fire, but substitute, for the open fire, close stoves, all over England." .

(I must risk the seeming impertinence of an interruption to remind the reader that this is good wine, and must be taken in sips, to get its flavor; for instance, the mock gravity of the "very desirable publication," and the sarcastic echoes of science in " great principle," and of sentiment in "never any more." Farther down, the " prosperity," proved by the high price of coal, alludes to previous scornful analysis of an economic fallacy; and the vegetable soup of Theseus is a standing mystification throughout the first three years of " Fors.")

" Now observe.   There was once a dish, thought peculiarly English — Roast Beef. And once a place, thought peculiarly English — the Fireside. These two possessions are now too costly for you.

Your England, in her unexampled prosperity, according to the 'Morning Post,' can no longer afford her roast beef — or her fireside. She can only afford boiled bones, and a stove-side.

"Well. Boiled bones are not so bad things, neither. I know something more about *them* than the writer of the penny cookery book. Fifty years ago, Count Rumford perfectly ascertained the price, and nourishing power, of good soup; and I shall give you a recipe for Theseus' vegetable diet, and for Lycurgus' black and Esau's red pottage, for your better pot-luck. But what next?

"To-day, you cannot afford beef — to-morrow, are you sure that you will be still able to afford bones? If things are to go on thus, and you are to study economy to the utmost, I can beat the author of the penny cookery book even on that ground. What say you to this diet of the Otomac Indians; persons quite of our present English character?

"'They have a decided aversion to cultivate the land, and live almost exclusively on hunting and fishing. They are men of a very robust constitution, and passionately fond of fermented liquors. While the waters of the Orinoco are low, they subsist on fish and turtles, but at the period of its inundations (when the fishing ceases) they eat daily, during some months, three quarters of a pound of clay, slightly hardened by fire' — (probably stewable in your modern stoves with better effect). 'Half, at least' (this is Father

Gumilla's statement, quoted by Humboldt), 'of the bread of the Otomacs and the Guamoes is clay — and those who feel a weight on their stomach purge themselves with the fat of the crocodile, which restores their appetite, and enables them to continue to eat pure earth!' 'I doubt,' Humboldt himself goes on, 'the manteca de caiman being a purgative. But it is certain that the Guamoes are very fond, if not of the fat, at least of the flesh, of the crocodile!'

"We have surely brickfields enough to keep our clay from ever rising to famine prices, in any fresh accession of prosperity; and though fish can't live in our rivers, the muddy waters are just of the consistence crocodiles like; and, at Manchester and Rochdale, I have observed the surfaces of the streams smoking, so that we need be under no concern as to temperature. I should think you might produce quite 'streaky' crocodile, — fat and flesh concordant, — St. George becoming a bacon purveyor, as well as seller,[1] and laying down his dragon in salt (indeed, it appears, by an experiment made in Egypt itself, that the oldest of human words is Bacon); potted crocodile will doubtless, also, from countries unrestrained by

---

[1] Allusion to the blunder of Emerson, who confused the St. George of Cappadocia and Venice and England with the Arian bacon-selling bishop of Cilicia. The oldest word was what the Egyptian babies said, whom Psammetichus isolated from their birth for his famous experiment in comparative philology (Herodotus ii. 2), — βέκο-s; pronounced, with more distinctively neuter termination, Baco-n.

religious prejudices, be imported, as the English demand increases, at lower quotations; and for what you are going to receive, the Lord make you truly thankful."

I do not call those classical allusions pedantic; for they are the spontaneous suggestions of an imaginative and scholarly mind.   I do not call the quotations from Humboldt coarse; for they are the plain speech of an outraged sense of decency, — outraged in a way which less delicate natures cannot comprehend, in the proposals, not very fully set forth in the passage quoted, but often noticed in " Fors," to do away with the last remnants of the comforts of home, and the graces of life, in order to accommodate the impoverished laborer to his still more impoverished lot.   Nor do I call the conclusion profane; for it is a counter-blast of indignation against the well-meant but mistaken preaching which recommended, as a religious duty, acquiescence in remediable injustice, and the hypocrisy of gratitude for stones instead of daily bread.

But this mingling of jest and earnest was misunderstood.   After a while the author learned too painfully the danger of trifling with cherished beliefs.   He forswore levity, but soon relapsed into the old style, out of sheer sincerity; for he was too much in earnest not to be himself all over in his utterances, without writing up to, or down to, any other person's standard.   With all the declamation, and all the wit, there was substance enough of solid and reasonable purpose to knit the work together. It was not, as one of his old friends said, his mind's wastepaper basket; but the unfolding of wrappings, perhaps unnecessary, round a definite proposal. He began by declining all connection with ordinary political life in any form; he said that the existing order of things was wholly wrong, and just for that reason the existing methods of government could not set them right, by acts of a parliament which he simply declined to recognize as efficient to cope with the question. Instead of that, rescue was to come from individuals, as it has always done before in times of barbarism and anarchy. If men would, each in his place, carry out the rudiments of justice and social morality, — doing good work well, helping others, harming none, and showing themselves law-worthy, — if such-minded men and women would withdraw from the struggle for success in the world and set the example of better things in a wholesome country life; that, he felt, would really effect a change. It was like the old scheme of St. Benedict, — the formation of agricultural communities, by which Europe was, even more than by the feudal and chivalric institutions imitated in " Time and Tide," founded and civilized out of swampy forests and lawless barbarism.

Mr. Ruskin did not wish to lead a colony or to head a revolution. He had been pondering for fifteen years the cause of poverty and crime, and the conviction had grown upon him that modern commercialism was at the root of it all. Other men in other lands were being gradually led to the same conclusion by different ways; and French communism, German socialism, Russian anarchism were the expressions of a kindred movement,— but very differently developed. On the Continent the wrong was open and obvious, in the form of tyrannical government in church and state; the remedy suggested by precedent was violent rebellion. Here, in England, with apparent liberty of conduct and opinion, the same evils took a more subtle shape; and were practiced by the kindliest men and women with the best intentions. The slow and sure pace of our constitutional reforms accustomed us to a grumbling content, and a disinclination for extreme measures.

Mr. Ruskin's attacks on commercialism — his analysis of its bad influence on all sections of society — were too vigorous and uncompromising for the newspaper editors who received " Fors," and even for most of his private friends. We don't like agitators.

There were, however, some who saw what he was aiming at; and let it be remarked that his first encouragement came from the highest quarters. Just as Sydney Smith, the chief critic of earlier days, had been the first to praise " Modern Painters," in the teeth of adverse opinion, so now Carlyle spoke for " Fors."

5 CHEYNE ROW, CHELSEA,
April 30, 1871.

DEAR RUSKIN, — This "Fors Clavigera," Letter 5th, which I have just finished reading, is incomparable ; a quasi-sacred consolation to me, which almost brings tears into my eyes! Every word of it is as if spoken, not out of my poor heart only, but out of the eternal skies ; words winged with Empyrean wisdom, piercing as lightning, — and which I really do not remember to have heard the like of. *Continue*, while you have such utterances in you, to give them voice. They will find and force entrance into human hearts, *whatever* the "angle of incidence" may be ; that is to say, whether, for the degraded and *in*human Blockheadism we, so-called "men," have mostly now become, you come in upon them at the broadside, at the top, or even at the bottom. Euge, Euge !

Yours ever,

T. CARLYLE.

Others, like Sir Arthur Helps, joined in this encouragement. And the old struggle with the newspapers began over again.

They united in considering the whole business insane, though they did not doubt his sincerity when Mr. Ruskin put down his own money, the tenth of what he had, as he recommended his adherents to do. By the end of the year he had set aside £7000 toward establishing a company to be called of "St. George," as representing at once England and agriculture. Sir Thomas Dyke Acland and the Right Hon. W. Cowper-Temple (afterwards Lord Mount Temple), though not pledging themselves to approval of the scheme, undertook the trusteeship of the fund. A few friends subscribed ; in June, 1872, after a year and a half of "Fors," the first stranger sent in his contribution, and at the end of three years £236 13s. were collected to add to Mr. Ruskin's £7000, and a few acres of land were given. A start was made, of which we shall have to trace the fortunes in the sequel.

Meanwhile Mr. Ruskin practiced what he preached. He did not preach renunciation; he was not a pessimist any more than an optimist. Sometimes he felt he was not doing enough; he knew very well that others thought so. I remember his saying, in his rooms at Oxford, in one of those years: "Here I am, trying to reform the world, and I suppose I ought to begin with myself. I am trying to do St. Benedict's work, and I ought to be a saint. And yet I am living between a Turkey carpet and a Titian, and drinking as much tea" — taking his second cup — "as I can *swig!*"

That was the way he put it to an undergraduate; to a lady friend he wrote later on, "I 'm reading history of early saints, too, for my Amiens book, and feel that I ought to be scratched, or starved, or boiled, or something unpleasant; and I don't know if I 'm a saint or a sinner in the least, in mediæval language. How did the saints feel themselves, I wonder, about their saintship!"

It is very easy to preach, and not so difficult to practice the great renunciation. But what then? It is very hard to see clearly, and infinitely hard to follow, the straight path of even-handed justice, and the fulfillment of duty to all the complex claims of life in the midst of a crooked and perverse generation.

If he had forsaken all and followed the vocation of St. Francis, — he has discussed the question candidly in " Fors " for May, 1874, — would not his work have been more effectual, his example more inspiring? Conceivably; but that was not his mission. His gospel was not one of asceticism; it called upon no one for any sort of suicide, or even martyrdom. He required of his followers that they should live their lives to the full in "admiration, hope, and love," and not that they should sacrifice themselves in fasting and wearing of camels'-hair coats. He wished them to work, to be honest and just, in all things immediately attainable. He asked the tenth of their living, — not the widow's two mites; and it was deeply painful to him to find, sometimes, that they had so interpreted his teaching: as when he wrote, later, to Miss Beever: "One of my poor 'Companions of St. George' who has sent me, not a widow's but a parlor-maid's (an old schoolmistress) 'all her living,' and whom I found last night, dying, slowly and quietly, in a damp room, just the size of your study (which her landlord won't mend the roof of), by the light of a single tallow candle, — dying, I say, *slowly* of consumption, not yet near the end, but contemplating it with sorrow, mixed partly with fear lest she should not have done all she could for her children!

The sight of this and my own shameful comforts, three wax candles and blazing fire and dry roof, and Susie and Joanie for friends! Oh me, Susie, what *is* to become of me in the next world, who have in this life all my good things!"

All? No, not nearly all. But even of what he had, no man was ever readier to spend and sacrifice.

After carrying on "Fors" for some time his attention was drawn by Mr. W. C. Sillar to the question of "usury." At first he had seen no crying sin in interest. He had held that the "rights of capital" were visionary, and that the tools should belong to him that can handle them, in a perfect state of society; but he thought that the existing system was no worse in this respect than in others, and his expectation of reform in the plan of investment went hand-in-hand with his hope of a good time coming in everything else. So he quietly accepted his rents, as he accepted his professorship, for example, thinking it his business to be a good landlord and spend his money generously, just as he thought it his business to retain the existing South Kensington drawing school, and the Oxford system of education, — not at all his ideal, — and to make the best use of them.

A lady who was his pupil in drawing, and a believer in his ideals of philanthropy, Miss Octavia Hill, undertook to help him in 1864 in efforts to reclaim part — though a very small part — of the lower-class dwellings of London. Half a dozen houses in Marylebone left by Mr. Ruskin's father, to which he added three more in Paradise Place, as it was euphemistically named, were the subjects of their experiment. They were ridiculed at first; but by the noblest endeavor they succeeded, and set an example which has been followed in many of our towns with great results. They showed what a wise and kind landlord could do by caring for tenants, by giving them inhabitable dwellings, recreation ground, and fixity of tenure, and requiring in return a reasonable and moderate rent. Mr. Ruskin got five per cent. for his capital, instead of twelve or more, which such property generally returns, or at that time returned.

But when he began to write against rent and interest there were plenty of critics ready to cite this and other investments as a damning inconsistency. He was not the man to offer explanations at any time. It was no defense to say that he took less and did more than other landlords. And so he was glad to part with the whole to Miss Hill; nor did he care to spend upon himself the £3500 which, I believe, was the price. It went right and left in gifts; till one day he cheerfully remarked,

> "It 's a' gane awa'
> Like snaw aff a wa'."

"Is there really nothing to show for it?" he was

asked. " Nothing," he said, " except this new silk umbrella."

The tea-shop was one of Mr. Ruskin's " experiments " in connection with " Fors." He himself dislikes the word, because it savors of failure. But words are what we make of them ; and in this case he made experiment mean success. He had talked so much of the possibility of carrying on honest and honorable retail trade that he felt bound to exemplify his principles. He took a house, No. 19 Paddington Street, with a corner shop, near his Marylebone property, and set himself up in business as a tea-man. Mr. Arthur Severn painted the sign, in neat blue letters ; the window was decked with fine old china, bought from a cavaliere near Siena, whose unique collection had been introduced to notice by Professor Norton ; and Miss Harriet Tovey, an old servant of Denmark Hill, was established there, like Miss Mattie in " Cranford," or rather like one of the salaried officials of " Time and Tide," to dispense the unadulterated leaf to all comers. No advertisements, no self-recommendation, no catch-penny tricks of trade were allowed ; and yet the business went on, and, I am assured, prospered with legitimate profits.

At first, various kinds of the best tea only were sold ; but it seemed to the tenant of the shop that coffee and sugar ought to be included in the list. This was not at all in Mr. Ruskin's programme, and there were great debates at home about it.

At last he gave way, on the understanding that the shop was to be responsible for the proper roasting of the coffee according to the best recipe.

After some time Miss Tovey died. And when, in the autumn of 1876, Miss Octavia Hill proposed to take the house and business over and work it with the rest of the Marylebone property, the offer was thankfully accepted.

Another of his principles was cleanliness; "the speedy abolition of all abolishable filth is the first process of education." Indeed, it was one of his chief differences with an ill world that fouled its own nest — with sewage in its rivers and smoke in its lungs. There was "nothing so small and mean," as his George Herbert had said, that it did not come into his province. If the prophet had bidden us do some great thing! But his teaching was to attack the enemy in detail, and carry on a guerrilla warfare with all the powers of darkness.

It was a very unimportant outpost of the devil, it might appear, that he attacked when he undertook to keep certain streets, not crossings only, cleaner than the public seemed to care for, between the British Museum and St. Giles's. But that labor came to his hand, and he did it with his might. He took the broom himself, for a start, put on his gardener, Downs, as foreman of the job, and engaged a small staff of helpers. The work began, as he promised, in a humorous letter to the " P. M. G.," upon New Year's Day,

1872, and he kept his three sweepers at work for eight hours daily " to show a bit of our London streets kept as clean as the deck of a ship of the line."

There were some difficulties, too. One of the staff was an extremely handsome and lively shoe-black, picked up in St. Giles's. It turned out that he was not unknown in the world ; he had sat to artists — to Mr. Edward Clifford, to Mr. Severn ; and went by the name of " Cheeky." Every now and then Mr. Ruskin "and party " drove round to inspect the works. Downs could not be every-where at once; and Cheeky used to be caught at pitch and toss or marbles in unswept Museum Street. Mr. Ruskin never gives anybody " the sack ; " but street-sweeping was not good enough for Cheeky, and so he enlisted. The army was not good enough, and so he deserted ; and was last seen disappearing into the darkness, after calling a cab for his old friends one night at the Albert Hall.

The Oxford diggings and St. George's farms afterwards claimed Downs's services. Enough, however, had been done to set the example, and to show that

> " Who sweeps a — street — as for Thy laws,
> Makes that — and the action — fine."

One more escapade of this most unpractical man, as they called him. Since his fortune was rapidly melting away, he had to look to his works as an ultimate resource; they have actually become his only means of livelihood. One might suppose that he would be anxious to put his publishing business on the most secure and satis-factory footing; to facilitate sale, and to ensure profit. But he had views. He objected to advertising; though he thought that in his St. George's scheme he would have a yearly book gazette drawn up by responsible authorities, indicating the best works. He distrusted the system of *unacknowledged* profits and percentages, though he fully agreed that the retailer should be paid for his work, and wished, in an ideal state, to see the shopkeeper a salaried official. He disliked the bad print and paper of the cheap literature of that day, and knew that people valued more highly what they did not get so easily. He had changed his mind with regard to one or two things — religion and glaciers chiefly — about which he had written at length in earlier works.

So he withdrew his most popular books — " Modern Painters " and the rest — from circulation, though he was persuaded by the publisher to reprint " Modern Painters " and " Stones of Venice " once more, — " positively for the last time," as they said the plates would give no more good impressions. He had his later writings printed in a rather expensive style; at first by Smith & Elder, after two years by Messrs. Watson & Hazell (now Hazell, Watson & Viney, Ltd.); and the method of publication is illustrated in the history of " Sesame and Lilies," the first volume of these "collected works." It was issued by Smith & Elder, May, 1871, at seven shillings, to the trade only, leaving the retailer to fix the price to the public. In September, 1872, the work was also supplied by Mr. George Allen, and the price was raised to nine shillings and sixpence (carriage paid) to trade and public alike, with the idea that an extra shilling, or nearly ten per cent., might be added by the bookseller for his trouble in ordering the work. If he did not add the commission, that was his own affair, though with postage of order and payment, when only one or two copies at a time were asked for, this did not leave much margin. So it was doubled, by the simple expedient of doubling the price!—or, to be accurate, raising it to eighteen shillings (carriage paid) for twenty shillings over the counter. It was freely prophesied by business men that this would not do; however, at the end of fifteen years the sixth edition of this work in this form was being sold, in spite of the fact that, five years before, a smaller edition of the same book had been brought out at five shillings, and was then in its fourth edition of 3,000 copies each.

Compared with the enormous sale of sensational novels and schoolbooks, this is no great matter; but for a didactic work, offered to the public without advertisement, and in the face of the almost universal opposition of the book-selling trade, it means not only that, as an author, Mr. Ruskin had made a secure reputation, but also that he deserved the curious tribute once paid him by the journal of a big modern shop (Compton House, Liverpool) as a " great tradesman."

His high prices were a stumbling-block to most of his readers; and indeed he has withdrawn his objection to cheapness, since finding that it does not mean bad printing, and that there are many people who, though they cannot afford the old-fashioned scholar's library, have the old-fashioned scholar's respect for books. Formerly, when clerks from Glasgow or working men from Manchester wrote to say that they really wanted to read him, but really could not afford, he replied with a growl that if a child in the gutter wanted a picture book he would say, " Come out of that first !" Which, though a hard saying, truly represented his attitude. He distrusted people who lamented their dismal lot, and showed no courage to mend it; who protested a thirst for nature and art, and yet took no steps to enjoy what they could get, or to get what they could enjoy,— " So here we sit sullen in the black slime "—*or ci attristiam nella belletta negra.* If they bought anything of his, there was " Fors," in which he was giving his best, at the price, as he said, of two pots of beer a month!

CHAPTER III.

OXFORD TEACHING.

(1872–1875.)

> " How should he care what men may say,
>   Who see no heaven day by day,
>   And dream not of his hidden way?
>
> " For though betwixt dull earth and him
>   Such clouds and mists deceptive swim,
>   That to his eyes life's ways look dim ;
>
> " Yet when on high he lifts his gaze
>   He sees the stars' untroubled ways
>   And the divine of endless days."
>   *To " the Ethereal Ruskin " (Spectator*, June 5, 1875).

EARLY in 1872, after bringing out " Munera
Pulveris " and the essays he had written ten years
before for " Fraser " on economy ; after getting
those street-sweepers to work near the British
Museum, where he was making studies of animals
and Greek sculpture ; and after once more ad-
dressing the Woolwich cadets, this time on the
Bird of Calm (the mythology of the Halcyon),
Professor Ruskin went to Oxford to give a course
of ten lectures on the relation of natural science
to art, afterwards published under the title of
" The Eagle's Nest." He wrote to Professor Norton, " I am, as usual, unusually busy. When I

get fairly into my lecture work at Oxford I always find the lecture would come better some other way, just before it is given, and so work from hand to mouth. I am always unhappy, and see no good in saying so. But I am settling to my work here — recklessly — to do my best with it; feeling quite sure that it is talking at hazard, for what chance good may come. But I attend regularly in the schools as mere drawing-master, and the men begin to come in one by one, about fifteen or twenty already; several worth having as pupils in any way, being of temper to make good growth of."

Why was he always unhappy? It was not that Mr. W. B. Scott criticised "Mr. Ruskin's Influence" in that March; or that by Easter he had to say farewell to his old home on Denmark Hill, and settle "for good" at Brantwood. Nor that he could go abroad again for a long summer in Italy with Mr. and Mrs. Severn and the Hilliards and Mr. Albert Goodwin; though it was a busy time they spent. They started about the middle of April, and on the journey out he wrote, beside his "Fors," which always went on, a preface to the Rev. R. St. John Tyrwhitt's "Christian Art and Symbolism." He drew the apse at Pisa, half-amused and half-worried by the little ragamuffin who varied the tedium of watching his work by doing horizontal bar tricks on those railings which, the tourist knows, fence the cathedral green. Then to Lucca, where, to show his friends something of Italian landscape, he took them for rambles through the olive farms and chestnut woods, among which Miss Hilliard lost her jeweled cross. Greatly to Mr. Ruskin's delight, for he is a firm believer in Italian peasant-virtue, it was found and returned without offer of reward.

At Rome they visited old Mr. Severn, and then went homeward by way of Verona, where Mr. Ruskin wrote an account of the Cavalli monuments for the Arundel Society, and Venice, where he returned to the study of Carpaccio. At Rome he had been once more to the Sistine, and found that the ceiling and the Last Judgment had taken his attention on earlier visits too exclusively. Now that he could look away from Michelangelo he became conscious of the claims of Botticelli's frescoes, which represent, in the Florentine school, somewhat the same kind of interest that he had found in Carpaccio. He became enamored of Botticelli's Zipporah, and resolved to study the master more closely. On reaching home he had to prepare " The Eagle's Nest " for publication; in the preface he gave special importance to Botticelli, and amplified it in lectures on early engraving, that autumn ;[1] in which he quoted with appreciation the passage on the Venus Anadyomene from Mr. Pater's " Studies in the Renaissance," just published.

This sudden enthusiasm about an unknown painter amused the Oxford public; and it became

---

[1] *Ariadne Florentina.* Mr. Ruskin's first mention of Botticelli was in the course on landscape, Lent term, 1871.

a standing joke among the profane to ask who was Ruskin's last great man. It was in answer to that, and in expression of a truer understanding than most Oxford pupils attained, that Bourdillon of Worcester wrote on " the Ethereal Ruskin," — that was Carlyle's name for him : —

> " To us this star or that seems bright,
>   And oft some headlong meteor's flight
>   Holds for awhile our raptured sight.

> " But he discerns each noble star;
>   The least is only the most far,
>   Whose worlds, may be, the mightiest are."

The critical value of this course, however, to a student of art-history, is impaired by his using, as illustrations of Botticelli and of the manner of engraving which he took for standard, certain plates which were erroneously attributed, and impressions of them which perhaps misrepresent their original condition as intended by the artist. " It is strange," he wrote in despair to Professor Norton, " that I hardly ever get anything stated without some grave mistake, however true in my main discourse." But in this case a fate stronger than he had taken him unawares. The circumstances do not extenuate the error of the professor, but they explain the difficulties under which his work was done.

For on his return to England this August, 1872, an event had happened, too important in its consequences to be left unnoticed, though too painful for more than a passing allusion.

Many of his readers know, and many more must suspect, that there was some reason for his being "always unhappy,"—that something at this period came to a crisis, that it turned out unfortunately, and wrecked, " on a low lee shore," a career which though stormy had been prosperous, and was now approaching the desired haven. The cloud that rested on his own life was, without doubt, the result of a strange and wholly unexpected tragedy in another's.

It was an open secret — his attachment to a lady who had been his pupil, and was now generally understood to be his *fiancée*. She was far younger than he; but at fifty-three he was not an old man; and the friends who fully knew and understood the affair favored his intentions, and joined in the hope, and in auguries for the happiness which he had been so long waiting for, and so richly deserved. But now that it came to the point the lady finally decided that it was impossible. He was not at one with her in religious matters. He could speak lightly of her evangelical creed, — it seemed he scoffed in " Fors " at her faith. She could not be unequally yoked with an unbeliever. To her, the alternative was plain; the choice was terrible: yet, having once seen her path, she turned resolutely away. It cost her life. Three years after, as she lay dying, he begged to see her once more. She sent to ask whether he could yet say that he loved God better than he loved her; and when he said " No," her door was closed upon him forever.

Meanwhile, in the bitterest despair, he sought refuge, as he had done before, in his work. He accepted the lesson, though he, too, could not recant; still he tried to correct his apparent levity in the renewed seriousness and more earnest tone of " Fors," speaking more plainly and more simply, but without concession. He wrote on the next Christmas Eve to an Aberdeen Bible-class teacher : —

" If you care to give your class a word directly from me, say to them that they will find it well, throughout life, never to trouble themselves about what they ought *not* to do, but about what they *ought* to do. The condemnation given from the Judgment Throne — most solemnly described — is all for the *undones* and not for the *dones*. People are perpetually afraid of doing wrong; but unless they are doing its reverse energetically, they do it all day long, and the degree does not matter.

" Make your young hearers resolve to be honest in their work in this life. Heaven will take care of them for the other."

That was all he could say; he did not *know* there was another life ; he *hoped* there was ; and yet, if he were not a saint or a Christian, was there any man in the world who was nearer to the kingdom of heaven than this stubborn heretic?

His heretical attitude was singular. He was just as far removed from adopting the easy antagonism of science to religion as from siding with religion against science. In a singularly interesting — and in his biography important — paper on the " Nature and Authority of Miracle," read to the Metaphysical Society (February 11, 1873), he tried to clear up his position.

" The phenomena of the universe," he said, "with which we are acquainted, are assumed to be, under general conditions, constant, but to be maintained in that constancy by a supreme personal mind; and it is farther supposed that, under particular conditions, this ruling Person interrupts the constancy of these phenomena, in order to establish a particular relation with inferior creatures." He thought that the religious mind was sometimes hasty in claiming that miracles were worked for private advantage, — but he believed that miracles have happened and do happen. "A human act may be super-doggish, and a Divine act super-human, yet all three acts absolutely natural. . . . We can only look for an imperfect and interrupted, but may surely insist on an occasional manifestation of miraculous credentials by every minister of religion. . . . ' These signs shall follow them that believe ' are words which admit neither of qualification nor misunderstanding; and it is far less arrogant in any man to look for such Divine attestation of his authority as a teacher, than to claim, without it, any authority to teach. And assuredly it is no proof of any unfitness or unwisdom in such expectations that, for the last thousand years, miraculous powers seem to have been withdrawn from, or at least, indemonstrably possessed by, a church which, having been again and again warned by its Master that Riches were deadly to Religion, and Love essential to it, has nevertheless made wealth the reward of theological learning, and controversy its occupation."

With that year expired the term for which he had been elected to the Slade professorship, and in January, 1873, he was reëlected. In his first three years he had given five courses of lectures designed to introduce an encyclopædic review and reconstruction of all he had to say upon art. Beginning with general principles, he had proceeded to their application in history, by tracing certain phases of Greek sculpture, and by contrasting the Greek and the Gothic spirit as shown in the treatment of landscape, from which he went on to the study of early engraving. The application of his principles to theory was made in the course on science and art (" The Eagle's Nest"). Now, on his reëlection, he proceeded to take up these two sides of his subject, and to illustrate his view of the right way to apply science to art, by a course on birds, in nature, art and mythology, and next year by a study of Alpine forms. The historical side was continued with lectures on Niccola Pisano and early Tuscan sculpture, and in 1874 with an important, though unpublished, course on Florentine art.

It is to this cycle of lectures that we must look

for that matured Ruskinian theory of art which his early works do not reach ; and which his writings between 1860 and 1870 do not touch. Though the Oxford lectures are only a fragment of what he ought to have done, they should be sufficient to a careful reader; though their expression is sometimes obscured by diffuse treatment, they contain the root of the matter, thought out for fifteen years since the close of the more brilliant, but less profound, period of " Modern Painters."

The course on birds, Lent term, 1873, was given in the drawing school at the University Galleries. The room was not large enough for the numbers that crowded to hear Professor Ruskin, and each of these lectures, like the previous and the following courses, had to be repeated to a second audience. Great pains had been given to their preparation, — much greater than the easy utterance and free treatment of his theme led his hearers to believe. For these lectures and their sequel, published as " Love's Meinie," he collected an enormous number of skins — to compare the plumage and wings of different species; for his work was with the outside aspect and structure of birds, not with their anatomy. He had models made, as large as swords, of the different quill-feathers, to experiment on their action and resistance to the air. He got a valuable series of drawings by H. S. Marks, R. A., and made many careful and beautiful studies himself of feathers and of birds, at the Zoölogical Gardens and the

British Museum ; and after all, he had to conclude his work saying, " It has been throughout my trust that if death should write on these, ' What this man began to build, he was not able to finish,' God may also write on them, not in anger, but in aid, ' A stronger than he cometh.' "

The lectures on birds were repeated at Eton before the boys' literary and scientific society and their friends ; and between this and 1880 Mr. Ruskin often went to address the same audience, with the same interest in young people that had taken him in earlier years to Woolwich.

After a long vacation at Brantwood, the first spent there, he went up to give his course on Niccola Pisano (" Val d'Arno "). The lectures were printed separately and sold at the conclusion, and the first numbers were sent to Carlyle, whose unabated interest in his friend's work was shown in his letter of October 31st: " After several weeks of eager expectation I received, morning before yesterday, the sequel to your kind little note, in the shape of four bright quarto lectures (forwarded by an Aylesbury printer) on the Historical and Artistic Development of Val d'Arno. Many thanks to you for so pleasant and instructive a gift. The work is full of beautiful and delicate perceptions, new ideas, both new and true, which throw a brilliant illumination over that important piece of History, and awake fresh curiosities and speculations on that and on other much wider subjects. It is all written with the old nobleness and fire, in which no other living voice, to my knowledge, equals yours. *Perge, perge ;* — and, as the Irish say, ' more power to your elbow!'

"I have yet read this ' Val d'Arno' only once. Froude snatched it away from me yesterday; and it has then to go to my brother at Dumfries. After that I shall have it back."

During that summer and autumn Mr. Ruskin suffered from nights of sleeplessness or unnaturally vivid dreams, and days of unrest and feverish energy, alternating with intense fatigue. The eighteen lectures in less than six weeks, a "combination of prophecy and play-acting," as Carlyle had called it in his own case, and the unfortunate discussion with an old-fashioned economist who undertook to demolish Ruskinism without understanding it, added to the causes of which we are already aware, brought him to New Year, 1874, in "failing strength, care, and hope." He sought quiet at Ilfracombe, but found modern hotel-life intolerable; he went back to town and tried the pantomimes for distraction, — saw Kate Vaughan in Cinderella, and Violet Cameron in Jack in the Box, over and over again, and found himself " now hopelessly a man of the world ! — of that woeful outside one, I mean. It is now Sunday; half-past eleven in the morning. Everybody else is gone to church, — and I am left alone with the cat, in the world of sin." Thinking himself better, he went to Oxford, and announced a course on Alpine form ; but after a week was obliged to retreat and go home to Coniston, still hoping to return and give his lectures. But it was no use. The gloom without deepened the gloom within; and he took the wisest course in trying Italy, alone this time with his old servant Crawley.

The greater part of 1874 was spent abroad, — first traveling through Savoy and by the Riviera to Assisi, where he fell dangerously ill again, as at Matlock in 1871. He dreamed in his illness that they had made him a brother of the third degree of the order of St. Francis, — a fancy that took strong hold of his mind ; and he wrote his " Fors " for May under great temptation to follow St. Francis, not in adopting his creed, but in imitating his renunciation. But saving common-sense reminded him of his duties to his pupils at Oxford, and he contented himself with playing at monks with the last survivors of the great Franciscan convent. He wrote to Miss S. Beever : —

" The Sacristan gives me my coffee for lunch in his own little cell, looking out on the olive woods; then he tells me stories of conversions and miracles, and then perhaps we go into the sacristy and have a reverent little poke-out of relics. Fancy a great carved cupboard in a vaulted chamber full of most precious things (the box which the Holy Virgin's veil used to be kept in, to begin with), and leave to rummage in it at will ! Things that are only shown twice in the year or so, with fumigation ! all the congregation on their knees — and the sacristan and I having a great heap of them on the table at once, like a dinner service! I really looked with great respect on St. Francis's old camel-hair dress."

Thence he went to visit Mrs. and Miss Yule at Palermo, deeply interested in Scylla and Charybdis, Etna and the metopes of Selinus. His interest in Greek art had been shown, not only in a course of lectures, but in active support to archæological explorations. He said once, " I believe heartily in diggings, of all sorts." Meeting General L. P. di Cesnola and hearing of the wealth of ancient remains in Cyprus, then newly discovered, Mr. Ruskin placed £1000 at his disposal. In spite of the confiscation of half the treasure-trove by the local government, General di Cesnola was able, in April, 1875, to announce that he had shipped a cargo of antiquities, including many vases, terra-cottas, and fragments of sculpture, which proved most valuable as illustrations of the growth of Greek art from the earliest Egypto-Assyrian form into the later periods.

The landscape of Theocritus and the remains of ancient glories roused him to energetic sketching, — a sign of returning strength, which continued when he reached Rome, and enabled him to make a very fine copy of Botticelli's Zipporah, and other details of the Sistine frescoes.

The account of this journey can be gathered, in more detail than we can spare it here, in " Hortus Inclusus" and " Fors." Late in October he reached England, just able to give the promised lectures on Alpine forms, — I remember his curious attempt to illustrate the névé-masses by pouring flour on a model, — and a second course on the æsthetic and mathematic schools of Florence; and a lecture on Botticelli at Eton, of which the literary and scientific society's minute-book contains the following report : —

"On Saturday, December 12th (1874), Professor Ruskin lectured before a crowded, influential, and excited audience, which comprised our noble society and a hundred and thirty gentlemen and ladies, who eagerly accepted an invitation to hear Professor Ruskin 'talk' to us on Botticelli.

"It is utterly impossible for the unfortunate secretary of the society to transmit to writing even an abstract of this address; and it is some apology for him when beauty of expression, sweetness of voice, and elegance in imagery defy the utmost efforts of the pen."

Just before leaving for Italy he had been told that the Royal Institute of British Architects intended to present him with their gold medal in acknowledgment of his services to the cause of architecture; and during his journey official announcement of the award reached him. He dictated from Assisi, where he was at the moment (June 12, 1874) seriously ill, a letter to Sir Gilbert Scott, explaining why he declined the honor intended him. He said in effect, that if it had been offered at a time when he had been writing on architecture it would have been welcome; but

it was not so now that he felt all his efforts to have
been in vain and the profession as a body engaged
in work — such as the "restoration" of ancient
buildings — with which he had no sympathy.
"That I have myself failed, I have, as you tell me,
again and again confessed.   That I have made
the most fatal mistakes, I have also confessed.
That I have received no help, but met the most
scornful opposition in every effort I have ever
made which came into collision with the pecuniary
interests of modern builders, may, perhaps in a
degree more than I know, have occasioned my
failure."   It had been represented to him that his
refusal to accept a royal medal would be a reflec-
tion upon the royal donor.   To which he replied, " Having entirely loyal feelings towards the
Queen, I will trust to her Majesty's true interpretation of my conduct ; but if formal justification
of it be necessary for the public, would plead that
if a peerage or knighthood may without disloy-
alty be refused, surely much more the minor grace
proceeding from the monarch may be without im-
propriety declined by any of her Majesty's subjects who wish to serve her without reward, under
the exigency of peculiar circumstances."

It was only the term before that Prince Leopold had been at Oxford, a constant attendant on
Mr. Ruskin's lectures, and a visitor to his drawing
school.   The gentle prince, with his instinct for
philanthropy, was not to be deterred by the utterances of " Fors " from respecting the genius of

A certain portion of the work of man must be for his bread : and that is his Labour; — with the sweat of his face, for accomplished as a daily task — and ended as a daily task — with the prayer — Give us each day our daily bread. But another portion of Man's work is that in which according to his own separate gift and strength, he carries forward the purposes Morality of Lord for his Race: accepts from his Sires their Knowledge and their Art; adds to this his store of true craftsmans cutting — bequeaths his own piece and a part of the Immortal of work of this World — to the Future. be it here

in his own place — our work of our hands; Establish thou it
this work is — And the

it is in Heaven   honestly, In our own life of today
And the toil of the hands, for this life —
is our 'labour'.
But the toil of hand and heart, honestly — for
the future of life of others — is our 'Opus; — of
which when well done — the angels may say;
Perfecit opus' — Perfected — Did it thoroughly. and
of which before his eyes are closed — the promise is
to every servant of God. 'He shall see of the travail
of his soul, and shall be satisfied':

the professor; and the professor, with his old-world, cavalier loyalty, readily returned the esteem and affection of his new pupil. A sincere friendship was formed, lasting until the prince's death, which nobody lamented more bitterly than the man who had found so much in him and hoped so much from him.

At the end of the next summer term (June, 1875) Princess Alice and her husband, with Prince Arthur and Prince Leopold, were at Oxford. Mr. Ruskin had just made arrangements completing his gifts to the university galleries and schools. The royal party showed great interest in the professor and his work. The princess, the Grand Duke of Hesse, and Prince Leopold acted as witnesses to the deed of gift; and Prince Arthur and Prince Leopold accepted the trusteeship.

With all the Slade professor's generosity, the Ruskin drawing school, founded in these fine galleries to which he had so largely contributed, in a palatial hall handsomely furnished, and hung with Tintoret and Luini, Burne-Jones and Rossetti, and other rare masters, ancient and modern; with the most interesting examples to copy, — at the most convenient of desks, we may add, — in spite of it all, the drawing school was not a popular institution. When the professor was personally teaching, he got some fifteen or twenty — if not to attend, at any rate to join. But whenever the chief attraction could not be counted on, the attendance sank to an average of two or three. The cause was simple. An undergraduate is supposed to spend his morning in lectures, his afternoon in taking exercise, and his evening in college. There is simply no time in his scheme for going to a drawing school. If it were recognized as part of the curriculum, if it counted in any way along with other studies, or contributed to a "school" akin to that of music, practical art might become teachable at Oxford ; and Professor Ruskin's gifts and endowments — to say nothing of his hopes and plans — would not be wholly in vain.

It could not be hid, also, that Professor Ruskin's heart was elsewhere, though he put so much work — and money — into the foundation of a drawing school: as it were, to excuse his waning interest in art-teaching, and growing disbelief in the value of lectures. He found, as he said to a Glasgow man who invited him to hold forth there, that everybody wanted to hear, — nobody to read, — nobody to think. " To be excited for an hour, and, if possible, amused ; to get the knowledge it has cost a man half his life to gather, first sweetened up to make it palatable, and then kneaded into the smallest possible pills, — and to swallow it homœopathically and be wise. . . . It is not to be done. A living comment quietly given to a class on a book they are earnestly reading, — this kind of lecture is eternally necessary and wholesome."

He really wanted to be the guide, philosopher, and friend of some of those " worth having in any

way, — of temper to make good growth of;" and
to attract, not the would-be amateurs and dilettanti, or the academically and professionally successful men, but those who were going to be the
real thinkers and workers.

As he could not make the undergraduates draw,
he made them dig. He had noticed a very bad
bit of road on the Hinksey side, and heard that it
was nobody's business to mend it; meanwhile the
farmers' carts and casual pedestrians were bemired.
He sent for his gardener Downs, who had been
foreman of the street-sweepers; laid in a stock of
picks and shovels; took lessons in stone-breaking
himself, and called on his friends to spend their
recreation times in doing something useful. In
spite of a good deal of ridicule, something useful
was actually done. More picks were broken and
more time was lost than a regular business-con-
tractor would have liked; but the men had their
lesson and the cottagers their road. It was mali-
ciously said that the "Hinksey diggings" were
abandoned because the rustics jeered at the dig-
gers. The work was stopped when the work was
finished; it was no part of the scheme to take all
the bad roads of the county off the surveyor's
hands. Of jeers, none were offered that I remember; I recollect an oration of encouragement
and thanks from one of the farmers, who explained
the reason why the road was neglected, and described the rights accruing to us by law or by
custom, for keeping it up. I believe we were

entitled to graze a cow on a common — or something of the sort; at the time, however, we did not
value the privilege as we ought, and I am afraid
it was we who jeered at the rustic; the professor
being absent, be it understood.

Many of the disciples met at the weekly open
breakfasts at the professor's rooms in Corpus;
and he was glad of a talk to them on other things
beside drawing and digging. Some were attracted
chiefly by the celebrity of the man, or by the
curiosity of his humorous discourse; but there
were a few who partly grasped one side or other
of his mission and character. The cleverest of
the circle was W. H. Mallock, known then as a
nephew of Mr. Froude and a Newdigate-winner;
afterwards more widely known as the author of
" Is Life Worth Living ? " He was the only
man, Professor Ruskin said, who really understood him, — referring to " The New Republic."
But while Mallock saw the reactionary and pessi-
mistic side of his Oxford teacher, there was a
progressist and optimistic side which does not
appear in his " Mr. Herbert." That was discovered by another man, whose career, short as it was,
proved even more influential. Arnold Toynbee
was one of the professor's warmest admirers and
ablest pupils; and in his philanthropic work the
teaching of " Unto this Last " and " Fors " was
illustrated, — not exclusively, — but truly. " No
true disciple of mine will ever be a Ruskinian "
(to quote " St. Mark's Rest "); " he will follow,

not me, but the instincts of his own soul, and the guidance of its Creator."

Like other energetic men, Mr. Ruskin was fond of setting other people to work. One of his plans was to form a little library of standard books (" Bibliotheca Pastorum ") suitable for the kind of people who, he hoped, would join or work under his St. George's Company. The first book he chose was the " Economist " of Xenophon, which he asked two of his young friends to translate. I look back with astonishment at his patience in the midst of preoccupying labor and severest trial; for just then he was lecturing on the Alps at the London Institution, reading a paper to the Metaphysical Society, writing the Academy Notes of 1875, and " Proserpina," etc., as well as his regular work at " Fors," and the St. George's Company was then taking definite form, — and all the while the lady of his love was dying under the most tragic circumstances, and he forbidden to approach her.

In spite of sorrow, with strange firmness of mind, he would meet his pupils and give his afternoons to them ; he would correct their blunders and discuss their readings, — not like a tutor, but rather like a fellow-student; and bring all his wide knowledge to bear on the side issues of the story, so that it grew into the most fascinating of lessons.

On the 29th of May she died. On the 1st of June the royal party honored the Slade professor with their visit, — little knowing how valueless to him such honors had become. He went north and met his translators at Brantwood to finish the Xenophon; and to help dig his harbor and cut coppice in his wood. He prepared a preface; but the next term was one of greater pressure, with the twelve lectures on Sir Joshua Reynolds to deliver; and he wrote after Christmas: —

" Now that I have got my head fairly into this Xenophon business, it has expanded into a new light altogether; and I think it would be absurd in me to slur over the life in one paragraph. A hundred things have come into my head as I arrange the dates, and I think I can make a much better thing of it, with a couple of days' work. My head would not work in town; merely turned from side to side, — never nodded (except sleepily). I send you the proofs just to show you I 'm at work. I 'm going to translate all the story of Delphic answer before Anabasis; and his speech after the sleepless night." Delphic answers and sleepless nights were becoming too frequent in his own experience; and yet he could stop to explain himself, with forbearance, in answer to remarks on the proofs : —

" I had no notion you felt that flaw so seriously, or would have written at once. I should never call inspired prophecy ' Classical,' — nor the Sermon on the Mount — nor the like of it. All inspired writing stands on a nobler authority. 'Hail thou that art highly favored ' does not contain constant truth, for all, — but instant truth — for

Mary. If we criticise it as *language*, or ' Scripture ' writing — you must do so in its *Greek* or *Roman* words. But ' quanto quisque sibi plura negaverit Ab Dîs plura feret ' is classic, Eternal truth, in the best possible words. Whereas, ' If thine eye offend thee, pluck it out ' is not constant truth unless received in a certain temper and admitting certain conditions. It is then much *more* than constant truth. ' Scripture ' and ' writing,' — ' picture ' and ' painting,' are always used by me as synonymous terms."

The lectures on Reynolds went off with *éclat*, in spite of less pains bestowed on their preparation. I remember distinctly the brilliancy of rhetoric, the magic of oratory, the astonishing reaches of thought, utterly unlike the teaching of either the scribes or the Pharisees of modern times. I have the manuscript before me, and wonder, with increasing admiration, at the genius which transmuted these scribbled jottings, hardly to be called even notes, — these hieroglyphs, blots, mere hints and winks at words, — into the magnificent flow of rolling paragraph and rounded argument, that thrilled a captious audience with unwonted emotion, and almost persuaded many a careless or cynic hearer to abjure his worship of muscle or of brain for the nobler gospel of " the Ethereal Ruskin." In spite of strangeness, and a sense of antagonism to his surroundings, which grew from day to day, he did useful work which none other could do in the university, and wielded an enormous influence for good. That this was then acknowledged was proved by his reëlection, early in 1876; but his third term of three years was a time of weakened health. The cause of it, the greatest sorrow of his life, we have just revealed ; at the time the public put it down to disappointed egotism, or whatever they fancied. But repeated absence from his post and inability to fulfill his duties made it obviously his wisest course, at the end of that third term, to resign the Slade professorship.

CHAPTER IV.

ST. GEORGE AND ST. MARK.

(1875-1877.)

"A curious volume, patch'd and torn,
   That all day long, from earliest morn,
   Had taken captive her two eyes
   Among its golden broideries;
   Perplexed her with a thousand things, —
   The stars of Heaven, and angels' wings,
   Moses' breastplate, and the seven
   Candlesticks John saw in Heaven,
   The winged lion of St. Mark,
   And the Covenantal Ark."

KEATS.

IN the book his Bertha of Canterbury was reading at twilight on the Eve of St. Mark, Keats might have been describing "Fors." Among its pages, fascinating with their golden broideries of romance and wit, perplexing with mystic vials of wrath as well as all the Seven Lamps and Shekinah of old and new covenants commingled, there was gradually unfolded the plan of "St. George's Work."

The scheme was not easy to apprehend; it was essentially different from anything then known, though superficially like several bankrupt Utopias. Mr. Ruskin did not want to found a phalanstery, or to imitate Robert Owen or the Shakers. That would have been practicable — and useless.

He wanted much more. He aimed at the gradual introduction of higher aims into ordinary life; at giving true refinement to the lower classes, true simplicity to the upper. He proposed that idle hands should reclaim waste lands; that healthy work and country homes should be offered to townsfolk who would "come out of the gutter." He asked landowners and employers to furnish opportunities for such reforms; which would involve no elaborate organization nor unelastic rules, — simply the one thing needful, the refusal of commercialism.

As before, he scorned the idea that any good could be done by political agitation. Any government would work, he said, if it were an efficient government. No government was efficient unless it saw that every one had the necessaries of life, for body and soul; and that every one earned them by some work or other. Capital, that is, the means and material of labor, should therefore be in the hands of the government, not in the hands of individuals; this reform would result easily and necessarily from the forbidding of loans on interest. Personal property would still be in private hands; but as it could not be invested and turned into capital, it would necessarily be restricted to its actual use, and great accumulation would be valueless.

This is, of course, a very sketchy statement of

the groundwork of " Fors," but to most readers nowadays as comprehensible as, twenty years ago or less, it was incomprehensible. For when, long after " Fors " had been written, Mr. Ruskin found other writers advocating the same principles and calling themselves socialists, he said that he too was a socialist.

But the socialists of various sects have complicated, and sometimes confused, their simple fundamental principles with various ways and means, to which Mr. Ruskin could not agree. He had his own ways and means. He had his private ideals of life, which he expounded, along with his main doctrine. He thought, justifiably, that theory was useless without practical example; and so he founded St. George's Company (in 1877 called St. George's Guild) as his illustration.

The guild grew out of his call, in 1871, for adherents; and by 1875 began to take definite form. Its objects were to set the example of socialistic capital as opposed to a national debt, and of socialistic labor as opposed to competitive struggle for life. Each member was required to do some work for his living, — without too strict limits as to the kind, — and to practice certain precepts of religion and morality, broad enough for general acceptance. He was also required to obey the authority of the guild, and to contrib-ute a tithe of his income to a common fund, for various objects. These objects were, — first, to buy land for the agricultural members to cultivate, paying their rent, not to the other members, but to the company; not refusing machinery, but preferring manual labor. Next, to buy mills and factories, to be likewise owned by the guild and worked by members, using water power in preference to steam (steam at first not forbidden), and making the lives of the people employed as well spent as might be, with a fair wage, healthy work, and so forth. The loss on starting was to be made up from the guild store, but it was anticipated that the honesty of the goods turned out would ultimately make such enterprises pay, even in a commercial world. Then, for the people employed and their families, there would be places of recreation and instruction, supplied by the guild, and intended to give the agricultural laborer or mill-hand, trained from infancy in guild schools, some insight into literature, science, and art, — and tastes which his easy position would leave him free to cultivate.

So far the plan was simple. It was not a colony, but merely the working of existing industries in a certain way. Anticipating further development of the scheme, Mr. Ruskin looked forward to a guild coinage, as pretty as the Florentines had; a costume as becoming as the Swiss; and other Platonically devised details, which were not the essentials of the proposal, and never came into operation. But some of his plans were actually realized.

The chief objects of " St. George " come under

three heads, as we have just noticed: agricultural, industrial, and educational. The actual schools would not be needed until the farms and mills had been so far established as to secure a permanent attendance. But meanwhile provision was being made for them, both in literature and in art. The " Bibliotheca Pastorum " was to be a comprehensive little library, far less than the 100 books of the " Pall Mall Gazette," and yet bringing before the St. George's workman standard and serious writing of all times. It was to include, in separate volumes, the Books of Moses and the Psalms of David and the Revelation of St. John. Of Greek, the Xenophon; Hesiod, which Mr. Ruskin undertook to translate into prose. Of Latin, the first two Georgics and sixth Æneid of Virgil, in Gawain Douglas's translation. Dante; Chaucer, excluding the " Canterbury Tales," but including the " Romance of the Rose; " Gotthelf's " Ulric the Farmer," from the French version which Mr. Ruskin had loved ever since his father used to read it him on their first tours in Switzerland; and an early English history by an Oxford friend. Later were published Sir Philip Sidney's psalter, and Mr. Ruskin's own biography of Sir Herbert Edwardes, under the title of " A Knight's Faith."

These books were for the home library; reference works were bought to be deposited in central libraries, along with objects of art and science. It was not intended to keep the guild property centralized, but rather to spread it, as its other work was spread, broadcast. A number of books and other objects were bought with the guild money, and lent or given to various schools and colleges and institutions where work akin to the objects of the guild was being done. But for the time Mr. Ruskin fixed upon Sheffield as the place of his first guild museum, — being the home of the typical English industry, central to all parts of England, near beautiful hill-country, and yet not far from a number of manufacturing towns in which, if St. George's work went on, supporters and recruits might be found.

The people of Sheffield were already, in 1875, building a museum of their own, and naturally thought that the two might be conveniently worked together. But that was not at all what Mr. Ruskin wished. Not only was his museum to be primarily the storehouse of the guild, rather than one among many means of popular education, but the objects which he intended to place there were not such as the public expected to see. He had no interest in a vast accumulation of articles of all kinds. He wanted to provide for his friends' common treasury a few definitely valuable and interesting examples, — interesting to the sort of people that he hoped would join the guild or be bred up in it; and valuable according to his own standard and experience. The complete sets of stuffed animals or fossils, for example, that are found in any provincial museum; the ordinary

books and pictures and casts of the town library
and gallery; all that can be readily seen elsewhere
— not to say all that is of doubtful worth — was
to be excluded. Fine specimens of natural pro-
ducts, such as precious stones and the more beautiful minerals; casts from the best and least known
sculpture; expensive reference books; a few genuine pictures by old masters, plenty of good copies,
such as could now be produced by artists whom
he had trained, and records of architecture which
was rapidly passing away, — every separate object
separately noteworthy, — this was the kind of material which would interest the mind and stimulate
the imagination, more than a wearisome multitude of mediocrities.

In September, 1875, while traveling by short
stages from Brantwood to London, Mr. Ruskin
stayed a couple of days at Sheffield to inspect a
cottage at Walkley, in the outskirts of the town,
and to make arrangements for founding the museum, — humbly to begin with, but hoping for
speedy increase. He engaged as curator, at a
salary of £40 a year and free lodging on the
premises, his former pupil at the Working Men's
College, Henry Swan, who had done occasional
work for him in drawing and engraving. Swan
was a Quaker, and a remarkable man in his way;
enthusiastic in his new vocation, and interested in
the social questions which were being discussed in
" Fors." Under his care the museum remained
at Walkley, accumulating material in the tiny and

hardly accessible cottage, — being, so to speak, in embryo, until the way should be clear for its removal or enlargement, which took place in 1890.

When Mr. Ruskin came back on his posting tour of April, 1876, he stayed again at Sheffield, to meet a score of friends of Swan's, — Secularists, Unitarians, and Quakers, who professed communism. They had an interview (reported in the Sheffield " Daily Telegraph," April 28, 1876), which brought out rather curiously the points of difference between their opinions and his. They refused to join the guild because they would not promise obedience, and help in its objects. Mr. Ruskin, however, was willing to advance theirs. A few weeks afterwards he invited them to choose a piece of ground for their communist experiment. They chose Abbeydale, a farm of over thirteen acres at Dore and Totley, near Mickley; which the guild bought in 1877 at a cost of £2,287 16s. 6d. for their use, — the communists agreeing to pay the money back in installments, without interest, by the end of seven years ; when the farm should be their own.

When it was actually in their hands they found that they knew nothing of farming, and, besides, were making money at trades they did not really care to abandon. They engaged a man to work the farm for them ; and then another. They discovered that the land they had chosen was, for farming purposes, worthless. Their capital ran short; and they tried to make money by keeping a tea-garden. The original proposer of the scheme wrote to Mr. Ruskin, who sent £100. The others returned the money. Mr. Ruskin declined to take it back, and began to perceive that the communists were trifling. They had made no attempt to found the sort of community they had talked about; neither their plans nor his were being carried out. So when the original proposer and a friend of his named Riley approached Mr. Ruskin again, they found little difficulty in persuading him to try them as managers. The rest, finding themselves turned out by Riley, vainly demanded "explanations" from Mr. Ruskin, who then was drifting into his first attack of brain fever. So they declined further connection with the farm; the guild accepted their resignation, and undertook for the time nothing more than to get the land into good condition again.

This was not the only land held by the St. George's Guild. It acquired the acre of ground on which the Sheffield museum stood, and a cottage with a couple of acres near Scarborough. Two acres of rock and moor at Barmouth had been given by Mrs. Talbot in 1872; and in 1877 Mr. George Baker, then Mayor of Birmingham, gave twenty acres of woodland at Bewdley in Worcestershire, to which at one time Mr. Ruskin thought of moving the museum, before the present building was found for it by the Sheffield Corporation at Meersbrook Park. On the resignation of the original trustees, in 1877, Mr. Q. Talbot and Mr. Baker were offered the trust, and on the death of Mr. Talbot the trust was accepted by Mr. John Henry Chamberlain. After he died it was taken by Mr. George Thomson of Huddersfield, whose woolen mills, transformed into a coöperative concern, though not directly in connection with the guild, have given a widely known example of the working of principles advocated in " Fors."

In the middle of 1876, Mr. Egbert Rydings, the auditor of the accounts which, in accordance with his principles of "glass pockets," Mr. Ruskin published in " Fors," proposed to start a homespun woolen industry at Laxey, in the Isle of Man, where the old women who formerly spun with the wheel had been driven by failure of custom to work in the mines. The guild built him a water mill, and in a few years the demand for a pure, rough, durable cloth, created by this and kindred attempts, justified the enterprise. Mr. Ruskin set the example, and had his own gray clothes made of Laxey stuffs, — whose chief drawback is that they never wear out. A little later a similar work was done, with even greater success, by Mr. Albert Fleming, another member of the guild, who introduced old-fashioned spinning and hand-loom weaving at Langdale. The new material was speedily taken up by the public, not only as a staple of domestic use, but as a fine material for embroidery and lace-work; and employment was found for a great number of idle hands. At present the headquarters of the Ruskin Linen Industry, as it is called, are moved to Keswick; but the work goes on in several places, with no signs of failure: showing that the seed of "Fors," where it fell on good ground, was capable of bearing an abundant harvest.

To return from Mr. Ruskin's work to his life. We left him at Sheffield, posting northwards, in April, 1876, after his interview with the communists. The story of that journey was told many years afterwards, at the opening of the new Sheffield museum, by Mr. Arthur Severn, a famous *raconteur*, whose description of the adventures of their cruise upon wheels includes so bright a picture of Mr. Ruskin, that I must use his words as they were reported on the occasion in the magazine "Igdrasil": —

. . . "With the professor, who dislikes railways very much, it was not a question of traveling by rail. He said, 'I will take you in a carriage and with horses, and we will drive the whole way from London to the North of England. And I will not only do that, but I will do the best in my power to get a postilion to ride, and we will go quite in the old-fashioned way.'[1] . . . The professor went so far that he actually built a carriage for this drive. It was a regular posting carriage, with good strong wheels, a place behind for the luggage, and

[1] The old-fashioned way in which he used to travel with his parents (see *ante*, p. 22). It was for "auld lang syne," and not for any affectation of old-fashioned life or ordinary romantic sentiment, that he took these tours. And I cannot tell how much of it was mixed up in his choice of Yorkshire and of Sheffield for the museum, together with memories of Turner, who in his old age could never talk of the dales without emotion.

cunning drawers inside it for all kinds of things that we might require on the journey. We started off one fine morning from London, — I must say without a postilion, — but when we arrived at the next town, about twenty miles off, having telegraphed beforehand that we were coming, there was a gorgeous postilion ready with the fresh horses, and we started off in a right style, according to the professor's wishes.

"After many pleasant days of traveling, we at last arrived at Sheffield, and I well remember that we created no small sensation as we clattered up to the old posting inn. I think it was the King's Head. We stayed a few days, and visited the old museum at Walkley; and I remember the look of regret on the professor's face when he saw how cramped the space was there for the things he had to show. However, with his usual kindliness, he did not say much about it at the time, and he did not complain of the considerable amount of room it was necessary for the curator and his family to take up in that place. We stayed about two days looking at the beautiful country, — and I am glad to say there was a good deal still left, — and then the professor gave orders that the carriage should be got ready to take us on our journey, and that a postilion should be forthcoming, if possible. I remember leaving the luncheon table and going outside to see if the necessary arrangements were complete. Sure enough, there was the carriage at the door, and a still more gorgeous postilion than any we had had so far on our journey. His riding breeches were of the tightest and whitest I ever saw; his horses were an admirable pair, and looked like going. A very large crowd had assembled outside the inn, to see what extraordinary kind of mortals could be going to travel in such a way.

"I went to the room where the professor was still at luncheon, and told him that everything was ready, but that there was a very large crowd at the door. He seemed rather amused; and I said, 'You know, professor, I really don't know what the people expect — whether it is a bride and bridegroom, or what.' He said, 'Well, Arthur, you and Joan shall play at being bride and bridegroom inside the carriage, and I will get on the box.' He got Mrs. Severn on his arm, and had to hold her pretty tightly as he left the door, because when she saw the crowd outside she tried to beat a retreat. At last he got her into the carriage, I was put in afterwards, and he jumped up on the box. The crowd closed in, and looked at us as if we were a sort of menagerie. I was much amused when I thought how little these eager people knew that the real attraction was on the box ; I felt inclined to put my head out of window, and say, 'My good people, there is the man you should look at, — not us.' I did not like to do so ; and the professor gave the word to be off, the postilion cracked his whip, and we went off in grand style, amidst the cheers of the crowd.

" We very soon got to one of the steep hills which seem to abound here, and went up at a hand gallop. Towards the top of it one of the horses turned out to be very restless, and it was evidently a sort of jibber. The gorgeous postilion had great difficulty to control it ; and at last (I hardly like to mention such things), but in his efforts to control this wild Sheffield animal these gorgeous riding trousers went off 'pop.' They cracked like a sail in a gale of wind. The horse became still more restive, and at last the whole thing came to a standstill. We had to get out, and the professor got down from the box.

" He treats any little accident like that with the utmost coolness, and he seemed glad of the delay, because it enabled him to look at the view, which he was pleased to show us. We turned furtively round every now and then to see how the postilion was going on and what he was doing. He took the saddle off the horse he was riding, and put it on the restive one. We were amused at his cleverness, for whenever he saw we were looking towards him he always managed to get a horse between us and the accident which had happened to his trousers. When everything was ready we got in again, and at last arrived at Brantwood, after a most delightful three weeks and a half of traveling, getting there one sunny afternoon, and hardly knowing how we had reached there, the journey had been so pleasant. The professor took a chess-board on that occasion, and over some of the long, and to him rather dreary, Yorkshire moors, we used to play games at chess."

On one of these posting excursions, they came to Hardraw. (Mrs. Alfred Hunt tells the story in her edition of Turner's "Richmondshire;" but I give Mr. Severn's account, which is somewhat different.) After examining the fall, Mrs. Severn and Mr. Ruskin left Mr. Severn to sketch, and went away to Hawes to order their tea. When they were gone, a man who had been standing by came up and asked if that were Professor Ruskin. "Yes," said Mr. Severn, "it was; he is very fond of the fall, and much puzzled to know why the edge of the cliff is not worn away by the water, as he expected to find it after so many years." "Oh," said the other, "there are twelve feet of masonry up there to protect the rock. I'm a native of the place, and know all about it." "I wish," said Mr. Severn, absently, as he went on drawing, "Mr. Ruskin knew that; he would be so interested." And the stranger ran off. When the sketcher came in to tea he felt there was something wrong. "You're in for it!" said his wife. "Let us look at his sketch first," said Mr. Ruskin; and luckily it was a very good one. By and by it all came out; how the Yorkshireman had caught the professor, and eagerly described the horrible vandalism, receiving in reply some very emphatic language. Upon which he took off his hat and bowed low: " But, sir," he faltered, " the gentleman up there said I was to tell you, and you would be so interested ! " The professor, suddenly mollified, took off his hat in turn, and apologized for his reception of the news : " But," said he, " I shall never care for Hardraw waterfall again."

" The professor," said Mr. Severn, " dislikes railways very much ; " and on his arrival at Brantwood after that posting journey he wrote a preface to " A Protest against the Extension of Railways in the Lake District," by Mr. Robert Somervell. Mr. Ruskin's dislike of railways has been the text of a great deal of misrepresentation, and his use of them, at all, has been often quoted as an inconsistency. As a matter of fact, he has never objected to main lines of railway communication ; but he has strongly objected, in common with a vast number of people, to the introduction of railways into districts whose chief interest is in their scenery: especially where, as in the English Lake district, the scenery is in miniature, easily spoiled by embankments and viaducts, and by the rows of ugly buildings which usually grow up round a station ; and where the beauty of the landscape can only be felt in quiet walks or drives through it. Many years later, after he had said all he had to say on the subject again and again, and was on the brink of one of his illnesses, he wrote in violent language to a correspondent who tried to " draw " him on the subject of another proposed railway to Ambleside. But his real opinions are simple enough, and consistent with a practicable scheme of life, — as can be read in the preface to Mr. Somervell's tract, reprinted in " On the Old Road," vol. i., p. 682.

In August, 1876, he left England for Italy. He traveled alone, accompanied only by his new servant Baxter, who had taken and still holds the place vacated by Crawley, Mr. Ruskin's former valet of twenty years' service. He crossed the Simplon to Venice, where he was welcomed by an old friend, Mr. Rawdon Brown, and a new friend, Prof. C. H. Moore of Harvard. He met two Oxford pupils, Mr. J. Reddie Anderson (whom he set to work on Carpaccio), and Mr. Whitehead, — " So much nicer they all are," he wrote in a private letter, " than I was at their age; " also his pupil Mr. Bunney, at work on copies of pictures and records of architecture, the legacy of St. Mark to St. George. Two young artists were brought into his circle, during that winter, — both Venetians, and both singularly interesting men : Giacomo Boni, the capo d' opera of the ducal palace, who was doing his best to preserve, instead of " restoring," the ancient sculptures ; and Angelo Alessandri, a painter of more than usual seriousness of aim and sympathy with the fine qualities of the old masters.

Mr. Ruskin had been engaged on a manual of drawing for his Oxford schools, which he now

MURANO

By John Ruskin, 1876

meant to complete in two parts: "The Laws of Fésole," teaching the principles of Florentine draughtsmanship; and "The Laws of Rivo Alto," about Venetian color. Passages for this second part were written. But he found himself so deeply interested in the evolution of Venetian art, and in tracing the spirit of the people as shown by the mythology illustrated in the pictures and sculptures, that his practical manual became a sketch of art history, "St. Mark's Rest," — as a sort of companion to "Mornings in Florence," which he had been working at during his last visit to Italy. His intention in this work was to supersede "Stones of Venice" by a smaller book, giving more prominence to the ethical side of history, which should illustrate Carpaccio as the most important figure of the transition period, and do away with the exclusive Protestantism of his earlier work.

He set himself to this task, — with Tintoret's motto, "Sempre si fa il mare maggiore," — and worked with feverish energy, recording his progress in letters home (with which the reader may compare letters to Miss Beever in "Hortus Inclusus," pages 36–46).

"13 *Nov.* — I never was yet, in my life, in such a state of hopeless confusion of letters, drawings, and work; chiefly because, of course, when one is old, one's *done* work seems all to tumble in upon one, and want rearranging, and everything brings a thousand old as well as new thoughts.

My head seems less capable of accounts every year. I can't *fix* my mind on a sum in addition, — it goes off, between seven and nine, into a speculation on the seven deadly sins or the nine muses. My table is heaped with unanswered letters, — MS. of four or five different books at six or seven different parts of each, — sketches getting rubbed out, — others getting smudged in, — parcels from Mr. Brown unopened, parcels *for* Mr. Moore unsent; my inkstand in one place, — too probably upset, — my pen in another; my paper under a pile of books, and my last carefully written note thrown into the waste-paper basket."

" 3 *Dec.* — I 'm having nasty foggy weather just now, — but it 's better than fog in London, — and I 'm really resting a little, and trying not to be so jealous of the flying days. I 've a most *cumfy* room [at the Grand Hotel] — I 've gone out of the very expensive one, and only pay twelve francs a day; and I 've two windows, one with open balcony and the other covered in with glass. It spoils the look of window dreadfully, but gives me a view right away to Lido, and of the whole sunrise. Then the bed is curtained off from rest of room like that [sketch of window and room], with fine flourishing white and gold pillars, — and the black place is where one goes out of the room beside the bed."

" 9 *Dec.* — I hope to send home a sketch or two which will show I 'm not quite losing my head yet. . . . I must show at Oxford some reason for my staying so long in Venice."

After studies in the Chapel of St. George, he had Carpaccio's Dream of St. Ursula taken down — it had been "skied" at the Academy until then — and placed in the sculpture gallery for him to copy; and he labored to produce a facsimile.

"24 *Dec.* — I do think St. Ursula's lips are coming pretty — and her eyelids — but oh me, her hair! Toni, Mr. Brown's gondolier, says she's all right — and he's a grave and close-looking judge, you know."

Christmas Day was a crisis in his life. He was attacked by illness; severe pain, followed by a dreamy state in which the vividly realized presence of St. Ursula mingled with memories of his dead lady, whose "spirit" had been shown him just a year before by a " medium " met at a country house. Since then he had watched eagerly for evidences of another life; and the sense of its conceivability grew upon him, in spite of the doubts which he had entertained of the immortality of the soul. At last, after a year's earnest desire for some such assurance, it seemed to come to him. What others call coincidences, and accidents, and states of mind flashed, for him, into importance; times and seasons, names and symbols, took a vivid meaning. His intense despondency changed for a while into a singular happiness, — it seemed a renewed health and strength; and instead of despair, he rejoiced in the conviction of guarding providences and helpful influences.

Readers of " Fors " had traced for some years back the reawakening of a religious tone, now culminating in a pronounced mysticism which they could not understand, and in a recantation of the skeptical judgments of his middle period. He found, now, new excellences in the early Christian painting; he depreciated Turner and Tintoret, and denounced the frivolous art of the day. He searched the Bible more diligently than ever for its hidden meanings, — and in proportion as he felt its inspiration, he recoiled from the conclusions of modern science, and wrapped the prophet's mantle more closely round him, as he denounced with growing fervor the crimes of our unbelieving age.

CHAPTER V.

DEUCALION AND PROSERPINA.

(1877–1879.)

"Quam pæne furvæ regna Proserpinæ
. . . . vidimus."
HORACE, Odes, II. 13.

THROUGHOUT Mr. Ruskin's life, but never more than in this period, we have had to trace different interests and lines of work, running at cross purposes, like the "cleavage planes" he has described in the Alps. To render the mere quantity of detail by which alone, as he says, the size of a subject can be suggested, and yet to keep the breadth of effect, and choose the leading lines that will give the whole truth in its proper relations and perspective, would need a Turner in literary art. But as the strict order of events is appended in the Chronology, we need not mind looking back, now and then, to retrace lines of work which have been perforce omitted.

In the summer of 1875, while his two pupils were harbor-digging and Xenophon-translating at Brantwood, Mr. Ruskin wrote: —

"I begin to ask myself, with somewhat pressing arithmetic, how much time is likely to be left me, at the age of fifty-six, to complete the various designs for which, until past fifty, I was merely collecting material. Of these materials I have now enough by me for a most interesting (in my own opinion) history of fifteenth-century Florentine art, in six octavo volumes; an analysis of the Attic art of the fifth century B. C., in three volumes; an exhaustive history of northern thirteenth-century art, in ten volumes; a life of Sir Walter Scott, with analysis of modern epic art, in seven volumes; a life of Xenophon, with analysis of the general principles of education, in ten volumes; a commentary on Hesiod, with final analysis of the principles of political economy, in nine volumes; and a general description of the geology and botany of the Alps, in twenty-four volumes." The estimate of volumes was — perhaps — in jest; but the plans for harvesting his material were in earnest.

"Proserpina" — so named from the Flora of the Greeks, the daughter of Demeter, Mother Earth — had been already begun in 1874. It was little like an ordinary botany book, — that was to be expected. It did not dissect plants; it did not give chemical or histological analysis; but with bright and curious fancy, with the most ingenious diagrams and perfect drawings, beautifully engraved by Burgess and Allen, illustrated the mystery of growth in plants and the tender beauty of their form. Though this was not science, strictly so called, it was a field of work which no one but Mr. Ruskin has cultivated. He was helped by a few scientific men like Professor Oliver, who saw a value in his line of thought, and showed a kindly interest in it.

"Deucalion " — from the mythical creator of human life out of stones — was begun as a companion work ; to be published in parts, as the repertory of Oxford lectures on Alpine form, and notes on all kinds of kindred subjects. For instance, before that hasty journey to Sheffield he gave a lecture at the London Institution on " Precious Stones " (February 17th, repeated March 28, 1876. A lecture on a similar subject was given to the boys of Christ's Hospital on April 15th.) For this lecture, as usual, he sought help from his pupils, and sent a pressing note by the college-messenger one morning to ask one of his younger friends to run to various professors and make inquiries about various details : " What else are the professors there for ? " he would say ; and he would be greatly impressed if we could answer his questions without appeal to the higher powers. The day after the first lecture he wrote : —

" Those French derivations are like them. No authorities on heraldry are of the slightest value after the fifteenth century — even Guillim is only good for something in the first edition, the rest nowhere. My pearl is all right, — I got it from the book of St. Albans, 1480, — but my shield is not absolutely in the old terms. I invent 'colombin,' for the old 'plumby,' and use 'écarlate' for

' tenné'— mine is to be the norma for St. George's heraldry, not a merely historical summary. I hope to be back on Saturday evening. . . . The lecture went well and pleased my audience — and pleased myself better than usual in that I really got everything said that I intended, of importance."

This lecture, called " The Iris of the Earth," stood first in Part III. of " Deucalion ; " and the work went on, in studies of the forms of silica, on the lines marked out ten years before in the papers on banded and brecciated concretions, — now carried forward with much kind help from the Rev. J. Clifton Ward, of the Geological Survey, and Mr. Henry Willett, F. G. S., of Brighton.

On the way home over the Simplon in May and June, 1877, traveling first with Signor Alessandri, and then with Mr. G. Allen, Professor Ruskin continued his studies of Alpine flowers for " Proserpina." In the autumn he gave a lecture at Kendal (October 1st, repeated at Eton College, December 8th) on " Yewdale and its Streamlets."

This lecture, reprinted as Part V. of " Deucalion," took an unusual importance in his own mind, not only because it was a great success as a lecture, — though I have heard a Kendalian complain that there was not enough " information " in it, — but because it was the first given since that Christmas at Venice, when a new insight had been granted him, as he felt, into spiritual things, and a new burden laid on him, to withstand the rash conclusions of " science falsely so called," and to preach in their place the presence of God in nature and in man.

Writing to Miss Beever about his Oxford course of that autumn, "Readings in Modern Painters,"[1] he said, on the 2d December: "I gave yesterday the twelfth and last of my course of lectures this term, to a room crowded by six hundred people, two-thirds members of the university, and with its door wedged open by those who could not get in; this interest of theirs being granted to me, I doubt not, because for the first time in Oxford I have been able to speak to them boldly of immortal life. I intended when I began the course only to have read 'Modern Painters' to them; but when I began, some of your favorite bits[2] interested the men so much, and brought so much larger a proportion of undergraduates than usual, that I took pains to re-inforce and press them home; and people say I have never given so useful a course yet. But it has taken all my time and strength."

He wrote again, on December 16th, from Herne Hill: "It is a long while since I 've felt so good-for-nothing as I do this morning. My very wristbands curl up in a dog's-eared and disconsolate manner; my little room is all a heap of disorder. I 've got a hoarseness and wheezing and sneezing and coughing and choking. I can't speak and I

---

[1] These lectures were never prepared for publication.

[2] Miss Beever had published early in 1875 the extracts from *Modern Painters* so widely known as *Frondes Agrestes.*

can't think; I'm miserable in bed and useless out of it; and it seems to me as if I could never venture to open a window or go out of a door any more. I have the dimmest sort of diabolical pleasure in thinking how miserable I shall make Susie by telling her all this; but in other respects I seem entirely devoid of all moral sentiments. I have arrived at this state of things, first by catching cold, and since trying to 'amuse myself' for three days." He goes on to give a list of his amusements, — Pickwick, chivalric romances, the " Daily Telegraph," Staunton's games of chess, and, finally, analysis of the Dock Company's bill of charge on a box from Venice.

Ten days after, he wrote from Oxford in his whimsical style: " Yesterday I had two lovely services in my own cathedral. You know the *Cathedral* of Oxford is the chapel of Christ Church College, and I have my high seat in the chancel, as an honorary student, besides being bred there, and so one is ever so proud and ever so pious all at once, which is ever so nice, you know: and my own dean, that 's the Dean of Christ Church, who is as big as any bishop, read the services, and the psalms and anthems were lovely; and then I dined with Henry Acland and his family; . . . but I do wish I could be at Brantwood too." Next day it was " Cold quite gone." But he was not to be quit so easily this time of the results of overwork and worry.

He had been passing through the unpleasant

experience of a misunderstanding with one of his most trusted friends and helpers. His work on behalf of the St. George's Guild had been energetic and sincere; and he had received the support of a number of strangers, among whom were people of responsible station and position. But he was surprised to find that many of his personal friends held aloof. He was still more surprised to learn, on returning from Venice, full of new hope and stronger convictions in his mission, that the caution of one upon whom he had counted as a firm ally had dissuaded an intending adherent from joining in the work. A man of the world, accustomed to overreach and to be overreached, would have taken the discovery coolly, and accepted an explanation. But Mr. Ruskin was never a man of the world; and now, much less than ever. He took it, not as an error, or even so much as a personal attack, but as treason to the great work of which he felt himself to be the missionary. It chilled his hopes and dashed his zeal; and as it is always the most generous of men whose suspicions, once aroused, are fiercest, he was quite unable to forgive and forget. Throughout the autumn and winter the discovery rankled, and preyed on his mind. As for the sake of absolute candor he had published in " Fors " everything that related to the guild work, — even his own private affairs and confessions, whatever they risked, — he felt that this too must out, in order that his supporters might judge of his conduct and that nothing affecting the enterprise might be kept back. And so, at Christmas, he sent the correspondence to his printers.

Years afterwards, by the intervention of friends, this breach was healed ; but what suffering it cost can be learned from the sequel. To Mr. Ruskin it was like the beginning of the end. His Aberdeen correspondent asked just then for the usual Christmas message to the Bible class ; and, instead of the cheery words of bygone years, received the couplet from Horace : —

> " Inter spem curamque, timores inter et iras,
> *Omnem* crede diem tibi diluxisse supremum."

" Amid hope and sorrow, amid fear and wrath, believe *every* day that has dawned on thee to be thy last."

From Oxford, early in January, 1878, Mr. Ruskin went on a visit to Windsor Castle, whence he wrote: "I came to see Prince Leopold, who has been a prisoner to his sofa lately, but I trust he is better; he is very bright and gentle under severe and almost continual pain." No less gentle, in spite of the severe justice he was inflicting upon himself even more than upon his friend, was the author of " Fors," as the letters of the time to his invalid neighbor, in " Hortus Inclusus," show. How ready to own himself in the wrong, — at that very moment, when he was being pointed at as the most obstinate and egotistic of men, — how placable he really was and open to rebuke, he showed, when from Windsor he went to Hawarden.   Nearly three years before he had written roughly of Mr. Gladstone; as a Conservative he was not predisposed in favor of the leader of the party to whom he attributed most of the evils he was combating.   Mr. Gladstone and he had often met, and by no means agreed together in conversation.   But this visit convinced him that he had misjudged Mr. Gladstone; and he promptly made the fullest apology in the current number of " Fors," saying that he had written under a complete misconception of his character.   In reprinting the old pages he not only canceled the offending passage, but left the place blank, with a note in the middle of it, as " a memorial of rash judgment."

He went slowly northward, seeking rest at Ingleton; whence he wrote, January 17th: " I 've got nothing done all the time I 've been away but a few mathematical figures [crystallography, no doubt, for " Deucalion,"], and the less I do the less I find I can do it; and yesterday, for the first time these twenty years, I had n't so much as a ' plan ' in my head all day."   Arrived at Brantwood, as rest was useless, he tried work.   Mr. Willett had asked him to reprint " The Two Paths," and he got that ready for press, and wrote a short preface.   At Venice, Mr. J. R. Anderson had been working out for him the myths illustrated by Carpaccio in the Chapel of S. Giorgio de' Schiavoni; and the book had been waiting for Mr. Ruskin's introduction until he was surprised

by the publication of an almost identical inquiry by
M. Clermont-Ganneau. He tried to fulfill his duty
to his pupil by writing the preface immediately;
most sorrowfully feeling the inadequacy of his
strength for the tasks he had laid upon it. He
wrote: " My own feeling, now, is that everything
which has hitherto happened to me, and been
done by me, whether well or ill, has been fitting
me to take greater fortune more prudently, and to
do better work more thoroughly. And just when
I seem to be coming out of school, — very sorry
to have been such a foolish boy, yet having taken
a prize or two, and expecting now to enter upon
some more serious business than cricket, — I am
dismissed by the Master I hoped to serve, with a
— ' That's all I want of you, sir.' "

In such times he found relief by reverting to
the past. He wrote in the beginning of February
a paper for the " University Magazine " on " My
First Editor," W. H. Harrison, and forgot himself
— almost — in bright reminiscences of youthful
days and early associations. Next, as Mr. Marcus
Huish, who had shown great friendliness and
generosity in providing prints for the Sheffield
museum, was now proposing to hold an exhibition of Mr. Ruskin's Turners at the Fine Art
Galleries in New Bond Street, it was necessary to
arrange the exhibits and to prepare the catalogue.
For the next fortnight he struggled on with this
labor, and with his last " Fors," — the last he was
to write in the long series of more than seven

years.[1] How little the thousands who read the preface to his catalogue, with its sad sketch of Turner's fate, and what they supposed to be its "customary burst of terminal eloquence," understood that it was indeed the cry of one who had been wounded in the house of his friends, and was now believing every day that dawned on him to be his last. He told of Turner's youthful picture of the Coniston Fells and its invocation to the mists of morning, bidding them "in honor to the world's great Author, rise," — and then how Turner's "health, and with it in great degree his mind, failed suddenly, with snap of some vital chord," after the sunset splendors of his last, dazzling efforts. "Morning breaks, as I write, along those Coniston Fells, and the level mists, motionless and gray beneath the rose of the moorlands, veil the lower woods, and the sleeping village, and the long lawns by the lake-shore.

"Oh that some one had but told me, in my youth, when all my heart seemed to be set on these colors and clouds, that appear for a little while and then vanish away, how little my love of them would serve me, when the silence of lawn and wood in the dews of morning should be completed; and all my thoughts should be of those whom, by neither, I was to meet more!"

The catalogue was finished, and hurried off to the printers. A week of agitating suspense at

---

[1] *Fors* was taken up again, at intervals, later on; but never with the same purpose and continuity.

home, and then it could no longer be concealed. Friends and foes alike were startled and saddened with the news of his "sudden and dangerous illness."

It was some form of inflammation of the brain, the result of overwork, but still more immediately of the emotional strain from which he had been suffering. It took him quite at unawares; for though he knew as well as others that he had lost that peace and strength which he had found in Venice, and that his mind was alternately stimulated to unwonted activity and depressed into helplessness, yet he had not received definite warning, as from any sort of headache, — to which he had always been a stranger, — nor from approach to the delirium which now was the chief feature of his disease.

On March 4th, the Turner exhibition opened, and day by day the bulletins from Brantwood announcing his condition were read by multitudes of visitors with eager and sorrowful interest. Newspapers all the world over copied the daily reports; even in the towns of the Far West of America the same telegrams were posted, and they say even a more demonstrative sympathy was shown. Nor was the feeling confined to the English-speaking public. The Oxford Proctor in Convocation of April 24th, when, after the first burst of the storm, the patient was slowly drifting back into calmer waters, thought it worth while, in the course of his speech, to mention that in Italy, where he had lately been on an Easter vacation tour, he had witnessed a widespread anxiety about Mr. Ruskin, and heard prayers put up for his recovery: " Nec multum abfuit quin nuper desideraret Academia morbo letali abreptum Professorem, in sua materie unicum, Joannem Ruskin. ' Sed multæ urbes et publica vota vicerunt.' Neque id indignum memoratu puto quod nuperrime mihi in Italia commoranti contigit videre quantæ sollicitudines ob ejus salutem, quantæ preces moverentur, in ea terra cujus ille artes et monumenta tam disertissime illustraverit."

By May 10th he was so much better that he could complete the catalogue with some gossip about those Alpine drawings of 1842 (see vol. i., p. 100), which he regarded as the climax of Turner's work. The first — and best in some ways — of the series was the Splügen, which had been bought by Mr. Munro, of Novar, in the absence of Mr. Ruskin's father; and now he believed it had been sold lately at Christie's.

Without any word to him, the diligence of kind friends and the help of a wide circle of admirers traced the drawing and subscribed its price, — 1000 guineas, to which Mr. Agnew generously added his commission, — and it was presented to Mr. Ruskin as a token of sympathy and respect. It was a timely and very welcome tribute. It showed him that he still had the ear of the public; that they cared for himself, if not for his schemes. He would have preferred support for St. George's work, but he was not insensible to the personal compliment implied, and by way of some answer he spent the first few days of his convalescence in arranging and annotating a series of drawings by himself, and engravings, illustrating the Turners, to add to his show during the remainder of the season. When they were sent off (early in June) to Bond Street, he left home with the Severns to complete his recovery at Malham.

There was another reason why that spontaneous testimonial was welcome at the moment, for a curious and unaccustomed ordeal was impending for Mr. Ruskin's claims as an art critic. On his return from Venice after months of intercourse with the great Old Masters, he found the Grosvenor Gallery just opened for the first time, with its memorable exhibition of the different extra-academical schools. It placed before the public, in sharp contrast, the final outcome of Pre-Raphaelitism, for which Mr. Ruskin had fought many a year before, and samples of the last new fashion from Paris. The maturer works of Mr. Burne-Jones had been practically unseen by the public, and Mr. Ruskin took the opportunity of their exhibition to write his praise of the youngest of the Old Masters in the current number of " Fors," and afterwards in two papers on the " Three Colors of Pre-Raphaelitism " (" Nineteenth Century Magazine," November and December, 1878). But in the same " Fors " he dismissed with half a paragraph of contempt Mr. Whistler's eccentric sketch of Fireworks. Long before, in 1863, when he was working with various artists connected with the Pre-Raphaelite circle, Mr. Whistler had made overtures to the great critic through Mr. Swinburne, the poet; but he had not been taken seriously. Now he had become the missionary in England of the new French gospel of "impressionism," which to Mr. Ruskin was one of those half-truths which are ever the worst of heresies. Mr. Whistler appealed to the law. He brought an action for libel, which was tried on November 25th and 26th before Baron Huddleston, and recovered a farthing damages. Mr. Ruskin's costs — amounting to £386 12s. 4d. — were paid by a public subscription to which one hundred and twenty persons, including many strangers, contributed.

By that time Mr. Ruskin was fully recovering from his illness, back at Coniston, after a short visit to Liverpool. It was forbidden to him to attempt any exciting work. He had given up " Fors " and Oxford lecturing, and was devoting himself again to quiet studies for " Proserpina " and " Deucalion." On the first day of the trial the St. George's Guild was registered as a company; on the second day he wrote to Miss Beever : —

" I have entirely resigned all hope of ever thanking you rightly for bread, sweet odors, roses and pearls, and must just allow myself to be fed, scented, rose-garlanded and bepearled, as if I were a poor little pet dog, or pet pig. But my cold is better, and I *am* getting on with this botany; but it is really too important a work to be pushed for a week or a fortnight." Then he goes into details about the plans for his botany, which occupied him chiefly for the rest of the autumn.

Early in 1879 his resignation of the Slade professorship was announced; and he was more free than ever to spend his time in the researches which had always interested him, and which, he sometimes imagined, were his *forte*. The severe winter of 1878–79 was particularly favorable for watching the phenomena of icicles and ice-formation, and this study commended itself to him in a twofold sense. On the one hand it illustrated the great problem of crystallization in general, and on the other it touched the question of glaciers. Enough has been said (Book III., chap. iii.) to show the attitude he had taken for fifteen years past, as a disciple of Forbes, against the ordinary theory of glacial action, to which he had assented in " Modern Painters," vol. iv. But he was now confirmed in his views of what he, and a group of Forbes's friends, considered to be the unfair action of Professor Tyndall, whose contributions did not warrant, as they thought, his treatment of the pioneer, in this country, of Alpine investigations. Mr. Ruskin did not make the most of his position in the eyes of the public by inserting his remarks on Professor Tyndall, insufficiently supported with argument and illustration, among very different kinds of matter in " Fors," and by allowing himself to write at moments when the ill-health of three years left him — "the greatest gladiator of the age," as he has been called — hardly a match for the cool fence of his opponent.

But it was his wish now to go into the subject again, in " Deucalion." The following letter to a friend at Chamouni (July 25, 1879) will show, at any rate, the kind of method upon which he was intending to work, and the extreme views he had come to take : —

" Yes. Chamouni is as a desolated home to me — I shall never, I believe, be there more : I could escape the riffraff in winter and early spring ; but that the glaciers should have betrayed me, and their old ways know them no more, is too much.

. . . " I was gladly surprised to hear of your going to the Aiguille du Tour, if the whole field round it is still pure ; but all 's so wrecked ; perhaps it 's all mud and stones by this time.

" However, the thing I want of you is to get as far up the old bed of the Glacier des Bois as you can, and make a good graphic sketch for me of any bit of rock that you can find of the true bottom among the débris. *Graphic*, I say, — as opposed to colory or shadowy ; show me the edges and ins and outs, well — with any notes of the direction and effect of former ice on it you can make for yourself. You know I don't believe the ice ever moves at the *bottom* of a glacier at all, —

in a general way, but on so steep a slope as that of the Bois, it may sometimes have been dragged a little at the bottom, as it is ordinarily at the sides. Anyhow, sketch me a bit of the rocks and tell me how the boulders are lodged, whether merely dropped promiscuously, or driven into particular lines or corners.

" Please give my love to the big old stone under the Breven, a quarter of a mile above the village, unless they 've blasted it up for hotels."

A little later he planned to write a " Grammar of Ice," with the same pupil's help, and he plunged deep into the study of crystallization. I have before me a great quantity of letters to an assistant, discussing the mathematics of crystallography, sending specimens for microscopic examination, acknowledging drawings ; and all illustrated, on every page, with the cleverest pen-sketches of crystal forms. Somewhere at Brantwood there is a deep drawer full of material for " Deucalions " that never were published, for the storm-cloud came down upon him just as he was beginning to find his way out of the wood.

Whatever might have been the value of Mr. Ruskin's work on this subject, after the serious study of his later years, one book that he planned and began I take leave to regret. It was to be a manual of the actual forms, the phenomenology, of native gold and silver and other minerals which crystallize into fronds and twigs and tangles, and pretty, plant-like shapes, unregarded by the mathematician and quite unexplained by the elementary laws of crystallography.   Illustrated from the beautiful specimens in Mr. Ruskin's collection, with such exquisite drawings as he makes of these tiny still-life subjects, it would have been a fairy-book of science.   For that reason, perhaps, " Fata Morgana," or the " third Fors," was jealous, or perhaps " Proserpina " and " Deucalion " quarreled over these flowers of the under-world, and left them in the babies' limbo among the things that might have been.

CHAPTER VI.

THE DIVERSIONS OF BRANTWOOD.

(1879–1880.)

" In that Library I pass away most of the Days of my Life, and most of the Hours of the Day. In the Night I am never there. There is within it a Cabinet, handsome and neat enough, with a very convenient Fireplace for the Winter, and Windows that afford a great deal of light and very pleasant Prospects." — COTTON, *Montaigne.*

SIXTY years of one of the busiest lives on record were beginning to tell upon the hero of our story. He would not confess to old age, but his recent illness had shaken him severely. It was obvious that he could no longer stand to his post at Oxford; and though, in spite of everything, Oxford was loath to part with him, his resignation was accepted early in 1879.

The next three years were spent chiefly at Coniston, in comparative retirement; but neither in despair, nor idleness, nor loneliness. He had always lived a sort of dual life, — solitary in his thoughts, but social in his habits; liking company, especially of young people; ready, in the intervals of work, to enter into their employments and amusements, and curiously able to forget his cares in hours of relaxation. Sometimes, when earnest admirers made the pilgrimage to their

Mecca — "holy Brantwood," as a scoffing poet called it — they were surprised, and even shocked, to find the Prophet of " Fors " at the head of a merry dinner-table, and the Professor of Art among surroundings which a London or a Boston " æsthete " would have ruled to be in very poor taste.

Shall I take you for a visit there, — to Brantwood as it was in those old times ?

It is a weary way to Coniston, whatever road you choose. The inconvenience of the railway route was perhaps one reason of Mr. Ruskin's preference for driving, on so many occasions. After changing and changing trains, and stopping at many a roadside station, at last you see, suddenly, over the wild undulating country, the Coniston Old Man — Maen, stone; a survival of Celtic Cumbria — and its crags, abrupt on the left, and the lake, long and narrow, on the right. Across the water, tiny in the distance and quite alone amongst forests and moors, there is Brantwood; and beyond it everything seems uncultivated, uninhabited, except for one gray farmhouse high on the fell, where gaps in the ragged larches show how bleak and storm-swept a spot it is.

To come out of the station after long travel, and to find yourself face to face with magnificent rocks, and white cottages among the fir-trees, is a surprise like walking for the first time down the High Street of Edinburgh to Holyrood. And as you are whirled down through the straggling village, and along the shore round the head of the lake, the panorama, though not Alpine in magnitude, is almost Alpine in character. The valley, too, is not yet built up; it is still the old-fashioned lake country, almost as it was in the days of the "Iteriad;" still in touch with the past. You drive up and down a narrow, hilly lane, catching peeps of mountains and sunset through thick, overhanging trees; you turn sharp up through a gate under dark firs and larches; and the carriage stops in what seems in the twilight a sort of court, — a graveled space, one side formed by a rough stone wall crowned with laurels and almost precipitous coppice, the *brant* (or steep) wood above, and the rest is Brantwood, with a capital B.[1]

You expect that Gothic porch you have read of in " Lectures on Architecture and Painting," and you are surprised to find a stucco Doric portico in the corner, painted and *grained*, and heaped around with lucky horseshoes, brightly black-leaded, and mysterious rows of large blocks of slate and basalt and trap, —a complete museum of local geology, if only you knew it, — very unlike an ideal entrance; still more unlike an ordinary one. While you wait you can see through the glass door a roomy hall, lit with candles, and hung with large drawings by Burne-Jones and by the master of the house. His soft hat, and thick

---

[1] The archway supporting a great pile of new buildings did not exist in the time when this visit is supposed to be made.

gloves, and chopper, lying on the marble table, show that he has come in from his afternoon's woodcutting.

But if you are expected you will hardly have time to look round, for Brantwood is nothing if not hospitable. The honored guest, — and all guests are honored there, — after welcome, is ushered up a narrow stair, which betrays the original cottage, into the " turret room." It had been the professor's until after his illness, and he papered it with naturalistic pansies, to his own taste, and built out at one corner a projecting turret to command the view on all sides, with windows strongly latticed to resist the storms ; for Ruskin can say with Montaigne, " my House is built upon an Eminence, as its Name imports, and no part of it is so much expos'd to the Wind and Weather as that." There is old-fashioned solid comfort in the way of furniture ; and pictures, — a Dürer engraving, some Prouts and Turners, a couple of old Venetian heads, and Meissonier's Napoleon, over the fireplace — a picture which Mr. Ruskin bought for one thousand guineas, showed for a time at Oxford, and hung up here in a shabby little frame to be out of the way.[1] It gives you a curious sense of being in quite a new kind of place.

If you are a man, you are told not to dress ; if you are a lady, you may put on your prettiest gown. They dine in the new room, for the old

[1] Sold in 1882 for 5,900 guineas.

dining-room was so small that one could not get round the table. The new room is spacious and lofty compared with the rest of the house; it has a long window with thick red sandstone mullions — there at last is a touch of Gothicism — to look down the lake, and a bay window opens on the narrow lawn sloping steeply down to the road in front, and the view of the Old Man. The walls, painted "duck egg," are hung with old pictures: the Doge Gritti, a bit saved from the great Titian that was burnt in the fire at the ducal palace in 1557; a couple of Tintorets; Turner and Reynolds, each painted by himself in youth; Raphael by a pupil, so it is said; portraits of old Mr. and Mrs. Ruskin, and little John and his " boo hills." There he sits, no longer little, opposite; and you can trace the same curve and droop of the eyebrows (a Highland trait?) prefigured in the young face and preserved in the old, and a certain family likeness to his handsome young father.

Since Mr. Ruskin's illness his cousin, Mrs. Arthur Severn, has become more and more indispensable to him: she sits at the foot of the table and calls him " the coz." An eminent visitor was once put greatly out of countenance by this apparent irreverence. After obvious embarrassment, light dawned upon him towards the close of the meal. " Oh ! " said he, " it 's ' the coz ' you call Mr. Ruskin. I thought you were saying ' the *cuss !* ' "

There are generally two or three young people

staying in the house, salaried assistants[1] or amateur, occasional helpers; but though there is a succession of visitors from a distance there is not very frequent entertainment of neighbors.

A Brantwood dinner is always ample; there is no asceticism about the place; nor is there any affectation of "intensity" or of common-room cleverness. The neat things you meant to say are forgotten, — you must be hardened indeed to say them to Mr. Ruskin's face; but if you were shy, you soon feel that there was no need for shyness; you have fallen among friends; and before dessert comes in, with fine old sherry — the pride of your host, as he explains — you feel that nobody understands you so well, and that all his books are nothing to himself.

It is not a mere show, this kindliness and consideration. Two young visitors, once staying at Brantwood with Mr. Ruskin alone, mistook the time and appeared an hour late for dinner. Not

---

[1] The face most familiar at Brantwood in those times was "Laurie's." A strange, bright, gifted boy, — admirable draughtsman, ingenious mechanician, marvelous actor; the imaginer of the quaintest and drollest humors that ever entered the head of man; devoted to boats and boating, but unselfishly ready to share all labors and contribute to all diversions; painstaking and perfect in his work, and brilliant in his wit, — Laurence Hilliard was dearly loved by his friends, and is still loved by them dearly. He was Mr. Ruskin's chief secretary at Brantwood from January, 1876, to 1882, when the death of his father, and his own failing health, made him resign the post. He continued to live at Coniston, and was just beginning to be famous as a painter of still life and landscape when he died of pleurisy on board a friend's yacht in the Ægean, April 11, 1887, aged thirty-two.

a hint or a sign was given that might lead them to suspect their error; their hungry host was not only patient, but as charming as possible. Only next day they learned from the servants that the dinner and the master had waited an hour for them.

They don't sit over their wine, and smoking is not allowed. Mr. Ruskin goes off to his study after dinner — it is believed for a nap, for he was at work early and has been out all the afternoon. In the drawing-room you see pictures, — water-colors by Turner and Hunt, drawings by Prout and Ruskin, an early Burne-Jones, a sketch in oil by Gainsborough. The furniture is the old mahogany of Mr. Ruskin's childhood, with rare things interspersed, like the cloisonné vases on the mantelpiece.

Soon after nine Mr. Ruskin comes in with an armful of things that are going to the Sheffield museum, and while his cousin makes his tea and salted toast, he explains his last acquirements in minerals or missals, eager that you should see the interest of them; or displays the last studies of Mr. Rooke or Mr. Fairfax Murray, copies from Carpaccio or bits of Gothic architecture. (Mr. Ruskin about this time was anxious to secure memorials of old buildings and sculpture before "restoration." In 1880 he published an appeal for subscriptions towards work in St. Mark's, which was being restored; but he met with no response. Perhaps, in the opinion of the public,

Ongania's great work partly forestalled the necessity.)   Mr. Ruskin likes, you will find, to talk about the museum, lately honored by Prince Leopold's visit (October 23, 1879).   He will tell you why he put it at Sheffield, and why, after all, it is not at Sheffield, but so far out of the town — in order to entice workmen out of the smoke to study in a country retreat, where there will be always pretty things for them to see and light to read by.   He hopes to get it filled with men who will join to scientific teaching the study of art and nature, and, in short, to make it "a working-man's Bodleian library."   He plans also to join a school to the museum, where Sheffield girls and boys may be taught to carve from the natural leaves, instead of the conventional pattern-drawing which he considers the fallacy of modern popular art-teaching.

Then, sitting in the chair in which he preached his baby-sermon, he reads aloud a few chapters of Scott or Miss Edgeworth, or, with judicious omissions, one of the older novelists; or translates, with admirable facility, a scene of Scribe or George Sand.   When his next work comes out you will recognize this evening's reading in his allusions and quotations, perhaps even in the subjects of his writing, for at this time he is busy on the articles of " Fiction, Fair and Foul."

After the reading, music; a bit of his own composition, " Old Ægina's Rocks," or " Cockle-hat and Staff;" his cousin's Scotch ballads, or Christy

Minstrel songs; and if you can sing a new ditty, fresh from London, now is your chance. You are surprised to see the Prophet clapping his hands to "Camptown Races," or the "Hundred Pipers," —chorus given with the whole strength of the company; but you are in a house of strange meetings.

By about half-past ten his day is over; a busy day, that has left him tired out. You will not easily forget the way he lit his candle, — no lamps allowed, and no gas, — and gave a last look lovingly at a pet picture or two, slanting his candlestick and shading the light with his hand, before he went slowly upstairs to his own little room, literally lined with the Turner drawings you have read about in "Modern Painters."

In the morning you may be waked by a knock at the door, and "Are you looking out?" And pulling up the blind, there is one of our Coniston mornings, with the whole range of mountains in one quiet glow above the cool mist of the valley and lake. Going down at length on a voyage of exploration, and turning in perhaps at the first door, you intrude upon the Professor at work in his study, half sitting, half kneeling at his round table in the bay window, with the early cup of coffee, and the cat in his crimson arm-chair. There he has been working since dawn, perhaps, or on dark mornings by candlelight. Like Montaigne, he does not pass the night in his study, but he takes "to-day" by the forelock. And he does not seem to mind the interruption; after a welcome he asks you to look round while he finishes his paragraph, and writes away composedly.

A long, low room, evidently two old cottage-rooms thrown into one; papered with a pattern specially copied from an Old Master's drapery in the National Gallery; and hung with Turners. A great early Turner [1] of the Lake of Geneva is over the fireplace. You are tempted to make a mental inventory. Polished steel fender, very unæsthetic; curious shovel,—his design, he will stop to remark, and forged by the village smith; red mahogany furniture, with startling shiny emerald leather chair cushions; red carpet and green curtains; most of the room crowded with bookcases and cabinets for minerals, "handsome and neat enough;" scales in a glass case; heaps of mineral specimens; books on the floor; rolls of diagrams; early Greek pots from Cyprus; a great litter of things, and yet not disorderly nor dusty. "I don't understand," he once said, "why you ladies are always complaining about the dust; my bookcases are never dusty!"—the truth being that, though he rose early, the housemaid rose earlier.

Before you have finished your inventory he breaks off work to show you a drawer or two of minerals, fairyland in a cupboard; or some of his missals, or the original MS. of the Scott he was

---

[1] Since sold, and replaced by a Della Robbia Madonna.

reading last night; or, opening a door in a sort of secrétaire, pulls out of their sliding cases frame after frame of Turners, — the Bridge of Narni, the Falls of Terni, Florence or Rome, and many more, — to hold in your hand, and take to the light, and look into with a lens, — quite a different thing from seeing pictures in a gallery.

At breakfast, when you see the post-bag brought in, you understand why he tries to get his bit of writing done early. The letters and parcels are piled in the study, and after breakfast, at which, as in old times, he reads his last-written passages, — how much more interesting they will aways look to you in print! — after breakfast he is closeted with an assistant, and they work through the heap. Private friends, known by handwriting, he puts aside; most of the morning will go in answering them. Business he talks over, and gives brief directions. But the bulk of the correspondence is from strangers in all parts of the world, — admirers' flattery; students' questions; begging-letters for money, books, influence, advice, autographs, criticism on enclosed MS. or accompanying picture; remonstrance or abuse from dissatisfied readers, or people who object to his method of publication, or wish to convert him to their own religion, whatever it happens to be. And so the heap is gradually cleared, with the help of the waste-paper basket; the secretary's work cut out, his own arranged; and by noon a long row of letters and envelopes have been set out to dry, —

Mr. Ruskin uses no blotting-paper, and, as he dislikes the vulgar method of fastening envelopes, the secretary's work will be to seal them all with red wax, and the seal with the motto "To-day" cut in the apex of a big specimen of chalcedony.

One hesitates how far to go in these minutiæ of portrait painting: some may think the picture more finished for its details, and they may like to know that he writes on the flat table, not on a desk; that he uses a cork penholder and a fine steel pen, though he is not at all a slave to his tools, and differs from others rather in the absence of the *sine qua non* from his conditions. He can write anywhere, on anything, with anything; wants no penwiper, no special form of paper, or other "fad." Much of his work is written in bound note-books, especially when he is abroad, to prevent the loss and disorder of multitudinous foolscap. He generally makes a rough syllabus of his subject, in addition to copious notes and extracts from authorities, and then writes straight off; not without a noticeable hesitation and re-vision, even in his letters. His rough copy is transcribed by an assistant, and he usually does not see it again until it is in proof. He likes the type-writer, and employs it for fair-copying, of late years. Formerly he set no store by his MSS. His cousin says that her early recollections of Denmark Hill include a vision of crumpled fools-cap sticking out of the grate every morning; Mr. Ruskin's copy and proofs kept the housemaids in fire-lighting until she begged the interesting sheets. But there are no complete works of Ruskin in MS., as there are of Scott.

Printers' proofs are always a trial to Mr. Ruskin, and he is glad to shift the work on to an assistant's shoulders, such as Mr. Harrison, who saw all his early works through the press. Mr. Ruskin himself is not an accurate proof-reader; too pressed with other business to give attention, for he usually takes up a totally different subject when he has finished one piece of work, that is, while he is reading the proofs of it. But he is extremely particular about certain things, and knows how to calculate the effect on the reader of the look of his work in print. Mr. Jowett (of Messrs. Hazell, Watson, & Viney, Limited) says, in "Hazell's Magazine" for September, 1892, that Mr. Ruskin has made the size of the page a careful study, though he has adopted many varieties. The "Fors" page is different from, and not so symmetrical as that of the octavo "Works Series," although both are printed on the same sized paper, medium 8vo. Then there is the "Knight's Faith" and "Ulric," in both of which the type (pica *modern* — "this delightful type," wrote Mr. Ruskin) and the size of the page are different from any other; yet both are his choice. The "Ulric" page was imitated from an old edition of Miss Edgeworth. The first proof he criticised thus, — "Don't you think a quarter inch off this page, as enclosed, would look better? The type is very nice.   How delicious a bit of Miss Edge-worth's is, like this!"   "Ida" was another page of his choice, and greatly approved.   His title-pages, too, were arranged with great care; he used to draw them out in pen and ink, indicating the size and position of the lines and letters.   He objects to ornaments in print, and is very partic-ular about proportions and spacing and division of words.   Mr. Jowett tells that in issuing "Ulric" in parts, the word "stockings" happened to be divided; "and thus 'stock-' ended one part, and 'ings' began the next!   In all my correspondence with him," says Mr. Jowett, " I never knew Mr. Ruskin so annoyed.   'Dear Jowett, — I'm really a little cross with you — for once — for doing such an absurd thing as jointing a word between the two parts.   Did I really pass Part II. with half a word at the end?'   This unfortunately was fol-lowed by many weeks' silence and entire absti-nence from any kind of work.   The Master had been seriously ill!   The silence was broken by the following: 'My dear Jowett, — that unlucky extra worry with "Ulric" was just the drop too much, which has cost me a month's painful illness again.'"

But to return to Brantwood in 1880.

In the morning everybody is busy.   There are drawings and diagrams to be made, MS. to copy, references to look up, parcels to pack and unpack. Some one is told off to take you round, and you visit the various rooms and see the treasures, inspect the outhouse with its workshop for carpentry, framing and mounting, casting leaves and modeling; one work or another is sure to be going on; perhaps one of the various sculptors who have made Mr. Ruskin's bust is busy there. Down at the Lodge, a miniature Brantwood, turret and all, the Severn children live when they are at Coniston. Then there are the gardens, terraced in the steep, rocky slope, and the usual hot-houses, which Mr. Ruskin thinks a superfluity, except that they provide grapes for sick neighbors.

Below the gardens a path across a field takes you to the harbor, begun in play by the Xenophon translators and finished by the village mason, with its fleet of boats, — chief of them the Jumping Jenny (called after Nanty Ewart's boat in " Redgauntlet "), Mr. Ruskin's own design and special private water-carriage, which, you are told, one day in a big storm he insisted on rowing by himself up the lake, while all the household turned out on to the terrace to watch, in real terror. Laurie can imitate the cook to perfection : " Eh, dear, the Maister 's gone ! . . . Eh, now, look ye, there he is, riding on t' white horses ! Eh, there, he 's going ; he 's going ; he 's gone ! " An hour or so afterwards he walked in, drenched, but triumphant in the seaworthy qualities of his Jump.

Outside the harbor the sail-boats are moored, Mr. Severn's Lily of Brantwood, Hilliard's boat, and his Snail, an unfortunate craft brought from Morecambe Bay with great expectations that were

FOREGROUND DETAIL AT BRANTWOOD
By John Ruskin, 187–

never realized; though Mr. Ruskin always professed to believe in her, as a real sea-boat (see " Harbors of England ") such as he used to steer with his friend Huret, the Boulogne fisherman, in the days when he, too, was smitten with sea-fever.

After luncheon, if letters are done, all hands are piped to the moor. With billhooks and choppers the party winds up the wood paths, the professor first, walking slowly, and pointing out to you his pet bits of rock-cleavage, or ivied trunk, or nest of wild-strawberry plants. You see, perhaps, the ice-house — tunneled at vast expense into the rock and filled at more expense with the best ice; opened at last with great expectations and the most charitable intent, for it was planned to supply invalids in the neighborhood with ice, as the hothouses supplied them with grapes; and revealing, after all, nothing but a puddle of dirty water. You see more successful works, — the professor's little private garden, which he is supposed to cultivate with his own hands; various little wells and watercourses among the rocks, moss-grown and fern-embowered; and so you come out on the moor.

There great works go on. Juniper is being rooted up; boggy patches drained and cultivated; cranberries are being planted, and oats grown; paths engineered to the best points of view; rocks bared to examine the geology, — though you cannot get the professor to agree that every inch of his territory has been glaciated. These diversions

have their serious side, for he is really experiment-
ing on the possibility of reclaiming waste land;
perhaps too sanguine, you think, and not counting
the cost. To which he replies that, as long as
there are hands unemployed and misemployed, a
government such as he would see need never be
at a loss for laborers. If corn can be made to
grow where juniper grew before, the benefit is a
positive one, the expense only comparative. And
so you take your pick with the rest, and are almost persuaded to become a companion of St.
George.

Not to tire a new-comer, he takes you away
after a while to a fine heathery promontory where
you sit before a most glorious view of lake and
mountains. This, he says, is his " Naboth's vine-
yard; "[1] he would like to own so fine a point of
vantage. But he is happy in his country retreat,
far happier than you thought him; and the secret
of his happiness is that he has sympathy with all
around him, and hearty interest in everything,
from the least to the greatest.

Coming down from the moor after the round,
when you reach the front door, you must see the
performance of the waterfall; everybody must see
that. On the moor a reservoir has been dug and
dammed, with ingenious flood-gates, — Mr. Ruskin's device, of course, — and a channel led down
through the wood to a rustic bridge in the rock.
Some one has stayed behind to let out the water,

---

[1] Since then taken on a long lease from the friendly landlord.

and down it comes; first a black stream and then a white one, as it gradually clears; and the rocky wall at the entrance becomes for ten minutes a cascade. This too has its uses; not only is there a supply of water in case of fire (the exact utilization of which is yet undecided), but it illustrates one of his doctrines about the simplicity with which works of irrigation could be carried out among the hills of Italy.

And so you go in to tea and chess, for he loves a good game of chess with all his heart. He loves many things, you have found. He is different from other men you know, just by the breadth and vividness of his sympathies, by power of living as few other men can live, in admiration, hope, and love. Is not such a life worth living, whatever its monument be?

CHAPTER VII.

FORS CLAVIGERA RESUMED.

(1880–1881.)

> " How can he give his neighbor the real ground,
>   His own conviction ? "
>
> BROWNING, *Karshish.*

RETIREMENT at Brantwood, as the reader may suspect, was only partial. All Mr. Ruskin's habits of life made it impossible for him to be idle, much as he acknowledged the need of thorough rest. - And he was a man with a mission. His work was not of the sort that could be laid aside and done with. He could not be wholly ignorant of the world outside Coniston, though sometimes for weeks together he tried to ignore it, and refused to read a newspaper. The time when General Gordon went out to Khartoum was one of these periods of abstraction, devoted to mediæval study. Somebody talked one morning at breakfast about the Soudan. "And who *is* the Soudan?" he earnestly inquired, connecting the name, as it seemed, with the Soldan of Babylon, in crusading romance.

> " The man is apathetic, you deduce ?
>   Contrariwise, he loves both old and young,

> Able and weak, affects the very brutes
> And birds — how say I ? flowers of the field —
> As a wise workman recognizes tools
> In a master's workshop, loving what they make.
> Thus is the man as harmless as a lamb :
> Only impatient, let him do his best,
> At ignorance and carelessness and sin."

" Don't you know," he wrote to a friend (January 8, 1880), " that I am entirely with you in this Irish misery, and have been these thirty years? — only one can't speak plain without distinctly becoming a leader of Revolution? I know that Revolution *must come* in all the world — but I can't act with Danton or Robespierre, nor with the modern French Republican or Italian one. I *could* with you and your Irish, but you are only at the beginning of the end. I have spoken, — and plainly too, — for all who have ears, and hear."

If he had spoken plainly about "landlordism," as they call it, he had spoken plainly too on the subject of capital. Nowadays every well-informed person knows that a vast number of influential thinkers hold — rightly or wrongly — that the private exploitation of labor is an error, if not a crime. But even in 1880, the doctrine of collectivism was too strange, even to educated people, to be heard with anything but the extremest impatience. The author of " Fors " had tried to show that the nineteenth-century commercialist spirit was not new; that the tyranny of capital was the old sin of usury over again; and he asked why preachers of religion did not denounce it, — why, for example, the Bishop of Manchester did not, on simply religious grounds, oppose the teaching of the " Manchester school," who were the chief supporters of the commercialist economy. Not until the end of 1879 had Dr. Fraser been aware of the challenge; but at length he wrote, justifying his attitude. The popular and able bishop had much to say on the expediency of the commercial system and the error of taking the Bible literally; but he did not seem to have any conception of Mr. Ruskin's standpoint; he seemed unaware of the revolution in economical thought which " Unto this Last " and " Fors " had been pioneering.

" I 'm not gone to Venice yet," wrote Mr. Ruskin to Miss Beever, " but thinking of it hourly. I 'm very nearly done with toasting my bishop; he just wants another turn or two, and then a little butter." The toasting and the buttering, both neatly done, appeared in the " Contemporary Review " for February, 1880; reprinted in the " Old Road " (vol. ii., pp. 202–238); and if the reader have insight into the course of modern thought, he will see that Mr. Ruskin's rejoinder was much more than a bit of clever persiflage.

This incident led him to feel that the mission of " Fors " was not finished. If bishops were still unenlightened, there was yet work to do. And so he gave up Venice, and resumed his crusade.

Brantwood life was occasionally interrupted by short excursions to London or elsewhere. In the autumn Mr. Ruskin had heard Professor Huxley on the evolution of reptiles; and this suggested another treatment of the subject, from his own artistic and ethical point of view, in a lecture oddly called " A Caution to Snakes," given at the London Institution, March 17, 1880 (repeated March 23d, and printed in " Deucalion," part vii.). In the course of this address he gave some notes of his observations on the motion of snakes, and claimed to be the first to have explained how they did not creep or drag themselves along, but traveled by a sort of skating action. Whether he was right in believing this to be a discovery I cannot say; but it was the result of much watching of the ways of adders in freedom on his moor, in addition to study at the Zoölogical Gardens, where he used to get the cases opened, to " make friends " with the snakes.

Mr. Ruskin was not merely an amateur zoölogist and F. Z. S., but a devoted lover and keen observer of animals. It would take long to tell the story of all his dogs, from the spaniel Dash, commemorated in his earliest poems, and Wisie, whose sagacity is related in " Præterita," down through the long line of bulldogs, St. Bernards, and collies, to Bramble, the reigning favorite; and all the cats who made his study their home, or were flirted with abroad. To Miss Beever, from Bolton Abbey (January 24, 1875) he describes the Wharfe in flood, and then continues: " I came home (to the hotel) to quiet tea, and a black kitten called Sweep, who lapped half my cream-jugful (and yet I had plenty), sitting on my shoulder." Grip, the pet rook at Denmark Hill, is mentioned in " My First Editor," as celebrated in verse by Mr. W. H. Harrison.

Kindness to animals has often been noted as one of the most striking traits of Mr. Ruskin, — a sympathy with them which goes much deeper than benevolent sentiment, or the curiosity of science. He cared little about their organization and anatomy, much about their habits and characters. He had not Thoreau's powers of observation and intimate acquaintance with all the details of wild life, but his attitude towards animals and plants was the same; hating the science that murders to dissect; resigning his professorship at Oxford, finally, because vivisection was introduced into the university; and supporting the Society for the Prevention of Cruelty to Animals with all his heart. But, as he said at the annual meeting in 1877, he objected to the sentimental fiction and exaggerated statements which some of its members circulated. " They had endeavored to prevent cruelty to animals," he said, " but they had not enough endeavored to promote affection for animals. He trusted to the pets of children for their education, just as much as to their tutors."

It was to carry out this idea (to anticipate a little) that he founded the Society of Friends of Living Creatures, which he addressed, May 23, 1885, at the club, Bedford Park, in his capacity of — not president — but " papa." The members, boys and girls from seven to fifteen, promised not to kill nor hurt any animal for sport, nor tease creatures ; but to make friends of their pets and watch their habits, and collect facts about natural history.

I remember, on one of the rambles at Coniston in the early days, how we found a wounded buzzard, — one of the few creatures of the eagle kind that our English mountains still breed. The rest of us were not very ready to go near the beak and talons of the fierce-looking and, as we supposed, desperate bird. Mr. Ruskin quietly took it up in his arms, felt it over to find the hurt, and carried it, quite unresistingly, out of the way of dogs and passers-by, to a place where it might die in solitude or recover in safety. He often told his Oxford hearers that he would rather they learned to love birds than to shoot them ; and his wood and moor were harbors of refuge for hunted game or " vermin," and his windows the rendezvous of the little birds, — though, indeed, they hardly want a friend at Coniston as long as the Thwaite feeds them with lavish bounty.

Mr. Ruskin had not been abroad since the spring of 1877, and in August, 1880, felt able to travel again. He went for a tour among the northern French cathedrals, staying at his old haunts, — Abbeville, Amiens, Beauvais, Chartres, Rouen, — and then returned with Mr. A. Severn and Mr. Brabazon to Amiens, where he spent the greater part of October.   He was writing a new book — the " Bible of Amiens " — which was to be to the " Seven Lamps " what " St. Mark's Rest " was to " Stones of Venice."

Before he returned the secretary of the Chesterfield art school had written to ask him to address the students.   Mr. Ruskin, traveling without a secretary, and in the flush of new work and thronging ideas, put the letter aside ; he carried his letters about in bundles in his portmanteau, as he said in his apology, " and looked at them as Ulysses at the bags of Æolus."   Some wag had the impudence to forge a reply, which was actually read at the meeting in spite of its obviously un-Ruskinian style and statements : —

" HARLESDEN (!), LONDON, Friday.

" MY DEAR SIR, — Your letter reaches me here.   Have just returned [commercial English, not Ruskin] from Venice [where he had meant to go, but did not go] where I have ruminated (!) in the pasturages of the home of art (!) ; the loveliest and holiest of lovely and holy cities, where the very stones cry out, eloquent in the elegancies of iambics " (!!) — and so forth.

However, it deceived the newspapers, and there was a fine storm, which Mr. Ruskin rather enjoyed.   For though the forgery was clumsy enough, it embodied some apt plagiarism from a letter to the Mansfield art school on a similar occasion.[1]

---

[1] Printed as appendix to a *A Joy for Ever*.   The Chesterfield letter and correspondence are given *in extenso* in *Igdrasil* (vol. i., pp. 215, 216).

BEAUVAIS CATHEDRAL

By John Ruskin, 1880

Not long before, a forgery of a more serious kind had been committed by one of the people connected with St. George's Guild, who had put Mr. Ruskin's name to checks. The bank authorities were long in tracing the crime. They even sent a detective to Brantwood to watch one of the assistants, who never knew — nor will ever know — that he was honored with such attentions ; and certainly neither Mr. Ruskin nor any of his friends for a moment believed him guilty. He had sometimes imitated Mr. Ruskin's hand ; a dangerous jest. Fortunately the real culprit was discovered at last, and Mr. Ruskin had to go to London as a witness for the prosecution. " Being in very weak health," the " Times " report said (April 1, 1879), " he was allowed to give evidence from the bench." He had told the Sheffield communists that " he thought so strongly on the subject of the repression of crime that he dare not give expression to his ideas for fear of being charged with cruelty ; " but no sooner was the prisoner released than he took him kindly by the hand and gave the help needed to start him again in a better career. That sort of inconsistency in Ruskin I fully admit.

Though he did not feel able to lecture to strangers at Chesterfield, he visited old friends at Eton, on November 6, 1880, to give an address on Amiens. For once he forgot his MS., but the lecture was no less brilliant and interesting. It was practically the first chapter of his new work, the "Bible of Amiens,"—itself intended as the first volume of "Our Fathers have told us: Sketches of the History of Christendom, for Boys and Girls who have been held at its Fonts." The distinctly religious tone of the work was noticed as marking, if not a change, a strong development of a tendency which had been strengthening for some time past. He had come out of the phase of doubt, into acknowledgment of the strong and wholesome influence of serious religion; into an attitude of mind in which, without unsaying anything he had said against narrowness of creed and inconsistency of practice, without stating any definite doctrine of the after life, or adopting any sectarian dogma, he regarded the fear of God and the revelation of the Divine Spirit as great facts, and motives not to be neglected in the study of history, as the groundwork of civilization and the guide of progress.

Early in 1879 the Rev. F. A. Malleson, vicar of Broughton, near Coniston, had asked him to write, for the Furness Clerical Society's meetings, a series of letters on the Lord's Prayer. In them he dwelt upon the need of living faith in the Fatherhood of God, and childlike obedience to the commands of old-fashioned religion and morality. He criticised the English liturgy as compared with mediæval forms of prayer; and pressed upon his hearers the strongest warnings against evasion, or explaining away of stern duties and simple faiths. He concluded: "No man more than I has ever loved the place where God's honor dwells, or yielded truer allegiance to the teaching of His evident servants. No man at this time grieves more for the damage of the Church which supposes him her enemy, while she whispers procrastinating *pax vobiscum* in answer to the spurious kiss of those who would fain toll curfew over the last fires of English faith, and watch the sparrow find nest where she may lay her young, around the altars of the Lord."

But if the Anglican Church refused him, the Roman Church was eager to claim him. His interest in mediævalism seemed to point him out as ripe for conversion. Cardinal Manning, an old acquaintance, showed him special attention, and invited him to charming *tête-à-tête* luncheons. It was commonly reported that he had gone over, or was going. But two letters (of a later date) show that he was not to be caught. To a Glasgow correspondent he wrote in 1887: "I shall be entirely grateful to you if you will take the trouble to contradict any news gossip of this kind, which may be disturbing the minds of any of my Scottish friends. I was, am, and can be, only a Christian Catholic in the wide and eternal sense. I have been that these five-and-twenty years at least. Heaven keep me from being less as I grow older! But I am no more likely to become a Roman Catholic than a Quaker, Evangelical, or Turk." To another, next year, he wrote: " I fear you have scarcely read enough of

'Fors' to know the breadth of my own creed or communion. I gladly take the bread, water, wine, or meat of the Lord's Supper[1] with members of my own family or nation who obey Him, and should be equally sure it was His giving, if I were myself worthy to receive it, whether the intermediate mortal hand were the Pope's, the Queen's, or a hedge-side gypsy's."

At Coniston he was on friendly terms with Father Gibson, the Roman Catholic priest, and gave a window to the chapel, which several of the Brantwood household attended. But though he did not go to church, he contributed largely to the increase of the poorly-endowed curacy, and to the charities of the parish. The religious society of the neighborhood was hardly of a kind to attract him, unless among the religious society should be included the Thwaite, where lived the survivors of a family long settled at Coniston: Miss Mary Beever, scientific and political; and Miss Susanna, who won Mr. Ruskin's admiration and affection by an interest akin to his own in nature and in poetry, and by her love for animals, and bright, unfailing wit. Both were examples of sincerely religious life, " at once sources and loadstones of all good to the village," as he wrote in the preface to " Hortus Inclusus," the collection of his letters to them since first acquaintance

---

[1] Compare the lines in Longfellow's *Golden Legend :* —

> " A holy family, that makes
> Each meal a Supper of the Lord."

in the autumn of 1873. The elder Miss Beever died at an advanced age on the last day of 1883; Miss Susanna still retains, in spite of failing powers, the rare gifts of sympathy and imagination which made her, through so many years, the best loved of Mr. Ruskin's neighbors.

In children he took a warm and openly-expressed interest. He used to visit the school often, and delighted to give them a treat. On January 13, 1881, he gave a dinner to three hundred and fifteen Coniston youngsters, and the tone of his address to his young guests is noteworthy as taken in connection with the drift of his religious tendency during this period. He dwelt on a verse of the Sunday-school hymn they had been singing: "Jesu, here from sin deliver." "That is what we want," he said; "to be delivered from our sins. We must look to the Saviour to deliver us from our sin. It is right we should be punished for the sins which we have done; but God loves us, and wishes to be kind to us, and to help us, that we may not willfully sin." Words like these were not lightly spoken: we must take them, with their full weight, to represent his real convictions.

At this time he used to take the family prayers himself at Brantwood; preparing careful notes for a Bible-reading, which sometimes, indeed, lasted longer than was convenient to the household; and writing collects for the occasion, still existing in manuscript, and deeply interesting as the prayers of a man who had passed through so many wildernesses of thought and doubt, and had returned at last,—not to the fold of the Church, but to the footstool of the Father.

CHAPTER VIII.

THE RECALL TO OXFORD.

(1882–1883.)

"*Cras ingens iterabimus æquor.*"

Horace.

THIS Brantwood life came to an end with the end of 1881. Early in the next year Mr. Ruskin went for change of scene to stay with the Severns at his old home on Herne Hill. He seemed much better, and ventured to reappear in public. On March 3d he went to the National Gallery to sketch Turner's Python. On the unfinished drawing is written: " Bothered away from it, and never went again. No light to work by in the next month." An artist in the gallery had been taking notes of him for a surreptitious portrait, — an embarrassing form of flattery.

He wrote: " No — I won't believe any stories about overwork. It 's impossible, when one 's in good heart and at really pleasant things. I 've a lot of nice things to do, but the heart fails, — after lunch, particularly!" Heart and head did, however, fail again ; and another attack of brain fever followed. Sir William Gull brought him through, and won his praise as a doctor and esteem as a friend.   Mr. Ruskin took it as a great compliment when Sir William, in acknowledging his fee, wrote that he should keep the check as an autograph.

By Easter Monday the patient was better again, and plunging into work in spite of everybody. He wrote:[1] " The moment I got your letter to-day recommending me not to write books (I finished it, however, with great enjoyment of the picnic, before proceeding to act in defiance of the rest), I took out the last proof of last ' Proserpina ' and worked for an hour and a half on it; and have been translating some St. Benedict material since — with much comfort and sense of getting — as I said — head to sea again — (have you seen the article on modern *rudders* in the ' Telegraph '? Anyhow I 'll send you a lot of collision and other interesting sea-subjects by to-morrow's post). This is only to answer the catechism.

" Love and congratulations to the boys. Salute Tommy for me in an affectionate — and apostolic — manner, — especially since he carried up the lunch ! — Also, kindest regards to all the other servants. I daresay they 're beginning really to miss me a little by this time.

" What state are the oxalises in — anemones ? Why can't we invent seeing, instead of talking, by telegraph ?

[1] I quote the apparently irrelevant sentences as a specimen of a characteristic private letter. The reader will easily gather their meaning, and catch the kindliness of the writer and universal readiness of sympathy, in the midst of illness and business.

"I 've just got a topaz of which these are two contiguous planes! [sketch of sides nearly two inches long] traced as it lies — and the smaller plane is BLINDINGLY iridescent in sunshine with rainbow colors! I 've only found out this in Easter Sunday light."

Again: "I was not at all sure, myself, till yesterday, whether I *would* go abroad; also I should have told you before. But as you have had the (sorrowful?) news broken to you — and as I find Sir William Gull perfectly fixed in his opinion, I obey him, and reserve only some liberty of choice to myself — respecting, not only climate, — but the general appearance of the inhabitants, of the localities, where for antiquarian or scientific research I may be induced to prolong my sojourn. — Meantime I send you — to show you I have n't come to town for nothing, my last bargain in beryls, with a little topaz besides."

But the journey was put off week after week. There was so much to do, buying diamonds for Sheffield museum, and planning a series of models to show the normal forms of crystals, and to illustrate a subject which he thought many people would find interesting, if they could be got over its *pons asinorum*. Not only Sheffield was to receive these gifts and helps; some time before, Mr. Ruskin had become acquainted with the Rev. J. P. Faunthorpe, Principal of Whitelands College for Pupil Teachers, and had given various books and collections to illustrate the artistic side of education.   Now he instituted there the May Queen Festival, in some sort carrying out his old suggestion in " Time and Tide " (see page 342 of this work).   Mr. A. Severn designed a gold cross, and it was presented, with a set of volumes of Ruskin's works, sumptuously bound, to the May Queen and her maidens.   The pretty festival became a popular feature of the school, " patronized by royalty," and Mr. Ruskin has continued his annual gift to Whitelands, and kept up a similar institution at the high school at Cork.

At last, in August, he started for the Continent, and stayed at first at Avallon in central France, a district new to him.   There he met Mr. Frank Randall, one of the artists working for St. George's Guild, and explored the scenery and antiquities of a most interesting neighborhood.   He drove over the Jura in the old style, revisited Savoy, and after weeks of bitter *bise* and dark weather, a splendid sunset cleared the hills.   He wrote to Miss Beever: " I saw Mont Blanc again to-day, unseen since 1877 ; and was very thankful.   It is a sight that always redeems me to what I am capable of at my poor little best, and to what loves and memories are most precious to me.   So I write to *you*, one of the true loves left. The snow has fallen fresh on the hills, and it makes me feel that I must be soon seeking shelter at Brantwood and the Thwaite."

But he went forward, exhilarated by the drive through Savoy with a famous coachman, renowned for his whip-cracking and his dog Tom. He won the professor's heart by his dashing style and kindliness to his beasts; and on parting he gave the man twenty francs as a *bonne main*, and two francs, as he said, for a *bonne patte* to Tom.

At Annecy he was pleased to find the waiter at the Hotel Verdun remembered his visit twenty years before; everywhere he met old friends, and saw old scenes that he had feared he never would revisit. After crossing the Cenis and hastening through Turin and Genoa, he reached Lucca, to be awaited at the Albergo Reale dell' Universo by a crowd, every one anxious to shake hands with Signor Ruskin. No wonder! for instead of allowing himself to be a mere Number-so-and-so in a hotel, wherever he feels comfortable, — and that is everywhere except at pretentious modern hotels, — he makes friends with the waiter, chats with the landlord, finds his way into the kitchen to compliment the cook, and forgets nobody in the establishment, — not only in "tips," but in a frank and sympathetic address which must contrast curiously, in their minds, with the reserve and indifference of other English tourists.

At Florence he met Henry Roderick Newman, an American artist who had been at Coniston and was working for the guild. He introduced Mr. Ruskin to Mrs. and Miss Alexander. In these ladies' home he found his own aims, in religion, philanthropy, and art, realized in an unexpected way. Miss Alexander's drawing at first struck him by its sincerity. He had been always the enemy of that acquired skill and paraded cleverness which become so fatiguing to the experienced critic. He had always called out for human interest, the evidence of sympathy, the poetry of feeling, in art; and he found this in Miss Alexander, — not professionally learned, but full of observation and the tokens of affectionate interest in her subject. As to style, she fulfilled his own teaching of bygone years, — the combination of free point-work with the pure line (see *ante*, p. 314), without blotting and bungling; and her sense of color and texture compensated for any weakness in anatomy and composition. Not only did she draw beautifully, but she also wrote a beautiful hand; and it had been one of his old sayings that missal-writing, rather than missal-painting, was the admirable thing in mediæval art. The legends illustrated by her drawings were collected by herself, through an intimate acquaintance with Italians of all classes, from the nobles to the peasantry, whom she understood and loved, and by whom she was loved and understood. By such intercourse she had learned to look beneath the surface. In religious matters her American common-sense saw through her neighbors, — saw the good in them as well as the weakness, — and she was as friendly, not only in society but in spiritual things, with the worthy village-priest as with T. P. Rossetti,[1] the leader

[1] A cousin of the artist, and in his way no less remarkable a

of the Protestant "Brethren," whom she called her pastor. And Mr. Ruskin, who had been driven away from Protestantism by the Waldensians at Turin (see *ante*, p. 255), and had wandered through many realms of doubt and voyaged through strange seas of thought, alone, found harbor at last with the disciple of a modern evangelist, the frequenter of the poor little meeting-house of outcast Italian Protestants.

Ruskin's art-criticism fought its way to the front long ago. His economy is now practically accepted. His religious teaching has not yet been listened to. That must wait until this nineteenth century — as he put it in 1845 — "has, I cannot say breathed, but *steamed* its last."

One evening before dinner he brought back to the hotel at Florence a drawing of a lovely girl lying dead in the sunset; and a little note-book. "I want you to look over this," he said, in the way, but not quite in the tone, with which the usual MS. "submitted for criticism " was tossed to a secretary to taste. It was "The Story of Ida; written by her Friend." [1]

An appointment to meet Mr. E. R. Robson, who was making plans for an intended Sheffield museum, took Mr. Ruskin back to Lucca, to discuss Romanesque mouldings and marble facings.

man. It is hardly too much to say that he did for evangelical religion in Italy what Gabriel Rossetti did for poetical art in England: he showed the path to sincerity and simplicity.

[1] This title was altered by Mr. Ruskin to "The Story of Ida; Epitaph on an Etrurian Tomb. By Francesca."

Mr. Charles Fairfax Murray also met Mr. Ruskin at Lucca, with drawings commissioned for St. George's Guild. But he soon returned to his new friends, and did not leave Florence finally until he had acquired the wonderful collection of one hundred and ten drawings, with beautifully written text, in which Miss Alexander had enshrined " The Roadside Songs of Tuscany."

Returning homewards by the Mont Cenis he stayed a while at Talloires, a favorite haunt (see *ante*, p. 293), extremely content to be among romantic scenery, and able to work steadily at a new edition of his works in a much cheaper form, of which the first volumes were at this time in hand. He had been making further studies, also, in history and Alpine geology ; but at last the snow drove him away from the mountains. So he handed over the geology to his assistant, who compiled " The Limestone Alps of Savoy " (supplementary to " Deucalion ") " as he could, not as he would," while Mr. Ruskin wrote out the new ideas suggested by his visit to Citeaux and St. Bernard's birthplace. These notes he completed on the journey home, and gave as a lecture on "Cistercian Architecture " (London Institution, December 4, 1882), in place of the previously advertised lecture on crystallography.

He seemed now to have quite recovered his health, and to be ready for reëntry into public life. What was more, he had many new things to say. The attacks of brain fever had passed over him like passing storms, leaving a clear sky.

After his retirement from the Oxford professorship, a subscription had been opened for a bust by Sir Edgar Boehm, as a memorial of a university benefactor; and the clay model (now in the Sheffield museum) was placed in the drawing school pending the collection of the necessary £220. "The Oxford University Herald," in its article of June 5, 1880, no doubt expressed the general feeling, or at any rate the feeling of the clerical party, then still in the majority, in its praise as well as in its criticism of Professor Ruskin. He himself claimed to have "harked back" to old standards of thought, in opposition to contemporary religious and scientific enlightenment; and the reader, who has followed his course thus far, must judge his judges from a higher and more panoramic standpoint than perhaps was possible to them. But after reciting his benefactions to the university with becoming appreciation, the "Herald" continued : —

"Mr. Ruskin has enjoyed renown and felt the breath of high reputation in every possible form, in the highest possible perfection, and with the highest desert. He has been famous while young, which is proverbially a thing for gods; he has been one of the best abused men in England; he has been one of the best praised, and that in all forms, — critically and passionately, wisely and fanatically, — for his merits and for his frailties.

He has been an acknowledged chief among the chiefs of literature; he has been adored by girls and undergraduates; a large circle of friends has partly understood him, and still regards him with genuine admiration and affection; he has labored hard for laboring men, and dispersed abroad and given to the poor for more than fifty years of his life. His name and his work are indissolubly connected with Oxford, and it is a great pity he ever left us. He has of course suffered from his own powers, as all men, being human, must suffer. The intensity of his own perceptions always gave him difficulty in receiving any knowledge from others, and it has taken the form of subjectivity or egotism. He is unable to endure authority on any subject, or even to accept testimony. His life has been spoiled by his continual attempts to substitute a Christianity of his own for the Church of England; he has his own political economy; he has systematized an excellent botany of his own, a mineralogy of his own, a geology of his own; he has driven himself frantic by conducting a magazine of his own; he has separated himself from everybody whose mind is not a minute copy of his own.

" We know not what might have been the result if, during his residence here, Professor Ruskin had had the sympathy or genuine interest of men of his own age engaged in the work of the university, or if art had been admitted to be a part of that work. But in any case he has done Oxford great honor, and made great sacrifices for her, and it is time that some acknowledgment should be made to the foremost name in modern English literature strictly so called: to an Oxonian who has attempted and achieved beyond others; to the kindest heart and keenest benevolence in England; to the poet, painter, and interpreter of the Word of God in Nature, who is best worthy to succeed Wordsworth and Turner."

It was natural, therefore, that on recovering his health he should resume his post. Professor W. B. Richmond, the son of his old friend Mr. George Richmond, gracefully retired, and the "Oxford University Gazette" of January 16, 1883, announced the reëlection. On March 2d he wrote that he was "up the Old Man yesterday;" as much as to say that he defied catechism, now, about his health; and a week later he gave his first lecture. The "St. James's Budget" of March 16th gave an account of it in these terms: —

"Mr. Ruskin's first lecture at Oxford attracted so large an audience that, half an hour before the time fixed for its delivery, a greater number of persons were collected about the doors than the lecture-room could hold. Immediately after the doors were opened the room was so densely packed that some undergraduates found it convenient to climb into the windows and on to the cupboards. The audience was composed almost equally of undergraduates and ladies; with the exception of the vice-chancellor, heads of houses, fellows, and tutors were chiefly conspicuous by their absence.

"It is, no doubt, difficult to know what should be the plan of a lecture before such an audience. Mr. Ruskin's, if somewhat unconnected, was at any rate interesting. He carried his audience with him to the end, as well in his lighter as in his more impassioned periods. Perhaps the most interesting part of his lecture was the beginning, in which he spoke of the late Mr. Rossetti, and compared his work with that of Holman Hunt." I omit an abstract of the lecture, which can be read in full in "The Art of England." The reporter continued: "He had made some discoveries: two lads and two lasses, who, though not artists,[1] could draw in a way to please even him. He used to say that, except in a pretty, graceful way, no woman can draw; he had now almost come to think that no one else can. (This statement the undergraduates received with gallant, if undiscriminating, applause.) To many of his prejudices, Mr. Ruskin said, in the last few years the axe had been laid. He had positively found an American, a young lady, whose life and drawing were in every way admirable. (Again great and generous applause on the part of the undergraduates, stimulated, no doubt, by the

---

[1] "Though not artists" was a slip on the reporter's part, and contradicted by the subsequent "two young Italian artists." The reference was to Misses Alexander and Greenaway, and Messrs. Boni and Alessandri.

knowledge that there were then in the room two fair Americans, who have lately graced Oxford by their presence.) At the end of his lecture Mr. Ruskin committed himself to a somewhat perilous statement. He had found two young Italian artists in whom the true spirit of old Italian art had yet lived. No hand like theirs had been put to paper since Lippi and Leonardo.

"Mr. Ruskin concluded by showing two sketches of his own, harmonious in color, and faithful and tender in touch, of Italian architecture, taken from the Duomo of Lucca, to show that though he was growing older his hand had not lost its steadiness. And so he concluded a lecture which, though it seemed to lack some guiding principle, yet carried the audience with it throughout, and seemed all too short to those who were fortunate enough to hear it."

Three more lectures of the course were given in May, and each repeated to a second audience. Coming to London, Mr. Ruskin gave a private lecture on June 5th to some two hundred hearers at the house of Mr. W. H. Bishop, in Kensington, on Miss Kate Greenaway and Miss Alexander. "I have never, until to-day," he said, "dared to call my friends and my neighbors together to rejoice with me over any recovered good or rekindled hope. Both in fear and much thankfulness I have done so now; yet, not to tell you of any poor little piece of upgathered silver of my own, but to show you the fine gold which has been strangely trusted to me, and which before was a treasure hid in a mountain field of Tuscany." The "Spectator" shared his enthusiasm for the pen-and-ink drawings of Miss Alexander's "Roadside Songs of Tuscany," and concluded a glowing account of the lecture by saying: "All Professor Ruskin's friends must be glad to see how well his Oxford work has agreed with him. He has gifts of insight and power of reaching the best feelings and highest hopes of our too indifferent generation which are very rare. Agree or disagree with some of his doctrines as we may, he constrains the least hopeful of his listeners to remember that man is not yet bereft of that 'breath of life' which enables him to live in spiritual places that are not yet altogether depopulated by the menacing army of physical discoverers."

With much encouragement in his work, he returned to Brantwood for the summer, and resolved upon another visit to Savoy, for more geology and another breath of health-giving Alpine air. But he found time only for a short tour in Scotland before returning to Oxford to complete the series of lectures on Recent English Art. During this term he was prevailed upon to allow himself to be nominated as a candidate for the rectorship of the University of Glasgow. He had been asked to stand in the Conservative interest in 1880, and he had been worried into a rather rough reply to the Liberal party, when after some correspondence they asked him whether he sympathized with Lord Beaconsfield or Mr. Gladstone. "What, in the devil's name," he exclaimed, "have *you* to do with either Mr. Disraeli or Mr. Gladstone? You are students at the university, and have no more business with politics than you have with rat-catching. Had you ever read ten words of mine with understanding, you would have known that I care no more either for Mr. Disraeli or Mr. Gladstone than for two old bag-pipes with the drones going by steam, but that I hate all Liberalism as I do Beelzebub, and that, with Carlyle, I stand, we two alone now in England, for God and the Queen." After that, though he might explain [1] that he never, under any conditions of provocation or haste, would have said that he hated Liberalism as he did *Mammon*, or Belial, or Moloch; that he "chose the milder fiend of Ekron as the true exponent and patron of Liberty, the God of Flies;" still the matter-of-fact Glaswegians were minded to give the scoffer a wide berth. He was put up as an independent candidate in the three-cornered duel; and, as such candidates usually fare, he fared badly. The only wonder is that three hundred and nineteen students were found to vote for him, instead of siding, in political orthodoxy, with Mr. Fawcett or the Marquis of Bute.

At last a busy and eventful year came to a close

[1] Epilogue to *Arrows of the Chace*.

at Coniston, with a lecture at the village institute on his old friend Sir Herbert Edwardes (December 22d), and in kindly intercourse with young friends in his mountain home and theirs. His interest in the school and the school children was unabated, and he was always planning new treats for them, or new helps to their lessons. He had set one of the assistants to make a large hollow globe, inside of which one could sit and see the stars as luminous points pricked through the mimic "vault of heaven," painted blue and figured with the constellations. By a simple arrangement of cogs and rollers the globe revolved, the stars rose and set, and the position of any star at any hour of the year could be roughly fixed. But the inclement climate of Coniston, and the natural roughness of children, soon wrecked the new toy. Perhaps some day a more suitable place may be found for it than the school-playground, and then there would be no difficulty about restoring it to working order and real educational value.

About this time he was anxious to get the village children taught music with more accuracy of tune and time than the ordinary singing-lessons enforced. He made many experiments with different simple instruments, and fixed at last upon a set of bells, which he wanted to introduce into the school. It was difficult, though, to interfere with the routine of studies prescribed by the code, and Mr. Ruskin's theories of education could have been carried out only on completely independent ground. Considering, too, that he scorned "the three R's," a school after his own heart would have been a very different place from any that earns the government grant; and he very strongly believed that if a village child learned the rudiments of religion and morality, sound rules of health and manners, and a habit of using its eyes and ears in the practice of some good handicraft or art and simple music, and in natural philosophy, taught by object lessons, — then book-learning would either come of itself, or be passed aside as unnecessary or superfluous. This was his motive in a well-known incident which has sometimes puzzled his public. Once, when new buildings were going on, the mason wanted an advance of money, which Mr. Ruskin gave him, and then held out the paper for him to sign the receipt. A great deal of hesitation and embarrassment ensued, somewhat to Mr. Ruskin's surprise, as he knows a north-countryman a great deal too well to expect embarrassment from him. At last the man said, in dialect: "Ah mun put ma mark!" He could not write. Mr. Ruskin rose at once, stretched out both hands to the astonished rustic, with the words: "I am proud to know you. Now I understand why you are such an entirely good workman."[1]

Unlike Wordsworth, who wrote about the peasantry without much direct intercourse with them

[1] I tell the story as it has already appeared in print in an article by Miss Wakefield in *Murray's Magazine*, November, 1890.

(after his school-days), Mr. Ruskin was fond of visiting his neighbors in their homes, and took a very genuine interest in their lives and affairs. Many of them who knew little or nothing about *his* life and affairs, and were puzzled at first by his manner, — so different from anything they had known, — came at last to regard him as a real friend; to some of them he was as much of a hero as he was to the undergraduates at Oxford. At first they asked, "What is he? where does he come from?" with the northern distrust of a stranger. They found out that "he stoodied a deal," and that accounted for anything; and by and by one heard here and there a phrase that meant more than much newspaper eulogy: "Eh! he's a grand chap, is Maisther Rooskin!"

CHAPTER IX.

THE STORM-CLOUD.

(1884–1888.)

" OF course I need n't wish you a *happy* Christmas," wrote Professor Ruskin (December 24, 1883). " I 'll wish you — what it seems to me most of us more need, and particularly my poor self — a *wise* one ! When are you coming — in search of wisdom, of course — to see *me ?* I ought to call first, ought n't I ? but I don't feel able for long days out just now. Could you lock up house for a couple of days over there, and come and stay with me over here ? It seems to me as if it would be rather nice. The house is — as quiet as you please. I 'd lock you both out of my study, and you might really play hide-and-seek in the passages about the nursery all day long. Will you come ? "

His great improvement in health had seemed to justify his two chief assistants in feeling that their constant attendance was no longer necessary to him. One set up house at Coniston, the other not far away, both ready to give what help was called for; while the main business correspondence was undertaken by Miss S. D. Anderson. During the Severns' absence Miss Anderson also was away for a holiday; and the loneliness, though only temporary, was tedious to him, and not good for him. He was not very well; put off the visitors, and wrote again: " I 'm better, and hope to be presentable on Monday. — I 'm sending the carriage for you. I wonder if the model [1] could come on the top of it? I 've got some very interesting junctions of schist and granite from Skiddaw, and a crystal or two for you to see."

Again: " Mind, you 're both due on Monday. Such colors! Such brushes! Such — everything waiting!"

The truant, recaptured, was soon set to work with Messrs. Newman's extra-luminous watercolors, specially prepared for the great diagrams of sunsets to illustrate the lecture, shortly to be given, on " The Storm-Cloud of the Nineteenth Century."

It had been a favorite subject of study with the author of " Modern Painters." His journals for fifty years past had kept careful account of the weather, and effects of cloud. He had noticed that since 1871 there had been a prevalence of chilly, dark *bise*, as it would be called in France;

---

[1] A geological model of the neighborhood of Coniston, which was being made under his direction.

but different in its phenomena from anything of his earlier days. The "plague wind," so he named it, — tremulous, intermittent, blighting grass and trees, — blew from no fixed point of the compass, but always brought the same dirty sky in place of the healthy rain-cloud of normal summers; and the very thunder-storms seemed to be altered by its influence into foul and powerless abortions of tempest. Landscape painting, under its lurid light which blanched the sun instead of reddening it, seemed to be deteriorating by the mere physical impossibility of seeing and studying the blue skies of his youth. Nature and art seemed to be suffering together; the times were out of joint; and these were but signs and warnings of a more serious gloom. For, feeling as he did the weight of human wrong against which it was his mission to prophesy, believing in a divine government of the world in all its literalness, he had the courage to appear before a London audience,[1] like any seer of old, and to tell them that

[1] London Institution, February 4, 1884; repeated with variations and additions a week later. The occupations of his remaining weeks in London are told in the following extracts from letters written to friends at Brantwood in February, 1884: —

"I want to know all about the bells, and what the children [at the school] are making of them: I bought the compass (seaman's on card), and another of needle, for the big school, yesterday; and another on card for the infants, and I want to know how the bricks get on. What a blessed time it takes to get anything done!"

"I had rather a day of it yesterday. Into National Gallery by half-past eleven — went all over it, noting things for lecture to the Academy girls on Saturday. Then a nice half-hour in a toy-shop, buying toys for the cabman's daughter [Miss Greenaway's little

this eclipse of heaven was — if not a judgment —
at all events a symbol of the moral darkness of a

model] — kaleidoscope, magnetic fish, and skipping-rope. Out to
Holloway — sate for my portrait to K. G. — cabman's daughter at
four — had tea, muffins, magnetic fishing, skipping, and a game at
marbles. Back across town to Sanger's Amphitheatre over Westminster Bridge. Saw pretty girl ride *haute école*, and beginning
of pantomime, but pantomime too stupid; so I came away at half-
past ten, walked a mile homewards in the moonlight — shower
coming on took cab up the hill, and had pretty —— to boil eggs
for my supper."

"I really shall be rather sorry to leave town; but there's something to be said for the country, too."

"Please find a catalogue of 108 or 110 minerals, written by me,
of my case at the British Museum. You'll easily guess which it is
among the MSS. in top drawer of study book-case, west side,
farthest from fire. I want it here by Monday, for I'm going on
Tuesday to have a long day at the case. They're going to ex-
hibit the two diamonds and ruby on loan, the first time they've
done so."

"I had rather a day of it yesterday. Out at half-past ten, to
china-shop in Grosvenor Place and glass-shop in Palace Road.
Bought coffee- and tea-cups for Academy girls to-morrow, and a
blue bottle for myself. Then to Boehm's, and ordered twelve
medallions: flattest bas-relief size-of-life profiles, chosen British
types — six men and six girls. Then to Kensington Museum, and
made notes for to-morrow's lecture. Then to British Museum, and
worked for two hours arranging agates. Then into city, and heard
Mr. Gale's lecture on British Sports at London Institution. Then
home to supper, and exhibited crockery, and read my letters before
going to bed."

"But I'm rather sleepy this afternoon — however, I'm going to
the Princess's to see *Claudian* (by the actor's request) — hope I
sha'n't fall asleep."

These are only scraps, to show that his prophetic function was
not all sackcloth and ashes. He was none the less a prophet for
being Jonah's opposite. He took a deep interest in the modern
Nineveh. The next letter ends: "What *is* the world coming to?
I wish I could stay to see!"

nation that had " blasphemed the name of God deliberately and openly; and had done iniquity by proclamation, every man doing as much injustice to his brother as it was in his power to do."

It sounded like a voice crying in the wilderness; to those that sat at ease, a jest; to many who, without his religious feeling and without his ardent emotional temperament, were yet working for the same ends of justice to the oppressed, it seemed like fanaticism, out of place in these latter days. But to him, growing old, and wearying for the Kingdom of Heaven which he despaired at last of seeing, there was but one reality, — the great fact, as he knew it, of God above, and man either obeying or withstanding Him. Civilization, art, science, and all the pride of human progress, he weighed in the balance against the stern law of right and wrong, which " our fathers have told us." It had always been the burden of his teaching; and amidst all minor interests and occupations, the note sounded louder and deeper than before, now that he had shaken off the hesitancy of philosophic doubt, and saw the space narrowing between him and " the earnest portal of eternity."

In the autumn, at Oxford, he took up his parable again. His lectures on " The Pleasures of England " he intended as a sketch of the main stream of history from his own religious standpoint. It was a noble theme, and one which his breadth of outlook and detailed experience would have fitted him to handle; but he was already nearing the limit of his vital powers. He had been suffering from depression throughout the summer, unrelieved by the energetic work for St. George's Museum, which in other days might have been a relaxation from more serious thought. He had been editing Miss Alexander's " Roadside Songs of Tuscany," and recasting earlier works of his own, incessantly busy; presuming upon the health he had enjoyed, and taking no hints nor advice from anxious friends, who would have been glad to have seen the summer spent in change of scene and holiday-making.

At Oxford he was watched with concern, — restless and excited, too absorbed in his crusade against the tendencies of the modern scientific party, too vehement and unguarded in his denunciations of colleagues, too bitter against the new order of things which, to his horror, was introducing vivisection in the place of the old-fashioned natural history he loved, and speculative criticism instead of " religious and useful learning."

He was persuaded to cancel his last three attacks on modern life and thought — " The Pleasures of Truth," of " Sense," and of " Nonsense " — and to substitute readings from earlier works, hastily arranged and re-written : and his friends breathed more freely when he left Oxford without another serious attack of brain-fever. He wrote on December 1, 1884, to Miss Beever: " I gave my fourteenth, and last for this year, lecture with

vigor and effect, and am safe and well (D. G.)
after such a spell of work as I never did before."
To another correspondent, a few days later:
" Here are two lovely little songs for you to put
tunes to, and sing to me. You 'll have both to
be ever so good to me, for I 've been dreadfully
bothered and battered here.   I 've bothered other
people a little, too, — which is some comfort!"

But in spite of everything, the vote was passed
to establish a physiological laboratory at the museum; to endow vivisection,— which to him meant
not only cruelty to animals, but a complete misunderstanding of the purpose of science, and defiance of the moral law.[1]   He resigned his professorship, with the sense that all his work had been
in vain, that he was completely out of touch with
the age, and that he had best give up the unequal
fight.

In former times when he had found himself
beaten in his struggles with the world, he had
turned to geology for a resource and a relief; but
geology, too, was part of the field of battle now.
The memories of his early youth and the bright
days of his boyhood came back to him as the only
antidote to the distresses and disappointments of

---

[1] Curious that Schopenhauer, whom Ruskin in 1853 called " the
last most ingenious and most venomous of German philosophers,"
should be at one with him on this — as it turned out — crucial
point: the Franciscan doctrine of the brotherhood of living beings.
See Schopenhauer on the subject,— as violent and more bitter
than Ruskin, — in *Parerga und Paralipomena* (translated by T.
B. Saunders in *Religion, and other Essays*).

his age, and he strove to forget everything in " bygones "—" Præterita." So far back as 1875 there had been a proposal for a biography, to be written by the Oxford pupil to whom we owe " Arrows of the Chace," and other valuable collections of Ruskiniana. But as he looked up materials, Mr. Ruskin felt it premature to place them in another's hands. It was Professor Norton, I believe, who suggested that he should write his own life; and he began to tell the story, bit by bit, in " Fors." On the journey of 1882, he made a point of revisiting most of the scenes of youthful work and travel, to revive his impressions; but the meeting with Miss Alexander gave him new interests, and his return to Oxford, starting him, so to say, on a new lease of life, put the autobiography into the background.

Now, at last, he collected the scattered notes, and completed his first volume, which brings the account up to the time of his coming of age. It is not a connected and systematic biography; it omits many points of interest, especially the steps of his early successes and mental development; but it is the brightest conceivable picture of himself and his surroundings — "scenes and thoughts perhaps worthy of memory," as the title modestly puts it — told with inimitable ease and graphic power. Readers who knew him as a landscape-painter in prose were surprised at his insight into human character, and his skill in portraiture. Nothing could be livelier in anecdote, or happier in humorous expression, — the more surprising when one knows the difficult circumstances under which the book was written. Above all, it reveals the pathetic side of the author's life — his early limitations and struggles — in a way which taught a new sympathy for the man whose position had been envied, whose self-reliance and gladiatorial energy had been admired and feared, by readers who little understood how much tenderness they masked, and how many trials they had surmounted.

We have traced, even more fully than he has told, a life which was a battle with adversities from the beginning; over-stimulus in childhood; intense application to work in youth and middle age, under conditions of discouragement, both public and private, which would have been fatal to many another man; and this, too, not merely hard work, but work of an intensely emotional nature, involving — in his view at least — wide issues of life and death, in which he was another Jacob wrestling with the angel in the wilderness, another Savonarola imploring reconciliation between God and man.

Without a life of singular temperance, — the evidence of which is seen in still undimmed clearness of eye and unfailing fullness of hair and beard, — without unusual moral principle and self-command, he would long ago have fallen in the race, like other men of genius of his passionate type. He outlived consumptive tendencies in youth; and the repeated indications of over-strain in later life, up to the time of his first serious breakdown in 1878, had issued in nothing more than the depression and fatigue with which most busy men are familiar. He had been accustomed to hear himself called mad, — the defense of Turner was thought by the *dilettanti* of the time to be only possible to a lunatic; the author of "Stones of Venice," we saw (*ante*, p. 174), was insane in the eyes of his critic, the architect; it was seriously whispered when he wrote on political economy that Ruskin was out of his mind; and so on. Every new thing he put forward "made Quintilian stare and gasp" and *soi-disant* friends shake their heads, until a still newer nine-days'-wonder appeared from his pen; the fact being that all along he was simply ahead of his public, one of the very few men of broad outlook, of panoramic genius (to quote Carlyle on Goethe) in a hive of clever critics and myopic specialists.

But the brain-fever of 1878, so difficult to explain to his public, made it appear that the common reproach might after all be coming true. The recurrence of a similar illness in 1881 made it still more to be feared. It seemed as though his life's work was to be invalidated by his age's failure; it seemed that the stale shallow reproach might only too easily be justifiable.

We cannot but ask, How far was there ground for this fear? This is hardly the place to discuss the general question of the connection of insanity with genius. That some obscure relation of the sort does exist, cannot be denied; at any rate, that the busy brain of a great man is more liable than others to fail, partially or wholly, finally or transiently. The business of the public — and more especially of the critics who assume to lead the public's judgment — is to distinguish between the normal career of genius and its aberrations. The dividing line is sometimes easy to draw. Nobody doubts the value of Kant's or Wordsworth's work, although there was a gloom over their later days. At other times the line is more difficult to lay down, as in the case of Turner. In some of his most brilliant work one feels the presence of morbid conditions long before they can be diagnosed with certainty.

But in the life of a thinker and leader of men, like Ruskin, the question becomes more than a matter of curiosity. We all admit him to be sincere; but is he sound? Or, if infallibility be put out of the question, is he more — or less — logical, rational, coherent in mental development, than other men to whom we listen, and in whom we trust for opinion and advice?

To this I think there is only one answer. The more I study his life the more I see that his work is not irresponsible and eccentric. The careful student should be able to trace his genius, down to the end, in continuous and rational progression. Passing over defined intervals of mental disease, and allowing for vehemence of expression, — partly characteristic, partly the temporary effect of the *penumbra* of the storm-cloud, — his mental development, I make bold to say, is normal and logical throughout his life. And I believe that when his work can be looked back upon as a whole, with proper understanding of its environment and with full knowledge of its circumstances, the common reproach of insanity made against each new manifestation of his mind will then be scorned as an exploded prejudice.

But these attacks of mental disease, which at his recall to Oxford seemed to have been safely distanced, after his resignation began again at more and more frequent intervals. Crash after crash of tempest fell upon him, — clearing away for a while only to return with fiercer fury, until they left him beaten down and helpless at last, to learn that he must accept the lesson and bow before the storm. Like another prophet who had been very jealous for the Lord God of Hosts, he was to feel tempest and earthquake and fire pass over him, before hearing the still small voice that bade him once more take courage, and live in quietness and in confidence, for the sake of those whom he had forgotten, when he cried, " I, even I only, am left."

From one who has been out in the storm the reader will not expect a cool recital of its effects. The delirium of brain-fever brings strange things to pass ; and, no doubt, afforded ground for the painful gossip, of which there has been more than enough,— much of it absurdly untrue, the romancing of ingenious newspaper - correspondents; some of it, the lie that is half a truth. For in these times there were not wanting parasites such as always prey upon creatures in disease, as well as weak admirers who misunderstood their hero's natural character, and entirely failed to grasp his situation.

Let such troubles of the past be forgotten; all that I now remember of many a weary night and day is the vision of a great soul in torment, and through purgatorial fires the ineffable tenderness of the real man emerging, with his passionate appeal to justice and baffled desire for truth. To those who could not follow the wanderings of the wearied brain it was nothing but a horrible or a grotesque nightmare. Some, in those trials, learned, as they could not otherwise have learned, to know him, and to love him as never before.

There were many periods of health, or comparative health, even in those years. While convalescent from the illness of 1885 he continued "Præterita" and "Dilecta," the series of notes and letters illustrating his life. In connection with early reminiscences, he amused himself by reproducing his favorite old nursery book, " Dame Wiggins of Lee." He edited the works of one or two friends, wrote occasionally to newspapers, — notably, on books and reading, to the " Pall Mall Gazette," in the "symposium" on the best hundred books. He continued his arrangements for the museum, and held an exhibition (June, 1886) of the drawings made under his direction for the guild.

He was already drifting into another illness when he sent the famous reply to an appeal for help to pay off the debt on a chapel at Richmond. The letter is often misquoted for the sake of raising a laugh, so that it is not out of place to reprint it as a specimen of the more vehement expressions of this period. The reader of his life must surely see, through the violence of the wording, a perfectly consistent and reasonable expression of Mr. Ruskin's views : —

BRANTWOOD, CONISTON, LANCASHIRE,
May 19, 1886.

SIR, — I am scornfully amused at your appeal to me, of all people in the world the precisely least likely to give you a farthing! My first word to all men and boys who care to hear me is "Don't get into debt. Starve and go to heaven, — but don't borrow. Try first begging, — I don't mind, if it's really needful, stealing! But don't buy things you can't pay for!"

And of all manner of debtors, pious people building churches they can't pay for are the most detestable nonsense to me. Can't you preach and pray behind the hedges — or in a sand-pit — or a coal-hole — first?

And of all manner of churches thus idiotically built, iron churches are the damnablest to me.

And of all the sects of believers in any ruling spirit, — Hindoos, Turks, Feather Idolaters, and Mumbo Jumbo, Log and Fire worshippers, who want churches, your modern English Evangelical sect is the most absurd, and entirely objectionable and unendurable to me! All which they might very easily have found out from my books — any other sort of sect would ! — before bothering me to write it to them.

> Ever, nevertheless, and in all this saying,
> Your faithful servant, JOHN RUSKIN.

The recipient of the letter promptly sold it for ten pounds. Only three days later, Mr. Ruskin was writing one of the most striking passages in " Præterita " (vol. ii., chap. 5), — indeed, one of the daintiest landscape pieces in all his works, describing the blue Rhone as it flows under the bridges of Geneva.

This energetic letter-writing made people stare; but a more serious result of these periods between strength and helplessness was the tendency to misunderstanding with old friends. Mr. Ruskin had spoiled many of them, if I may say so, by too uniform forbearance and unselfishness; and now that he was not always strong enough to be patient, difficulties ensued which they had not always the tact to avert. " The moment I have to scold people they say I 'm crazy," he said, piteously, one day. And so, one hardly knows how, he found himself at strife on all sides. Before he was fully recovered from the attack of 1886 there were troubles about the Oxford drawing school, and he withdrew most of the pictures he had there on loan. How little animosity he really felt against Oxford is shown from the fact that early in the next year (February, 1887) he was planning with his cousin, Mr. Wm. Richardson, to give £5000 to the drawing school, as a joint gift in memory of their two mothers (see pedigree, *ante*, p. 9). Mr. Richardson's death, and Mr. Ruskin's want of means, — for he had already spent all his capital, — put an end to the scheme. But the remaining loans, important and valuable drawings by himself at the school, he has not withdrawn, and it is to be hoped they may stay there to show not only the artist's hand but the friendly heart of the founder and benefactor.

In April, 1887, came the news of Laurence Hilliard's death in the Ægean, with a shock that intensified the tendency to another recurrence of illness. For months the situation caused great anxiety. In August he posted with Mrs. A. Severn towards the south, and took up his quarters at Folkestone, moving soon after to Sandgate, where he remained, with short visits to town, until the following summer, — better, or worse, from week to week, — sometimes writing a little for " Præterita," or preparing material for the continuation of unfinished books; but bringing on his malady with each new effort. In June, 1888, he went with Mr. Arthur Severn to Abbeville and made his headquarters for nearly a month at the Tête de Bœuf. Here he was arrested for sketching the fortifications, and examined at the police station, much to his amusement. At Abbeville, too, he met Mr. Detmar Blow, a young architect, whom he asked to accompany him to Italy. They stayed a while at Paris, — drove, as in 1882, over the Jura, and up to Chamouni, where Mr. Ruskin wrote the epilogue to the reprint of "Modern Painters;" then, by Martigny and the Simplon, they went to visit Mrs. and Miss Alexander at Bassano; and thence to Venice. They returned by the St. Gotthard, reaching Herne Hill early in December.

But this journey did not, as it had been hoped, put him in possession of his strength like the journey of 1882. Then, he had returned to public life with new vigor; now, his best hours were hours of feebleness and depression; and he came home to Brantwood in the last days of the year, wearied to death, to wait for the end.

What was the end to be?

CHAPTER X.

DATUR HORA QUIETI.

(1889–1892.)

But it shall come to pass, that at evening time it shall be light. —
ZECH. xiv. 7.

IN the summer of 1889, at Seascale, on the
Cumberland coast, Mr. Ruskin was still working
at " Præterita." He had his work planned out to
the finish; in nine more chapters he meant to
conclude his third volume with a review of the
leading memories of his life down to the year
1875, when the story was to close. Passages here
and there were written, material collected from
old letters and journals, and the contents and titles
of the chapters arranged; but the intervals of
strength had become fewer and shorter, and at
last, in spite of all his courage and energy, he
was brought face to face with the fact that his
powers were ebbing away, that head and hand
would do their work no more.

He could not finish " Præterita ; " but he could
not leave it without record of one companionship
of his life, which was, it seemed, all that was left
to him of the old times and the old folks at home.
And so, setting aside the plans he had made, he

devoted the last chapter, as his forebodings told him it must be, to his cousin, Mrs. Arthur Severn, and wrote the story of " Joanna's Care."

In his bedroom at Seascale, morning after morning, he still worked, or tried to work, as he had been used to do on journeys farther afield in brighter days. But now he seemed lost among the papers scattered on his table; he could not fix his mind upon them, and turned from one subject to another in despair; and yet patient, and kindly to those with him whose help he could no longer use, and who dared not show — though he could not but guess — how heart-breaking it was.

They put the best face upon it, of course: drove in the afternoons about the country, — to Muncaster Castle, to Calder Abbey, where he tried to sketch once more; and when the proofs of " Joanna's Care " were finally revised, to Wastwater for the night; but traveling now was no longer restorative.

It added not a little to the misfortunes of the time that two of his best friends in the outside world were disputing over a third. By nobody more than by Mr. Ruskin was Carlyle's reputation valued, and yet he acknowledged that Mr. Froude was but telling the truth in the revelations which so surprised the public; and much as he admired Mr. Norton, he deprecated the attack on Carlyle's literary executor, whose motives he understood and approved.

In August, after his return to Coniston, the

storm-cloud came down upon him once more. It was only in the summer of 1890 that he was able to get about again. But firmly convinced that his one chance lay in absolute rest and quiet, he has since wisely refused any sort of exertion, and for the last two years has been rewarded by a steady improvement in health and strength.

Nowadays he seems, in all but the power of resuming work, himself again, though aged and feeble. He comes downstairs late, walks out morning and evening by the lake shore, — not so often now climbing up the moor, or boating on the lake. He reads the newspapers and books, and spends the evening in the old way in the drawing-room, rarely without music and chess. He visits his neighbors, and is glad to see intimate friends and young people; but he has hardly strength for the distinguished stranger, or the admirer from a distance. Remembering all he has passed through, his friends should not be surprised if he shrinks from visits of curiosity and inspection, however kindly meant. He retains a vivid memory and interest in many things; and, when the company is genial and the subject rouses him, talks as brightly as of old. There are not wanting signs of reserve power which encourage the hope that many years are in store for him of rest after toil, and tranquil light at evening time.

In the mean time he has been obliged to hand over to others such parts of his work as others

John Ruskin in 1892

can do. The St. George's Guild still continues
in existence, though it naturally lost much of its
interest, and the whole of its distinctive mission,
when he ceased to be able to direct it on the lines
marked out in " Fors." Contributions from the
friends and companions of the guild have, at a
rough calculation from published accounts, nearly
equaled the original £7000 which he gave to
start the fund. The agricultural schemes have
been left in abeyance, but the educational side,
less important though more attainable, has prospered. Very many schools and colleges have
benefited by its gifts and loans, but the museum
at Sheffield is looked upon as its chief outward
and visible sign.

It had quite outgrown its cottage at Walkley,
never intended for more than temporary premises;
and for ten years there had been talk of new
buildings, at first on the spot, then on the guild's
ground at Bewdley, where, at one time, Mr. Ruskin planned a fairy palace in the woods, with clois-
tered hostelries for the wandering student. Such
schemes were stopped less by his illness than by
want of means. More careful of others' property
than his own, he kept half the fund, and bought
land and consols as a permanent endowment.
The rest he spent on pictures, books, casts, coins,
and minerals. If sometimes he bought objects
that seemed expensive, or paid liberally for work,
it must be remembered that the rule of the museum was to have only the best of everything, and

the rule of the guild was that the laborer is worthy of his hire. There was no waste in useless salaries or accumulated specimens. Mr. Ruskin's judgment as buyer was invaluable, and freely given, and, after all, what he spent was his own gift, to which he added in kind as time went on. So there was no money for building.

Sheffield, moreover, did not wish to lose the museum, and offered to house it if the guild would present it to the town. That was, of course, out of the question. But a new offer to take over the collection on loan, the guild paying a curator, was another matter, and was thankfully accepted. The corporation fulfilled their share of the bargain with generosity. An admirable site was assigned at Meersbrook Park, in a fine old hall surrounded with trees, and overlooking a broad view of the town and country. But even the spacious rooms of Meersbrook Hall were found insufficient to show the collection, which had been simply warehoused at Walkley, and this year (1892) additional space has been provided. On April 15, 1890, the museum was opened by the Earl of Carlisle, in presence of the corporation, the trustees of the guild, and a large assembly of Mr. Ruskin's friends and Sheffield townspeople. Since then the attendance of visitors and students shows that the collection is appreciated by the public, and it is to be hoped that though nominally a loan it will remain there in perpetuity, and that it will be maintained and used with due regard to the intentions of the founder.

Many other plans had to be modified, as Mr. Ruskin found himself less able to work, and was obliged to hand over his business to others. With his early books he had been dissatisfied, as expressing immature views. " The Stones of Venice " had been recast into two small volumes, and " St. Mark's Rest " written in the attempt to supplement and correct it. But the original book was obviously in demand, and a new edition was brought out in 1886.

" Modern Painters " had been also on the con-demned list. The strong Protestantism and the geological theories involved in his descriptions of mountains made him reluctant to reprint; more-over, at the time of the last edition published by Messrs. Smith & Elder (1873), he had been told that the plates, which he considered a very im-portant part of the work, would not stand another impression ; and so he destroyed nine of them, in order that no subsequent edition might be brought out in the original form. He reprinted vol. ii. in a cheap edition, and began to recast the rest, with annotations and additions, as " In Montibus Sanc-tis " and " Cœli Enarrant ; " while Miss S. Beever's selections (" Frondes Agrestes ') found a ready sale. But this did not satisfy the public, and there was a continual cry for a reprint, to which, at last, he yielded. Early in 1889 the " Complete Edition " appeared, with the canceled plates reproduced. Copies of the original edition had reached the price of £50, and their owners not unnaturally felt aggrieved at the depreciation of their property. But the new edition was not an exact reproduction of the old. No connoisseur would accept photogravure reproductions and modern copies as equivalent in value to auto-graph etchings and old masterpieces of engrav-ing, and the edition of " 1888 " (as it is dated), however useful to the general reader, cannot re-place the original on the shelves of the intelligent book-lover. Indeed, in spite of a rapid sale for the reprint, which shows the reality of the demand, the earlier edition is now regaining its value in the book market.

While working at " Præterita," Mr. Ruskin had looked up those old writings in verse with which he had made his first reputation in his youth. He had been often pressed to reprint his volume of poems; and with a natural interest in his "first-born," and in everything that recalled early days, he acceded to the demand, — the more readily that American " pirated " editions were already in the field, and verses falsely attributed to him were in circulation, both in print and in MS. Though he had never set great store by his verse-writing, he had never wished to destroy the evidences of his early industry. In 1849 he printed a thin quarto containing the " Scythian Guest," [1] with a

---

[1] Now excessively rare. I owe the notice to the kindness of Mr. T. J. Wise.

preface in which he said: "However unwilling I might be to stand for public judgment as a poet by bringing together those uncollected productions, I cannot pretend to think them so wholly bad that no sample should be rescued and preserved." Next year he printed a tolerably full collection. In "The Queen of the Air" he gave a specimen of his earliest attempts, and in "Præterita" quoted others, and alluded to many more. Now at last he handed over the carefully preserved MSS. to one of his assistants, and the Poems of John Ruskin appeared in 1891. The volumes form an authentic record of the development of a remarkable mind. "Præterita" tells what the old man thought of his boyhood; the Poems, without the self-consciousness of most diary-writers, reveal him as he really was. Taken in this light, they are unique in literary history; taken as literature, they hardly claim to figure among the sixty-odd accredited poets of the period.

These volumes were the first published by Mr. Ruskin after the passing of the American copyright act. He had always felt it a grievance that the enormous popularity of his works in America meant an enormous piracy. Towards the end of the "fifties," Mr. Wiley of New York had begun to print cheap Ruskins; not, indeed, illegally, but without any acknowledgment to the author, and without any reference to the author's wishes as to form and style of production. An artist and writer on art, insisting on delicacy and refinement as the first necessity of draughtsmanship, and himself sparing no trouble or expense in the illustrations of his own works, was naturally dissatisfied with the wretched "artotypes" with which the American editions caricatured his beautiful plates.   Not only that, but it was a common practice to smuggle these editions, recommended by their cheapness, into other countries.   Mr. Wiley sent, on an average, five hundred sets of " Modern Painters " to Europe every year, the greater number to England.   His example was followed by other American publishers, so that in New York alone there are now half a dozen houses advertising Ruskin's works, and many more throughout the cities of the States.   Mr. Wiley, the first in the field, proposed to pay up a royalty upon all the copies he had sold if Mr. Ruskin would recognize him as accredited publisher in America. The offer of so large a sum would have been tempting, had it not meant that Mr. Ruskin must condone what he had for years denounced, and sanction what he strongly disapproved.   The case would have been different if proposals had been made to reproduce his books in his own style, under competent supervision.   This was done in 1890, when Mr. Allen made arrangements with Messrs. Charles E. Merrill & Co., of New York, to bring out the " Brantwood " edition of Ruskin, under the editorship of Professor C. E. Norton.

Though the sale of Mr. Ruskin's books in

America has never, until so recently, brought him any profit, his own business in England, started in 1872 at such disadvantage, has singularly prospered. It is impossible to reckon the total number of copies of Ruskin's works throughout the world; but a rough estimate gives the number of bound volumes published by Messrs. Smith & Elder and Mr. George Allen, exclusive of parts and pamphlets, as about 300,000. For the first few years there was a loss upon the Orpington business; then the scale turned, as the new system of publishing became better known. It was found that the booksellers were not indispensable, and that business could be done through the post as well as over the counter. In spite of occasional difficulties, such as the bringing out of works in parts, appearing irregularly or stopping outright at the author's illnesses, there has been a steady increase of profit, bringing in an income of two to three thousand pounds a year.

Fortunate it was for Mr. Ruskin that his bold attempt succeeded. The £200,000 he inherited from his parents have gone, — chiefly in gifts and in attempts to do good. The interest he used to spend on himself; the capital he gave away until it totally disappeared, except what is represented by the house he lives in and its contents. The sale of his books yields his only income, and a great part of that goes to an army of pensioners to whom in the days of his wealth he pledged himself, needy relatives and friends, discharged servants, institutions in which he took an interest at one time or other. But he has sufficient for his wants, and need not now fear poverty in his old age.

Though he no longer reads proofs nor writes business letters, he takes an interest in all that goes on. His desire, often expressed, is to see his works completely accessible to the public, and as cheap as possible, consistent with good form. He has deputed two of his nearest friends to manage the details of business, without giving him unnecessary trouble; but his readers may be assured that those in charge are acting under his eye, and sincerely endeavoring to consult his wishes and interests, which constant intercourse gives them every opportunity of understanding.

In this quiet retreat at Brantwood the echoes of the outer world do not sound very loudly. Mr. Ruskin has been too highly praised and too roundly abused, during fifty years of public life, for him to care now what magazine critics and journalists say of him. He was surprised, indeed, to read kindly notices in leading papers on the appearance of his juvenile poems; and often looks with pleasure at letters and tributes from high and low, all the world over, which he does not trust himself to answer; as, on the other hand, he longs sometimes, when great questions are in debate, to rush once more into the fray. Other men of his standing can solace themselves, if it be solace, in the consciousness that a grateful country has recognized their talents or their services. But civic and academic honors are not likely to be showered on a man who has spent his life in strenuous opposition to academicism in art and letters, and in vigorous attacks upon both political parties, and upon the established order of things.

Any distinction conferred on him has been, so to say, in spite of himself. Oxford and Cambridge have awarded him the highest honors in their gift.[1] In 1873 the Royal Society of Painters in Watercolors voted him honorary member, a recognition which gave him great pleasure at the time. At different dates he has been elected to various societies, — geological, zoölogical, architectural, horticultural, historical, anthropological, metaphysical; and to the Athenæum and Alpine clubs. But he has not sought distinctions, and he has even declined them, as in the case of the medal of the Royal Institute of British Architects. Many years before, in his youth, he received the diploma of a great Italian academy. He was very busy at the moment, traveling, and not sure of his Italian or the proper form of reply, — so he told me once, — and he put off his acknowledgment until he forgot all about it. Long after, he recollected the discourtesy with shame; but it was too late, then, to repair the slip, and he was glad to hear no more of the onerous compliment. He appears, however, in

---

[1] He was honorary student of Christ-Church, Oxford, already in 1859, not elected in 1869, as I have stated, *ante*, p. 375.

1877, as honorary associate of the Academy of Venice.

His works have not been popularized abroad by translations, to which he is opposed, feeling not only that his style would be difficult to render, but that the audiences they would address could hardly be open to the appeal he makes so distinctly to the mind and associations of an English-speaking race. But his name is well enough known in Italy, and not unknown in France. In 1864 M. Joseph Milsand, Browning's friend, in his " Esthétique Anglaise," more recently M. Ernest Chesneau in his " Ecole Anglaise,"[1] and M. Marcel Fouquier, have introduced him to their countrymen, not without appreciation, though their standpoint in art criticism was very different from his. The diplomas of honorary membership lately received from the Royal Academies of Antwerp and Brussels show that he is not unknown in Belgium.

A more striking form of distinction than empty titles is the fact that Mr. Ruskin was the first writer whose contemporaries, during his lifetime, formed societies to study his work. There may be question of the usefulness of their meetings, lectures, and publications; but there can be no doubt that they represent real enthusiasm on the part of readers. The first Ruskin society was

---

[1] The English translation of which was edited by Mr. Ruskin. He commissioned M. Chesneau to write a life of Turner, which after much preparation and expense was abandoned.

founded in 1879 at Manchester, and was followed by the societies of London, Glasgow, and Liverpool, still in working. In 1887 the Ruskin Reading Guild was formed in Scotland, with many local branches in England and Ireland, and a journal, subsequently re-named "Igdrasil," to promote study of literary and social subjects in Ruskin, and in writers like Carlyle and Tolstoï taking a standpoint similar to his. Though this society has since generalized its title into "The Reading Guild," as a disclaimer of the narrow Ruskinism which he more than any one deprecates, it still continues its work on the same lines.

A number of other societies for philanthropic purposes — such as the social unions in some large cities — trace their motive power chiefly to Ruskin, through many able thinkers and workers who are making themselves a place in the front rank in modern life. For though he looks fondly back to old times for his personal ideals, Ruskin's teaching is essentially modern. Its atmosphere is that of the time coming; its ideas are those that commend themselves to the vanguard of progress, — not the "progress" of old-fashioned liberalism, but of an age which has been born since Ruskin's voice began to fail, and which is now beginning to realize that he is its true father and pioneer.

Take, for instance, an anecdote of the London strikes in 1890 (from the "Pall Mall Gazette"). A man in the audience at a "labor-meeting" passes up a slip of paper to the platform: "Will

Mr. John Burns inform the writer whether, as foreman, he is willing to accept the same pay as an ordinary workman?" Back comes another slip: "Mr. Ruskin says that the laborer should be paid more than the landscape painter" (a doubtful statement, by the way; see *ante*, p. 290). But the dissentient replies: "The writer does not want to know what Mr. Ruskin says. *He has read him at home.*" For somehow, in spite of prohibitive prices the works of Ruskin have found their way among all classes, and his thoughts, more or less understood, and often unacknowledged, have become a part of the national mind.

Some Ruskin missionary-preaching has been done by the University Extension. Undergraduates, who listened to him in spite of their tutors' criticisms, are lecturers in their turn; and they find Ruskin a subject for the masses, who eagerly listen to his social doctrines. And his art teaching, so long called irresponsible and contradictory, now, by the first writer who has given us an adequate History of Æsthetic,[1] is treated as the work of a great thinker.

Not long since, talking over his failures, Mr. Ruskin said it was some comfort to him that he was not without successors, and he instanced Count Leo Tolstoï as one who was, in a way, carrying out the work he had hoped to do. Last June, in the "Cornhill Magazine," in which "Unto this Last" appeared over thirty years ago, a con-

---

[1] *History of Æsthetic.* By B. Bosanquet, M. A., LL. D., etc. 1892.

tributor reported his talk with the great Russian: " Ruskin he thought one of the greatest men of the age; and it pained him to notice that English people generally were of a different opinion. But ' no man is a prophet in his own country,' and the greatest men are seldom recognized in their own times, for the very reason that they are so much in advance of the age. Their contemporaries are unable to understand them."

So Tolstoï speaks; so all the best men of his time have spoken about Ruskin; and after theirs, what testimony can be added? Last words are often lost words; and, indeed, the last word cannot be spoken yet, nor can this story be brought to an end, I trust, for many a year to come, — unless in the phrase of the fairy-tale, " They lived happily ever after."

For now the storm-cloud has drifted away, and there is light in the west, a mellow light of evening time, such as Turner painted in his pensive Epilogue. " Datur Hora Quieti: " there is more work to do, but not to-day. The plough stands in the furrow; and the laborer passes peacefully from his toil, homewards.

APPENDIX

CHRONOLOGY.

(1860–1892.)

1860. — Leaving home, May 22, John Ruskin was
Age 41. on June 18 at Geneva; met W. J.
Stillman; wrote "Unto this Last," July
and Aug., at . . . . . Chamouni.

" Early in Sept. returned and spent the
winter at . . . . . . Denmark Hill.

1861. — March 23, gave Turner drawings to Ox-
Age 42. ford; May, gave Turner drawings to
Cambridge.

" April 2, Address, St. George's Mission . —

" April 19, Lecture, "Tree Twigs "(Roy.
Inst). . . . . . . —

" June 6, Address on "Illuminated Missals"
(Burlington House, Society of Anti-
quaries) . . . . . . —

" Went to Savoy, and during autumn wrote
" Munera Pulveris " . . . . Mornex.

" Dec. 2, letter to W. Thornbury from . Lucerne.

1862. — Feb. 17, home to examine Turners at
Age 43. National Gallery . . . . . Denmark Hill.

" May 31, starting from home, *via* Lucerne, '
for . . . . Milan.

" Aug. 31, after study of Luini, with Couttet and Allen at . . . . . Mornex.

" Middle of Nov., home; Nov. 29, address
at Working Men's College . . . Denmark Hill.

" By Christmas had returned to . . . Mornex.

1863. —	May, studying limestone Alps at . .	Talloires.
Age 44.	June 5, Lect. at Royal Inst., "Stratified Alps"	Denmark Hill.
"	June 8, evidence before R. A. commission	—
"	Summer, at Winnington and Wallington (Aug. 18).	
"	Sept. 20, Chamouni; Oct. with Bunney at Hotel Städthof . . .	Baden (Switz.).
"	Nov. 3, Lauffenburg; about Christmas returned to	Denmark Hill.
1864. —	Jan. 30, Lect. Working Men's College .	—
Age 45.	March 3, his father died; April 19, Miss Agnew (Mrs. A. Severn) came to live at	—
"	Lecture on "Traffic" (" Crown of Wild Olive ") given at	Bradford.
"	Dec. 6, Lect. " Kings' Treasuries " .	Manchester.
"	Dec. 7, address, Grammar School . .	—
"	Dec. 14, Lect. " Queens' Gardens " (" Sesame and Lilies ") . . .	—
1865. —	Jan. 24, Lect. " Work and Play " (" Crown	
Age 46.	of Wild Olive ") Camberwell . .	Denmark Hill.
"	Feb. 18, address, Working Men's Coll. .	—
"	May 15, address to R. I. B. A., " Study of Architecture "	—
"	Nov. 18, Lect. " Art," Working Men's Coll.	—
"	Dec., Lect. " War," Royal Military Academy	Woolwich.
1866. —	April 22, started with the Trevelyans	
Age 47.	abroad; April 26 at Paris; (Lady Trevelyan died, Neuchatel;) May 21, Thun; May 24, Interlaken; working at geology and botany in the early part of June at Giessbach; Lauterbrunnen, Lucerne, Schaffhausen, Neuchatel, Berne; July 2, Vevey; 4, Geneva; 16, reached home, Denmark Hill.	Switzerland.
"	Sept. 5, spoke at meeting of Eyre Defence Committee	Denmark Hill.

1867. — Feb. 4, began "Time and Tide" . . Denmark Hill.
Age 48. May 24, Rede Lecture . . . . Cambridge.
" June 7, Lect. "Modern Art," Royal Inst. Denmark Hill.
" July 17-30, Keswick; Aug. 9, Amble-
side ; 20, left . . . . . Keswick.
" Sept., Queen's Hotel, Norwood; Nov. 1,
home at . . . . . . Denmark Hill.
1868. — May 13, Lect. "Mystery of Life" ("Se-
Age 49. same and Lilies") . . . . . Dublin.
" Stayed on the way home at . . . Winnington.
" July 4 and 15, spoke at Social Science
Meetings (John St., Adelphi) . . Denmark Hill.
" July 18, address, "Three-legged Stool of
Art" (Jermyn St.) . . . . —
" Sept. 4-7, Namur ; 9, Dinant; 17, Huy;
with W. Ward . . . . . Belgium.
" A month at Abbeville, with Prof. Norton
and others; then to . . . Amiens.
1869. — Jan. 29, Lect. "Flamboyant Architec-
Age 50. ture of the Somme" (Royal Inst.) . Denmark Hill.
" March 9, Lect. "Greek Myths of Cloud
and Storm" (Univ. Coll.) . . . —
" March 15, Lect. "Hercules of Cama-
rina" (S. Lambeth Art School) . . —
" April 27, Paris with A. Burgess; 28,
Dijon; 29 . . . . . . Neuchatel.
" April 30, Vevey; May 5, Simplon; 7,
Milan; 8, Verona after 17 years' ab-
sence; 10 . . . . . . Venice.
" Aug. 10, elected Slade Professor; re-
ceived the offer at . . . . Verona.
" Early in Sept., home . . . . Denmark Hill.
" Dec. 14, Lect. "Future of England," at . Woolwich.
1870. — Feb. 4, Lect. "Verona and its Rivers"
Age 51. (Royal Inst.) . . . . . Denmark Hill.
" Feb. 8-23, First course of Lectures on
Art, at . . . . Oxford.
" April 27, Boulogne with the Hilliards
and Miss Agnew; April 30, Geneva;
May 7, Vevey; 10, Martigny; 20, Mi- Italy.
lan; 25, at Venice; June 21, to Flor-

1870.	ence ; 25, Siena, with Prof. Norton ;	
Age 51.	June 28, Florence ; June 30, Pisa ; July 4, Milan ; 5, Como ; 7, St. Gothard ; 10	Giessbach
"	July 31, returned home ; working at coins at Brit. Mus.	Denmark Hill.
"	Nov. 24–Dec. 10, Second course, "Aratra Pentelici," at	Oxford.
"	Dec. 13, Lect. "Story of Arachne," at the Arsenal	Woolwich.
1871.—Jan. 1, published "Fors Clavigera," No. I.		Denmark Hill.
Age 52.	Jan. 18, at meeting of French Relief Fund, Mansion House	—
"	Jan. 20–Feb. 24, Course on Landscape at	Oxford.
"	Summer at Matlock ; in Aug. dangerously ill at	Matlock.
"	Sept. 11, left home with the Hilliards ; Sept. 12, viewed Brantwood . . .	Coniston.
"	Sept. 21, Keswick ; short journey in Scotland ; Oct. 2–7 at Coniston ; Oct. 10 at	Denmark Hill.
"	Nov. 22, endowment of Mastership of drawing at Oxford accepted . .	—
"	Nov. 23, elected Lord Rector of St. Andrew's University	—
"	Dec. 5, his mother died	—
1872.—Jan. 13, Lect. "The Bird of Calm". .		Woolwich.
Age 53.	Feb. 8–March 9, Course "Eagle's Nest," at	Oxford.
"	March 29, left Denmark Hill ; in residence at Corpus Christi Coll. . .	—
"	April, with Mr. and Mrs. A. Severn, until the beginning of May at Pisa ; May 7, Lucca ; May 12, Rome ; June 10, Florence ; June 18, Verona ; June 22, to	Italy.
	Venice ; returned in August to . .	Herne Hill.
"	Sept. 2, first residence at . . .	Brantwood.
"	Oct. 30, to Oxford ; Nov. 2–Dec. 7, Course "Ariadne Florentina" . .	Oxford.
1873.—Jan. 14, reëlected Slade Professor . .		Brantwood.
Age 54.	Feb. 11, Paper on "Nature and Authority of Miracle," Grosvenor Hotel .	London.

1873. — March 15 and 19, Lect. on "Robin"
Age 54. ("Love's Meinie"), at . . . . Oxford.
" Easter at Brantwood; May 2 and 5, Lect.
  "Swallow" . . . . . . —
" May 9 and 12, Lect. "Chough" . . —
" May 10 and 17, Lectures on "Swallow"
  and "Chough," at . . . . Eton.
" June at Brantwood; June 15, London;
  June 21, Croydon; then . . . Brantwood.
" Oct. 20–Nov. 20, Course "Val d'Arno,"
  at . . . . Oxford.
1874. — Jan. 11, Ilfracombe; Feb. 4, Oxford;
Age 55. Feb. 23, to . . . . . Brantwood.
" March 30, left Herne Hill for Paris; by
  Mont Cenis; April 12 . . . Assisi.
" April 15, to Rome; April 21, to . . Sicily.
" May 6, began the Zipporah . . . Rome.
" June 8, left Rome for Assisi; studying
  Giotto's frescoes at . . . . Assisi.
" July 26–Sept. 25, at Lucca and . . Florence.
" Oct. 1, Mont Cenis; 19, Geneva; 20,
  Paris; 25 . . . . . . London.
" Oct. 27–Nov. 6, Course "Alps and
  Jura" . . . . Oxford.
" Nov. 10–Dec. 4, Course "Schools of
  Florentine Art" . . . . —
" Dec. 12, Lect. "Botticelli" . . . Eton.
1875. — Jan. 24, from Brantwood to Bolton Ab-
Age 56. bey, thence through . . . . Derbyshire.
" Feb. 9, Herne Hill; March 11, Lect.
  "Glacial Action" (Royal Inst.) . . Herne Hill.
" Easter at Brantwood; May and June at
  Herne Hill and . . . . . Oxford.
" July 8, after traveling through Derby-
  shire and Yorkshire, at . . . Brantwood.
" Sept., posting through Yorkshire; Sept.
  27 . . . . Herne Hill.
" Oct., at Broadlands, Romsey; and Cowley
  Rectory . . . . . . Uxbridge.
" Nov. 2–27, Course "Sir J. Reynolds" Oxford.

1875. — Nov. 27, evening, Lect. "Spanish Chap-
Age 56.   el " . . . . . . Eton.
    "   Dec., spent in visiting various friends;
         returning to . . . . . . Herne Hill.
1876. — Feb. 17 and March 28, Lect. "Precious
Age 57.   Stones" (London Institution) . . —
    "   Feb. 26, reëlected Slade Professor . . Oxford.
    "   April 13, Lect. "Stones" (Christ's Hos-
         pital).
    "   April 18, Lect. "Minerals" . . . Woolwich.
    "   April, posting from London; April 27,
         Sheffield; May 7 . . . . . Brantwood.
    "   Aug. 1, Barmouth; Aug. 21, Aylesbury;
         Aug. 26 . . . . . . Paris.
    "   Aug. 27, Geneva; 30, Martigny; Sept.
         12 at . . . . Venice.
1877. — Until May 23, studying Carpaccio at . —
Age 58.   May 24, Milan; June 6, Simplon; June
         15, Paris; June 16, home; 28, Oxford,
         then . . . . Herne Hill.
    "   July 10, speech at Society for Prevention
         of Cruelty to Animals . . . . —
    "   July 13, to Birmingham (Mr. G. Baker's);
         July 16, to . . . . . . Brantwood.
    "   Oct. 1, Lect. "Yewdale and its Stream-
         lets " . . . . Kendal.
    "   Nov. 6–Dec. 1, Course "Readings in
         Modern Painters" . . . . Oxford.
    "   Dec. 8, Lect. "Streams of Westmore-
         land " at . . . . . . Eton.
    "   Dec. 12, Herne Hill; Christmas at . Oxford.
1878. — Jan. 2, Windsor Castle; Jan. 13, Hawar-
Age 59.   den; Jan. 21 . . . . . Brantwood.
    "   Feb. and March (Turner Exhibition at
         Bond Street); illness at . . . —
    "   July, visit to Malham; Sept. and Oct. at —
    "   Nov. 9 . . . . Liverpool.
    "   (Nov. 25, 26, Whistler v. Ruskin) . . Brantwood.
1879. — March, short visit to London; Oct. 22, re-
Age 60.   ceived Prince Leopold at St. George's
         Museum . . . . . . Sheffield.

<table>
<tr><td>1879.—</td><td>Autumn at Herne Hill, returning for</td><td></td></tr>
<tr><td>Age 60.</td><td>Christmas to . . . . .</td><td>Brantwood.</td></tr>
<tr><td>1880.—</td><td>Feb. 12–16 . . . . . .</td><td>Sheffield.</td></tr>
<tr><td>Age 61.</td><td>March 17, 23, Lect. " Snakes " (London
Inst.) . . . .</td><td>Herne Hill.</td></tr>
<tr><td>"</td><td>April to Aug. 12, at Brantwood; Aug. 21,
left Herne Hill for . . . .</td><td>Dover.</td></tr>
<tr><td>"</td><td>Aug. 26–28, Abbeville; 30, Amiens to
Beauvais; Sept. 2, to Paris; 8, Chartres;
17, to . . . .</td><td>Paris.</td></tr>
<tr><td>"</td><td>Sept. 23, to Rouen; Oct. 11, with Messrs.
Severn and Brabazon to . . .</td><td>Amiens.</td></tr>
<tr><td>"</td><td>Nov. 4, to Herne Hill; Nov. 6, Lect.
" Amiens " . . . . . .</td><td>Eton.</td></tr>
<tr><td>"</td><td>Dec. 1, returned to . . . . .</td><td>Brantwood.</td></tr>
<tr><td>1881.—</td><td>July 25, for a few days at Seascale; re-</td><td></td></tr>
<tr><td>Age 62.</td><td>turning to . . . . . .</td><td>—</td></tr>
<tr><td>1882.—</td><td>Feb., to Herne Hill; March 3, copying</td><td></td></tr>
<tr><td>Age 63.</td><td>at Nat. Gall. . . . . .</td><td>Herne Hill.</td></tr>
<tr><td>"</td><td>(April 9, Rossetti died; May 11, Dr.
John Brown died) . . . .</td><td>—</td></tr>
<tr><td>"</td><td>Aug.–Dec., abroad with W. G. Colling-
wood; Laon, Reims; Aug. 21–30, at .</td><td>Avallon.</td></tr>
<tr><td>"</td><td>Sept. 9, Geneva; 11, Sallenches; 23,
Turin; 24, to . . . . .</td><td>Pisa.</td></tr>
<tr><td>"</td><td>Sept. 30, at Lucca; Oct., met Miss Alex-
ander at . . . . . .</td><td>Florence.</td></tr>
<tr><td>"</td><td>Returned to Lucca; by Mont Cenis to
(Nov. 13) . . . . . .</td><td>Talloires.</td></tr>
<tr><td>"</td><td>Nov. 22, Geneva; Paris; returning (Dec.
1) . . . .</td><td>Herne Hill.</td></tr>
<tr><td>"</td><td>Dec. 4, Lect. " Cistercian Architecture "
(Lond. Inst.) . . . . .</td><td>—</td></tr>
<tr><td>1883.—</td><td>Jan., to Brantwood; March 9, Lect. " Art</td><td></td></tr>
<tr><td>Age 64.</td><td>of England," I. . . . . .</td><td>Oxford.</td></tr>
<tr><td>"</td><td>Easter at Brantwood; May, 12–30, " Art
of England," II.–IV. . . . .</td><td>—</td></tr>
<tr><td>"</td><td>(May 25, Osborne Gordon died.)</td><td></td></tr>
<tr><td>"</td><td>June 5, Lect. on F. Alexander and K.
Greenaway . . . . . .</td><td>Kensington.</td></tr>
<tr><td>"</td><td>June to Aug. . . . . . .</td><td>Brantwood.</td></tr>
</table>

1883. — (Aug. 25, Rawdon Brown died.)

Age 64. Sept., tour to Abbotsford, Whithorn, etc. . . Scotland.

Nov. 7–21, Lect. "Art of England," V. and VI. . . . . . . Oxford.

" Dec. 22, Lect. on Sir H. Edwardes (Coniston) . . . . Brantwood.

" (Dec. 31, Miss Mary Beever died.)

1884. — Feb. 4 and 11, Lect. "Storm Cloud"

Age 65. (Lond. Inst.) . . . . . Herne Hill.

" Feb. 15, Lect. to Academy Girls . .

" March, returned to . . . . . Brantwood.

" Oct. at Canterbury; Oct. 18–Dec. 1, Course, "Pleasures of England" . . Oxford.

" Middle of December, returned to . . Brantwood.

1885. — May 7, to . . . . . . Herne Hill.

Age 66. May 23, address to Society of Friends of Living Creatures . . . . Bedford Park.

" Middle of June, returned to . . . Brantwood.

1886. — Working at "Præterita," vol. II.; illness at . . . . —

Age 67. Sept., at Heysham, near Lancaster; returning (Oct.) to . . . . . —

1887. — Aug. 18, posted with Mrs. A. Severn to

Age 68. St. Albans; thence to . . . . Folkestone.

" Nov., Sandgate; Dec. 7, in London; returning to . . . . . . Sandgate.

1888. — April 21, at private view of Watercolor

Age 69. Exhibition, etc. . . . . . London.

" April, visits to Chislehurst and Orpington, returning to . . . . . Sandgate.

" June 10, with Mr. A. Severn to . . Abbeville.

" July 3, Crecy; July 5, to Beauvais; Aug. 6, to . . . . Paris.

" Aug. 27, with Mr. Blow by the Jura to (Sept. 13) . . . . . . Chamouni.

" Sept. 18, to Martigny; by the Simplon to visit the Alexanders (Sept. 25) . Bassano.

" Oct. 6, to Venice; 17, to Milan; 18, to . Fluelen.

" Oct. 29, to Berne; Nov. 29, to Paris; Dec. 8, to . . . . . . Herne Hill.

" Dec. 29, returned to . . . Brantwood.

CHRONOLOGY.

1889. — In June, to Seascale (last " Præterita ") ;
Age 70.   returning to   .   .   .   .   . Brantwood.
1892. — Still residing at Brantwood.
Age 73.

xi

BIBLIOGRAPHY.

(1860–1892.)

1860. —[Unto this Last], four essays on the first principles of
Political Economy (*Cornhill Magazine*); reprinted as "Unto
this Last," 1862 (Smith, Elder, & Co.), and five subsequent
editions (George Allen). With this may be named: "The
Rights of Labour according to John Ruskin," arranged by
Thomas Barclay (extracts from "Unto this Last," with a
letter from Mr. Ruskin), 1887 (C. Merrick, Leicester);
edition 2 (n. d.); edition 3, 1889 (W. Reeves).

1861. —"Tree Twigs" (Proceedings of the Royal Institution),
reprinted separately; also in "On the Old Road."

1862–63. —[Munera Pulveris]: Essays in Political Economy (*Fraser's Magazine*); reprinted as "Munera Pulveris;" three
editions (George Allen).

1863. —"Forms of the Stratified Alps of Savoy" (Proceedings of
the Royal Institution), reprinted separately: also reprinted
with variations in "The Geologist" for July, 1863; and reported fully in French in the *Journal de Genève*, Sept. 2,
1863; also in "On the Old Road."

1865. —"Sesame and Lilies;" four editions (Smith, Elder); and
six editions (Allen) in original form. Revised and enlarged
by the addition of lecture on "The Mystery of Life" (printed
in Dublin Afternoon Lectures, 1869), in which form five
editions have appeared (Allen). The Lecture on the Queens'
Gardens was printed as a pamphlet in aid of the St. Andrew's
Schools Fund, 1864.

1865. —"Notes on the Shape and Structure of some parts of the
Alps," etc. (*Geol. Mag.* for Feb. and May).

1865–66. —"The Cestus of Aglaia;" nine papers in the *Art Journal*, partly reprinted in "On the Old Road" and in "The
Queen of the Air."

xii

BIBLIOGRAPHY.

1866. — "The Ethics of the Dust" (Smith, Elder), and four subsequent editions (Allen).

1866. — "The Crown of Wild Olive;" three editions (Smith, Elder), and five subsequent editions (Allen). Of these lectures were printed separately: "War," 1866; and "The Future of England," a paper read at the Royal Artillery Institution, Woolwich, 1869.

1867. — "Report on the Turner Drawings in the National Gallery" (Annual Reports, Nat. Gall.).

1867. — "Time and Tide by Weare and Tyne;" twenty-five letters first published in the *Manchester Examiner* and the *Leeds Mercury;* two editions (Smith, Elder), and three subsequent editions (Allen).

1867-70. — "On Banded and Brecciated Concretions;" seven papers in the *Geol. Mag.*

1868. — Introduction to "German Popular Stories," illustrated by Cruikshank (John Camden Hotten).

1868. — (First) "Notes on the General Principles of Employment for the Destitute and Criminal Classes;" two issues in the same year.

1869. — Catalogue of Pictures sold at Christie's.

1869. — Catalogue of Pictures in Illustration of Lecture on the Flamboyant Architecture of the Valley of the Somme.

1869. — "The Queen of the Air;" two editions (Smith, Elder), and three subsequently (Allen).

1870. — "Verona and its Rivers" (Proceedings of the Royal Institution), reprinted in "On the Old Road;" also

"Catalogue of Drawings and Photographs" (illustrating the above lecture), reprinted in "On the Old Road."

1870. — "Lectures on Art;" three editions (Clarendon Press), and small edition (Allen).

1870. — "Catalogue of Examples arranged for Elementary Study in the University Galleries" (Clarendon Press). With this may be named: "Catalogue of the Reference Series" (1871); "Catalogue of the Educational Series" (1871 and 1874); and "Instructions in Elementary Drawing" (1872), five editions.

1871. — "The Range of Intellectual Conception proportioned to the Rank in Animated Life;" a paper for the Metaphysical Society; also printed in the *Contemporary Review* for June, and in "On the Old Road."

1871-84. — "Fors Clavigera." Letters 1-84 published monthly

from Jan. 1, 1871, to Dec. 1, 1877. Letters 85–96 (1–12 of
the New Series) published at intervals from 1878 to 1884;
afterwards collected in eight volumes (Allen). With this
may be named: "Index to Vols. I. and II.," 1873; "Index
to Vols. III. and IV.," 1875 (Allen). Article on J. D. Forbes
chiefly from "Fors" No. 34, in Rendu's "Glaciers of Savoy,"
translated by Alfred Wills, Q. C. (Macmillan). "Letter to
Young Girls," from "Fors" Nos. 65 and 66; eighteen editions up to 1890 (Allen). Also the following publications
relating to St. George's Guild: "Abstract of the Objects and
Constitution," 1878; "Memorandum and Articles of Association," 1878; "Master's Report" for 1879, 1881, 1884, 1885;
"General Statement explaining the Nature and Purposes,"
1882, two editions (Allen); "Contents of large sliding
frames" (in Museum), 1879; "Catalogue of Drawings made
for the Guild and Exhibited at the Fine Art Society's Gallery," 1886; and "Catalogue of Minerals in the Museum."

1872. — "Aratra Pentelici," three editions (Allen).

1872. — "The Relation between Michael Angelo and Tintoret,"
three editions (Allen).

1872. — "The Eagle's Nest," three editions (Allen).

1872. — "Monuments of the Cavalli Family, Verona" (Arundel
Society); reprinted in "On the Old Road."

1872. — Preface to "Christian Art and Symbolism" by the Rev. R.
St. J. Tyrwhitt (Smith, Elder), reprinted in "On the Old
Road."

1873. — "The Nature and Authority of Miracle:" a paper for the
Metaphysical Society, reprinted privately; published in the
Contemporary Review for March, 1873, and in "On the Old
Road."

1873. — "Love's Meinie," Parts I. and II. published separately,
two editions; Part III. was issued in 1881. The complete
volume in 1882 (Allen).

1873. — "Ariadne Florentina," six lectures issued separately; subsequently as one volume, in two editions (Allen).

1874. — "Val d'Arno," ten lectures issued separately; subsequently
as one volume, in three editions (Allen).

1875. — "Notes on . . . the Royal Academy," four editions (Allen,
and Ellis & White).

1875-77. — "Mornings in Florence;" six parts issued separately,
in three editions (Allen). With this may be named: "The

Shepherd's Tower" (photographs of Giotto's Campanile), 1881 (William Ward).

1875-86. — "Proserpina," ten parts in several editions; collected into two volumes (Allen).

1875-83. — "Deucalion," eight parts, some of which ran to two editions; collected into two volumes (Allen). With this may be named: "Yewdale and its Streamlets," reprinted from the *Kendal Mercury*, 1877; "The Limestone Alps of Savoy," by W. G. Collingwood; edited with introduction by Mr. Ruskin as supplement to "Deucalion," 1884 (Allen).

1876. — "Modern Warfare" (*Fraser's Mag.* for July), reprinted in "Arrows of the Chace."

1876. — Preface and Notes to "The Art Schools of Mediæval Christendom," by Miss A. C. Owen (Mozley & Smith); reprinted in "On the Old Road."

1876. — Preface to "A Protest against the Extension of Railways in the Lake District," by Robert Somervell (J. Garnett, and Simpkin & Marshall); reprinted in "On the Old Road."

1876. — "Bibliotheca Pastorum," Vol. I.; "The Economist of Xenophon," translated by A. D. O. Wedderburn, and W. G. Collingwood; edited with preface by Mr. Ruskin (Ellis & White, and G. Allen).

1877. — "Bibliotheca Pastorum," Vol. II., "Rock Honeycomb;" Sir Philip Sidney's "Psalter," with Preface and Commentary by Mr. Ruskin (Ellis & White, and G. Allen). Vol. III. was not published.

1877. — "Guide to the Principal Pictures in the Academy of Fine Arts at Venice," in two parts; two editions (Venice, and G. Allen).

1877-84. — "St. Mark's Rest" in three parts; together with — Appendix, "Sanctus, Sanctus, Sanctus," by A. D. O. Wedderburn, 1882; First Supplement, "The Shrine of the Slaves" by Mr. Ruskin (also translated into Italian by Conte Cav. G. P. Zanelli, 1885); and Second Supplement, "The Place of Dragons" by J. R. Anderson, 1879 (the above published by G. Allen); and "Illustrative Photographs" (William Ward).

1877-78. — "The Laws of Fésole," in four parts in various editions; collected into one volume, 1879; edition 2, 1882 (Allen).

1878. — "An Oxford Lecture" (*Nineteenth Century* for Jan.), reprinted in "On the Old Road."

1878. — "My First Editor" (*University Magazine* for April), reprinted in "On the Old Road."

1878. — "Notes on the Turner Exhibition at the Fine Art Society's Galleries;" twelve issues and illustrated edition (Fine Art Society).

1878. — "The Three Colours of Pre-Raphaelitism" (*Nineteenth Century* for Nov. and Dec.), reprinted in "On the Old Road."

1879–80. — "Notes on the Prout and Hunt Exhibition;" four issues and illustrated edition (Fine Art Society).

1879–80. — "Circular respecting Memorial Studies at St. Mark's;" three issues (Fine Art Society).

1879–80. — "The Lord's Prayer and the Church:" Letters, etc. Edited by the Rev. F. A. Malleson, M. A. Three editions, varying in contents (Strahan & Co.). Mr. Ruskin's "Letters," reprinted in the *Contemporary Review* for December, 1879; also in "On the Old Road."

1880. — "Usury, a Reply and a Rejoinder" (*Contemporary Review* for February); reprinted in "On the Old Road."

1880. — "Elements of English Prosody" (Allen).

1880. — "Letters on a Museum or Picture Gallery" (*Art Journal* for June and August); reprinted in "On the Old Road."

1880. — "Arrows of the Chace;" letters to newspapers collected by A. D. O. Wedderburn, two vols. (Allen).

1880–81. — "Fiction, Fair and Foul:" five papers (in the *Nineteenth Century*); reprinted in "On the Old Road."

1880–85. — "The Bible of Amiens;" five parts, afterwards collected into one vol. ; separate travelers' edition of Chap. IV., 1881 (Allen).

1881. — "Catalogue of the Drawings and Sketches of J. M. W. Turner, R. A., at present in the National Gallery;" two editions and two special editions (Allen).

1883. — "The Art of England:" seven lectures issued separately ; afterwards collected into one vol.; two editions both of parts and vol. (Allen).

1883. — "Catalogue of Siliceous Minerals given to St. David's School" (Rev. W. H. Churchill), Reigate.

1883. — "Preface" to "The Story of Ida," by Francesca Alexander; four editions (Allen).

1883. — "Introduction" to "The Study of Beauty and Art in

Large Towns," by T. C. Horstall (Macmillan) ; reprinted in "On the Old Road."

1884. — "The Storm Cloud of the Nineteenth Century;" issued in two parts, afterwards in one volume (Allen).

1884. — "Catalogue of Minerals given to Kirkcudbright Museum."

1884. — "Catalogue of a Series of Specimens in the British Museum (Nat. Hist.), illustrative of the more common forms of native Silica" (Allen).

1884-85. — "The Pleasures of England:" four lectures issued separately (Allen). The course is reported in "Studies in Ruskin," by E. T. Cook, M. A., 1890 (Allen).

1885. — Preface and Notes to "Roadside Songs of Tuscany," by Miss Alexander (Allen).

1885. — Preface and Notes to "The English School of Painting," by E. Chesneau, three editions (Cassell).

1885. — Introduction to "Usury," by R. G. Sillar, two editions (A. Southey); reprinted in "On the Old Road."

1885. — "The Bishop of Oxford and Prof. Ruskin on Vivisection" (Victoria Street Society for the Protection of Animals from Vivisection).

1885. — "On the Old Road" (reprint of magazine articles), edited by A. D. O. Wedderburn (Allen).

1885. — "Bibliotheca Pastorum," Vol. IV. "A Knight's Faith" (life of Sir Herbert Edwardes); issued in three parts, collected into one volume (Allen).

1885-89. — "Præterita:" twenty-eight parts, of which twenty-four are collected into two volumes; Vol. I. has run to two editions (Allen).

1886-87. — "Dilecta:" correspondence, etc., illustrating "Præterita;" two parts (Allen).

1886-88. — Preface and Notes to "Ulric, the Farm Servant," by Gotthelf, translated by Mrs. Firth (Allen).

1887. — "Arthur Burgess" ("Century Guild Hobby Horse," for April).

1887. — "Hortus Inclusus:" letters to Misses Mary and Susanna Beever, edited by Albert Fleming, two editions (Allen).

1887-89. — "Christ's Folk in the Apennine," by Francesca Alexander, edited by Mr. Ruskin; six parts issued (Allen).

1888. — Preface and Notes to "A popular Handbook to the National Gallery," by E. T. Cook (Macmillan).

1888. — " The Black Arts: a Reverie in the Strand" (*Magazine
of Art* for January).

1890. — " Ruskiniana:" letters collected in " Igdrasil," and reprinted privately, supplementary to " Arrows of the Chace."

1891. — " The Poems of John Ruskin;" containing those above
mentioned, with additions; edited by W. G. Collingwood
(Allen).

CATALOGUE OF DRAWINGS BY MR. RUSKIN.

(1860–1889.)

1860. — Aiguilles by Moonlight (engraved but unpublished), perhaps this year; Moon-
light at Chamouni, large quarto .   .   Brantwood.

1861–62. — Mountains of Annecy from the Brezon
(color 4½ × 11 in.); The Brezon, and
other sketches in Savoy   .   .   .   —

Studies of Limestone Alps of this period
W. G. Collingwood.

St. Gothard, from near Fluelen (pen, 6¾
× 4¾ in.)   .   .   .   .   .   .   Prof. Norton.

Old Bridge at Lucerne, color (Cook's
" Studies in Ruskin ") .   .   .   .   Oxford.

Lucerne from the hills (pen, 8 × 11 in.);
Do. foreground (color, 7 × 10 in.)   .   Miss Hilliard.

1862. — Golden Sunshine, near Bonneville .   .   Prof. Norton.

Perhaps this year, Houses and Mountain,
Altorf, quarto   .   .   .   .   .   Sir J. Simon.

Copy of Luini's " St. Catherine " (color,
life-size figure) .   .   .   .   .   Oxford.

1863. — Mountains from Mornex .   .   .   .   Mr. F. Crawley.

Shell and tulip (color, 9 × 6 in.)   .   .   Mrs. Churchill.

Coldstream; Sketches of Baden and Lauffenburg .   .   .   .   Brantwood.

Perhaps this year, Farm on the Reuss
(" Poetry of Architecture ") .   .   .   —

And Lauffenburg from two points of view
(pencil) .   .   .   .   Harvard Coll.

1864. — (?) This year, Rouen Cathedral before
restoration .   .   .   .   .   T. W. Jackson, Esq.

And Portrait of Himself (see *Frontis-
piece*) .   .   .   .   Brantwood.

1865. — Study of Trees, from Turner .   .   .   Brantwood.
Evening at Norwood (cloud study, 10½ ×
9 in.) .   .   .   .   .   .   Prof. Norton.
1866. — Lady Trevelyan's grave, Neuchatel (pen
and pencil, 8 × 11 in.); Dawn, on the
morning of her death, and Storm on
the lake (both color, 5½ × 8½ in.)   .   Mrs. Churchill.
Lake of Brientz from the Giessbach   .   Brantwood.
1866. — Perhaps this year, Lucerne, from hill above
Reuss (Cook's "Studies") .   .   .   Oxford.
1867. — Agates for *Geological Magazine*.
1868. — Abbeville (*Poems*, 1891), and other drawings; Sunset at Abbeville ("Storm
Cloud" lecture) .   .   .   .   Brantwood.
St. Wulfran, and old house   .   .   Mr. G. Allen.
Place Amiral Courbet (Cook's "Studies
in Ruskin") .   .   .   .   .   Oxford.
Sunrise from Denmark Hill (sky on blue
paper), 9 × 4½ in.   .   .   .   Prof. Norton.
1869. — Geneva Cathedral and Salève; Montorio,
Verona (body color)   .   .   . F. W. Hilliard, Esq.
Old Vevey (pencil) .   .   .   .   Harvard Coll.
Perhaps this year, Approach to Venice   Sir J. Simon.
(tint, 10 × 7 in.); and the following
exhibited at the lecture on "Verona"
(Royal Inst.), 1870: Griffin on north
side of porch, Duomo, Verona; Lom-
bardic Lion, Venice; and Head of Dog,
Verona; Capital, St. Anastasia; Studies
of top and base of pilaster next Castel-
barco tomb; Piazza de' Signori, with
advertisement of " L'Homme qui Rit; "
Angel of Ducal Palace, looking seaward
from Piazzetta ; Hawthorn Leaves, S.
M. dei Miracoli, Venice; Tomb of Can
Grande; the same, general view; Sar-
cophagus and effigy of Can Grande;
The Two Dogs from Can Grande; Pattern on drapery of Can Mastino II.'s
tomb; Single niche and ironwork, tomb

<table>
<tr><td></td><td>of Can Signoria; Details from top of tomb of Can Signoria . . . .</td><td>Brantwood.</td></tr>
<tr><td>1870.—</td><td>Venice, Grand Canal (pencil), Cook's "Studies in Ruskin" . . . .</td><td>Oxford.</td></tr>
<tr><td></td><td>Perhaps this year, or 1872, Rialto (color, 6½ × 9 in.); and Front of Riva de' Schiavoni (color, 10 × 14 in.) . .</td><td>Miss Hilliard.</td></tr>
<tr><td>1871.—</td><td>Kingfisher, color (Cook's "Studies in Ruskin"); Wild Rose, Matlock .</td><td>Oxford.</td></tr>
<tr><td></td><td>Kingfisher's Foot, and Dormer Window, Abingdon . . . . .</td><td>Brantwood.</td></tr>
<tr><td>1872.—</td><td>Eagle's head, bird's wing, and head of Greek Statue; Stuffed Jackal; sketch of head; Verona (pencil, 10 × 9 in.); S. Giorgio de' Schiavoni (10 × 9½ in.)</td><td>Prof. Norton.</td></tr>
<tr><td></td><td>Moonlight at Venice (colored by moonlight, 5½ × 9½ in.); and Portrait of Miss C. Hilliard (pencil, 16½ × 13½ in.)</td><td>Mrs. Churchill.</td></tr>
<tr><td></td><td>Coliseum and St. Peter's, Rome; Oxford School Studies — Jampot, Candle, and others . . . . . .</td><td>Brantwood.</td></tr>
<tr><td>1872.—</td><td>Apse of Pisa Cathedral . . . .</td><td>Brantwood.</td></tr>
<tr><td>1873.—</td><td>Cyclamen, and two copies of Turner's "Bonneville" . . . . .</td><td>Prof. Norton.</td></tr>
<tr><td></td><td>The Old Man at Daybreak . . .</td><td>Mr. G. Allen.</td></tr>
<tr><td></td><td>Wild Strawberry . . . . .</td><td>Oxford.</td></tr>
<tr><td></td><td>Two Peacock's Feathers . . . .</td><td>Miss Beever.</td></tr>
<tr><td></td><td>Perhaps this year, Portrait of himself (quarto imp.) . . . . .</td><td>Prof. Norton.</td></tr>
<tr><td>1874.—</td><td>St. Francis, after Giotto (12¾ × 18); Lung' Arno (10½ × 7); and study for etching of Ponte Vecchio (4⅛ × 3¼) .</td><td>—</td></tr>
<tr><td></td><td>Spezia, sunset (color); Tomb of Frederick II., Palermo . . . .</td><td>Brantwood.</td></tr>
<tr><td></td><td>Etna; Taormina and Etna . . .</td><td>Oxford.</td></tr>
<tr><td></td><td>Etna at daybreak and twilight (color); many sketches of the Straits of Messina (pencil); Zipporah (large copy from Botticelli); several copies of Giotto, Perugino, and Botticelli; Fiesole, convent and Badia; Ponte Vecchio;</td><td></td></tr>
</table>

Annecy, passage Nemours; Bonneville;
Glacier des Bossons (*Poems*, 1891) . Brantwood.
Mont Blanc . . . . . . Oxford.
1875. — Fixed Cloud, Coniston . . . . Brantwood.
Gloomy vertical sunshine on the Old Man
($11 \times 3\frac{3}{4}$); perhaps this year, Portrait
of himself . . . . . . Prof. Norton.
1876. — Perhaps this year, Sunset at Herne Hill
("Storm Cloud") . . . . . Brantwood.
Brieg; Brieg, with bridge; Simplon
Mountains; Riva delle Zattere, Venice;
seven views in Venice . . . Prof. C. H. Moore.
Venetian match-box; Tassel of St. Ur-
sula's Pillow . . . . . Miss E. H. Moore.
St. Ursula's dream (small copy in color) . Oxford.
St. Ursula (actual size) . . . . Brantwood.
1877. — Other studies of Carpaccio and sketches
in Venice of architecture, etc. . . —
St. Andrea, Venice . . . . A. Fleming, Esq.
Alprose at Isella ("Proserpina") . . Brantwood.
1878. — Oak buds (study, 9×4 in.) . . . Prof. Norton.
1879. — Withered oak leaf; Seaweed (color) Sheffield Museum.
Byzantine Capital; Pheasant's feather;
Cotoneaster; Oak leaves (color) . . Harvard Coll.
Copy from study of the N. W. Porch of
St. Mark's . . . . . . Prof. Norton.
The original is at . . . . . Brantwood.
1880. — Sunset ("Storm Cloud" lecture); Calais;
Beauvais and Amiens (several sketches) —
1880. — Amiens . . . . Miss Gale.
1881. — Two drawings of Seascale Sands; and
Sunrise at Coniston (exhib. R. W. S.) Brantwood.
1882. — Sketch from Turner's "Python;" sketches
at Laon, Reims, Sens, Avallon; Porch
at Avallon; capital of pillar (color, half
imp.); sketches at Montreal, Citeaux,
Sallenches, etc.; studies of masonry and
sculpture at Pisa and Lucca; two half
imp. drawings, Lucca Cathedral (exhib.
R. W. S.); Lucca Mountains, late
afternoon (color); Ponte Vecchio in

   flood ; Ponte Vecchio, interior street
   (pencil) ; Ancient Walls of Fiesole, two
   sketches (color) ; Enlargement, $3\frac{1}{2}$ feet
   high, from sketch of Avallon ; various
   drawings of crystals about this time .   —
1888. — Sketches at Abbeville (colored sunrises,
   etc.) ; moulding at Beauvais . . . —
   Five sketches at Beauvais . . S. C. Cockerell, Esq.
1889. — Langdale Pikes from the Lower Moor
   (pencil) ; Calder Abbey ·. . . Brantwood.

[The above list contains only drawings to which dates can be
  affixed with more or less certainty. Many others exist which,
  being undated, have no direct biographical interest. In the
  Oxford Drawing-school there are upwards of one hundred
  drawings by Mr. Ruskin ; at Brantwood there are more than
  seven hundred, not counting scraps and sketchbooks.]

---

[1] Mrs. Orme (Miss Eliza Andrews), alluded to on page 40 as still living in Bedford Park, has died since this book was printed.